THE DEVIL'S BREATH

A DCI DANNY FLINT BOOK

TREVOR NEGUS

INKUBATOR
BOOKS

Published by Inkubator Books
www.inkubatorbooks.com

ISBN (eBook): 978-1-83756-012-7
ISBN (Paperback): 978-1-83756-013-4

PROLOGUE

10.00am, 2 November 1972
Entebbe Airport, Uganda

Aadesh Panchal drove his brand new station wagon into the airport. In the car with him were his wife Eashwari, his eighteen-year-old son Nabin, and his twelve-year-old daughter Padama.

The twenty-five-mile journey from their luxury detached house on Mayanja Drive, in the affluent suburb of Kawanda in Kampala, had been a fraught and dangerous one.

Three times Aadesh had managed to negotiate safe passage for his family through army roadblocks. As they neared Entebbe Airport, the troops manning the checkpoints had become more aggressive. The African soldiers manning them had displayed a fierce hatred towards the Asian family being expelled from Uganda on the direct orders of the country's president, Field Marshall Idi Amin Dada Oumee.

As Entebbe airfield came into view, Aadesh drove slowly

towards the airport buildings. In the far distance, he could see the early morning sun glistening off Lake Victoria, its beauty at odds with the ugly atmosphere pervading the airport. He steered the heavily laden station wagon towards the entrance marked 'Departures', and was dismayed to see a uniformed customs officer, flanked by two heavily armed soldiers, barring the vehicles' progress.

The barrel-chested customs officer waved the car into a parking area and approached the vehicle. He shouted for the family to get out of the car.

Aadesh turned to his family. 'Wait here until I tell you to get out. I'll see what he wants.'

Feeling scared, he got out of the vehicle turned to the African customs officer and said politely, 'Our flight to the UK is at eleven o'clock. I have the tickets, and we are British passport holders. As Gujarati Indians, we are following President Amin's order to leave the country.'

Now that he was up close to the customs officer, Aadesh could see that the man was heavily built and probably in his late forties, a little older than he was himself.

The African sneered cruelly, exposing a mouthful of gold crowns. He was sweating profusely, and there were dark sweat stains on his navy blue uniform. The two soldiers standing behind him wore angry expressions and pointed their rifles menacingly towards Aadesh's chest.

'Car keys,' snapped the customs officer.

In a voice full of appeasement, Aadesh said, 'You can have the car; I can't take it with me. I just want to get my wife and kids safely on the plane.'

Aadesh shouted for his wife and children to get out of the car. He unlocked the vast boot of the station wagon before giving the keys to the customs officer. He and his son, Nabin, began unloading the four large suitcases from the car.

The customs officer stepped in front of Aadesh and shoved him hard in the chest. 'What are you doing? Leave the cases in the car.'

'But that's all we have. Everything we own is in those cases.'

'Everything you own is what you have plundered from this country. The president has ordered us to ensure that you leave with nothing. Are you going to argue with the president?'

Hearing the raised voice of the customs officer, the two soldiers stepped forward towards Aadesh. Their evil intent was clear.

Eighteen-year-old Nabin stepped between his father and the soldiers, stuck his chest out and shouted, 'Leave my father alone! We've done nothing wrong!'

The first soldier raised his rifle and struck Nabin on his forehead with the butt. The force of the blow knocked the young Asian to the floor. His mother screamed and ran forward, helping her dazed son to his feet.

Aadesh held out his hands in a gesture of appeasement and said, 'Please take the cases, take everything. I'm begging you, just let us into the airport.'

A cruel smile once again played over the mouth of the customs officer, and he said, 'Let me see your passports and tickets.'

Aadesh held out the black British passports, which contained the air tickets, so that the African could see them. He gripped them tightly so the man couldn't take them from him.

In doing so, his jacket sleeve rode up, exposing his gold Rolex watch.

Seeing the valuable watch, the customs officer sneered, 'Give me the watch. Then you can go through.'

Aadesh shook his head. 'You've taken everything from me already. My house has been taken from me, now my car and luggage. This watch belonged to my father. It's the only thing of value I've got left; you're not having it.'

The bulky African stepped forward and gripped Aadesh by his throat, pushing him back over the bonnet of the car. Aadesh gasped for breath as the man's fat fingers squeezed his windpipe. One of the soldiers raised his rifle and cocked the weapon, ready to fire. His wife and daughter were screaming in panic, and Aadesh could feel his head beginning to spin as the African's grip tightened around his windpipe.

The man snarled and said, 'Give me the watch. I won't ask you a third time.'

The soldier who had raised his rifle began shouting at Aadesh in an unknown dialect and thrust the barrel of the rifle in his face.

Aadesh unclasped the gold watch and held it out to the customs officer, who snatched it from his hand as he released the grip on his neck.

Aadesh was gasping for breath. Helped by his wife, he staggered towards the airport buildings, followed by his two children. Behind them, the two soldiers had begun to force the locks on the large suitcases and were examining their plunder.

Once inside the airport buildings, the family walked to the British Airways desk and presented their passports and tickets to the stewardess.

She said robotically, 'You are on Flight 2735 to London Stanstead. The aeroplane leaves in one hour; make your way to the departure gate.'

As Aadesh and his family made their way across the tarmac to the aeroplane, he turned to his wife and children and said, 'Is everyone okay?'

His wife and daughter were still sobbing, and Nabin had a livid, purple bruise forming on his forehead where the rifle butt had struck him.

'Do you still have your belts?'

All three nodded.

It had been a calculated gamble by Aadesh, to argue about giving up the watch. He had heard stories of belongings being stolen at the airport, so he had stashed all the gold and cash the family owned in money belts he had purchased. He knew that somewhere on the journey to the airport, his car and any luggage they had would be seized by unscrupulous officials or soldiers.

They would arrive in the UK with their British passports, the clothes they were wearing and what valuables they had managed to hide on their persons. They climbed the steps onto the aircraft, and he showed the tickets to the stewardess. The family found their seats halfway down the plane. It was almost full, and every passenger on board was an Asian being unceremoniously expelled from the country.

He put his arm around his wife and said, 'Try not to worry; at least we're safe now. I'll be able to get work at a school or university in England. We'll be fine. Will your uncle be at the airport to meet us?'

Eashwari nodded. In between sobs, she said, 'He'll be there. He has said we can stay with him and my auntie in Nottingham until you can find decent work.'

As the aircraft accelerated down the runway and finally took off, Aadesh looked out of the window down at Kampala. He wondered if he would ever see his beloved Uganda again.

1

9.00am, 29 April 1988
23 Parkdale Road, Bakersfield, Nottingham

It was another delay that Ben Saunders could have done without. He wanted to crack on and get his round finished. The best thing about being a postman was that as soon as he had delivered all his letters and parcels, the day was his own.

He had been banging on the front door of the terraced house on Parkdale Road for five minutes. He was about to leave when he thought he heard a noise from inside the house.

Tutting loudly, he stepped away from the door and peered through the front window. It was difficult to see inside because of the heavy net curtains. It took a while for his brain to register what he was seeing.

In the gloomy room, he could just make out a man and a

woman sitting in armchairs and two children sitting on the settee. They were all totally unmoving, as if frozen in time. The flickering images from the television provided the only animation on their pale, still faces.

He stared harder and became aware that the room was infested with house flies. The black insects covered the net curtains.

As he slowly realised what he was seeing, he recoiled from the window in horror.

He now knew that the reason none of the people in the room were moving was because they were all dead.

He staggered away from the window, gasping for breath at the enormity of what he had discovered. Fighting back an overwhelming sense of nausea, he stepped out of the small front yard and frantically looked up and down the street. In the distance, he saw a red telephone box. Dropping his mailbag in the yard, he sprinted to the telephone box, praying it hadn't been vandalised.

To his relief, when he lifted the handset, he heard a dialling tone. He quickly dialled three nines and heard the operator say, 'Emergency. Which service do you require?'

He spluttered, 'I need the police urgently. I've found an entire family dead in their house.'

'Where are you, sir?'

'I'm on Parkdale Road at Bakersfield. The dead people are at number 23. Please hurry.'

'The police are on their way. What's your name, sir?'

'My name's Ben Saunders. I was trying to deliver a parcel. It's horrible. I could see a couple of young kids in there as well.'

'As I said, the police are on their way. Please make yourself known to them when they arrive.'

Ben replaced the handset and sprinted back towards the

house of death. After three minutes nervously pacing up and down outside the house, he heard the two-tone sirens of the approaching police cars.

2

11.00am, 29 April 1988
23 Parkdale Road, Bakersfield, Nottingham

Danny Flint parked his car behind the Scenes of Crime Ford Transit van. He opened the boot, quickly donned a forensic suit and picked up a pair of overshoes before walking towards the door of number 23. He could see Rob Buxton talking to a young constable standing outside the front door.

'Good morning, Rob. I understand the bodies were discovered at nine o'clock. Why all the delay to get inside?'

'The uniform sergeant who attended initially was worried there may have been a gas leak. He called out British Gas to clear the house first. When you see how the bodies are situated, you'll understand why he took that decision.'

'Okay. Let's have a look. Has the Home Office pathologist arrived yet?'

'Seamus Carter arrived ten minutes ago. He's already inside.'

Danny signed into the scene log and slipped on the overshoes before following Rob into the living room. He stepped inside the small lounge and saw the four bodies for the first time. It was a bizarre scene. They all appeared to be sitting watching the television. Even though the windows had now been opened, the stench of death inside the stuffy room was almost overpowering.

He could see Seamus Carter bent over the adult male, examining the man's face.

Danny turned to Rob and said, 'Do we know who they are yet?'

'We've done a basic Voters Register check. That check revealed that Robert and Kate Rawlings are listed as being resident here. The parcel that was being delivered by the postman was addressed to Mr R Rawlings, at this address.'

'And the children?'

'Early enquiries with neighbours suggest the children are Timothy, aged eleven, and Susan, aged eight. This hasn't been confirmed yet.'

'Do we have a next of kin?'

'Again, the same neighbour thinks Kate Rawlings has a brother. She thinks he lives somewhere at Beeston.'

'Okay. As a top priority, I want their identifications confirmed as soon as possible.'

Danny turned to Tim Donnelly, the Scenes of Crime supervisor, and said, 'Have you fingerprinted the television?'

'Yes. There's no marks of any value.'

'Let's switch the bloody thing off, then.'

Tim nodded, stepped forward and switched off the television. The silence in the room was now deafening.

It was broken by the pathologist, Seamus Carter, who said, 'This is a strange one, Danny.'

'In what way?'

'Well, I've made a preliminary examination of each of the bodies. I can see no obvious injuries anywhere. Let me show you the only thing I've found that's out of the ordinary. Look closely at the man's face.'

Danny stepped forward and looked at the face of the dead man.

Seamus said, 'Can you see that white residue around his mouth and on his chin?'

Danny could clearly see the foamlike substance the pathologist was referring to. 'I see it. Do you know what it is?'

'It's what we find sometimes when a person has ingested poison.'

Danny started to look closer at the woman's face. Carter said, 'It's the same on all the bodies. My best guess, right now, would be a poison or other toxic material. I'll obviously know more when I can examine the bodies properly.'

'Where will the post-mortems be held?'

'At the City Hospital. I've booked the examination room for four o'clock this afternoon.'

'That's good. We need to establish a cause of death as soon as possible. This could still be death by misadventure and not murder.'

'Quite so. As I say, I'll know more after the post-mortems.'

Danny turned to Rob and said, 'Is there any sign of a forced entry? Or a struggle anywhere?'

Rob shook his head. 'None.'

'Any suicide notes anywhere?'

'Not that we've found so far.'

Danny walked from the lounge into the small kitchen at the rear of the three-bedroomed terrace, followed by Rob and Tim. He could see the sink was full of unwashed plates, glasses, and pans. There were traces of uneaten food and drink on the crockery.

He turned to Tim and said, 'Bearing in mind what Seamus has just said, make sure you and your team get samples of every trace of food and drink in this kitchen. Check the fridge and the cupboards for any other food or drink that's been opened. If it's an ingested poison, as opposed to something they've inhaled, it will be in the food.'

'Got it.'

'I want everything photographed in situ before you take samples.'

'Understood.'

Danny walked back into the lounge and stared at the two dead children. His thoughts immediately turned to his own young daughter, who had recently survived meningitis. He pushed the thought of how close he had come to losing her to the back of his mind. He could hear his voice faltering as he asked, 'What have you organised so far, Rob?'

'I've got two pairs of detectives speaking to the immediate neighbours, trying to establish what we can about the victims. Rachel is currently at Carlton police station, getting a statement from the postman who found them.'

'Good work.'

Danny broke his gaze away from the children, turned to Seamus and said, 'How long do you think they've been dead?'

'Judging by the level of decomposition, I would estimate anywhere between three and seven days.'

'Will toxicology be viable after that length of time?'

'If it's a poison, the toxin could still be apparent in the stomach contents and in the liver, depending how quickly they died. They could have been in a comatose state for quite a while prior to death.'

'Thanks, Seamus. I'll see you later, at the City Hospital.'

Danny and Rob walked outside, signing out of the crime scene log.

Danny said, 'Stay here, and work the scene with Tim and

Seamus. I'll see you at the hospital for the post-mortems later. I'm going to get things organised at Carlton police station. I think we may as well use Carlton as a base rather than driving backwards and forwards from Mansfield every day. I'll get the rest of the team travelling to Carlton so we can get cracking on researching the names we've got. Before we do anything else, we need to confirm the identities of these people and establish their next of kin. We also need to establish whether we're investigating four murders or some bizarre accident. As soon as the detectives have finished talking to the neighbours, task them with mastering the local streets for the house-to-house enquiries we'll need to do. They can also make a start on checking the surrounding streets for any CCTV opportunities. It's residential, mainly, so I don't think there'll be too many cameras.'

Rob nodded. 'Will do. What's your first impression, boss?'

'I think it's still too early to call it yet. But I want to investigate these unexplained deaths in the same way we would a murder enquiry until it's proven they're not. I don't want to miss any opportunities for evidence just because we're unsure right now. I'll gather the team at Carlton for an initial briefing at two thirty this afternoon. I want you and Tim to both be there for that briefing. Once that's done, we'll travel to the City Hospital and see what the post-mortems turn up.'

'Okay, boss.'

Danny slipped off the plastic overshoes, took off the forensic suit, then made his way back to his car.

In his mind's eye, he could still see the blank expressions on the faces of the two children sitting, frozen in death, on the settee of their home. Inside his head, all he could hear was the voice of Seamus Carter: '*This is a strange one, Danny.*'

3

2.30pm, 29 April 1988
Carlton Police Station, Nottingham

The main briefing room at Carlton police station had been transformed. Danny had spoken to the chief superintendent commanding the division, and had gained permission to establish an incident room at his station.

Within a couple of hours, the technical support team had established a bank of computers along one wall and installed further telephones.

It made sense to base the incident room in this area of the city. Danny knew most of the enquiries that the MCIU would be undertaking would be in and around this location. The move would save time and money.

He had gathered the entire Major Crime Investigation Unit at Carlton for an initial briefing.

He raised his hands, and the murmuring chatter that had been a constant noise instantly fell silent.

Danny said, 'This is going to be our home for the foreseeable future. If any of you have any major issues about travelling here instead of to Mansfield every day, come and see me after this briefing, and I'll try to address them.'

He paused before continuing: 'We have the unexplained deaths of four people to investigate, two adults and two children. DC Jefferies, can you brief us on what we know about our victims so far?'

Fran Jefferies stood up, leaned on the walking stick she used constantly and said, 'Yes, sir. The identities of the four victims have all now been confirmed. The adult male is Robert Rawlings. He was thirty-one years of age and worked as a plastics injection operator at the Marden Brothers factory in Netherfield. The adult female is his wife, Kate Rawlings. She was thirty years old and worked part time as a dinner lady at Parkdale primary school. The male child is Timothy Rawlings, the couple's son. He was eleven years old and attended the Carlton le Willows school. The female child is Susan Rawlings, the daughter. She was just eight years of age and also attended Parkdale primary school. I've arranged for photographs of all four victims for our enquiry board; they should be arriving soon. They were the only four people living at that address. There are no other children.'

'Thanks, Fran, that's excellent work. I want you and Jeff to stay with that enquiry. I want you to establish everything we can about this family. The more knowledge we have about all of them, the more chance we have of getting to the bottom of their mysterious deaths. You both know what I'm looking for. Finances? State of their marriage? What type of people they were? Were they religious? Did they belong to any unusual groups or clubs? The list is endless. Keep me regularly informed how your enquiries are progressing, okay?'

The two detectives nodded.

Danny said, 'Have you managed to trace a next of kin for the formal identification yet?'

This time it was DC Jeff Williams who answered, 'Yes, sir. The nearest next of kin we've found is Kate Rawlings's brother. The parents of both Robert and Kate are all still alive, but they live down south. Robert's parents live in Watford, and Kate's in Deal. The brother is David Mackintosh; he lives locally. His address is Westward Avenue in Beeston.'

'Have you spoken to him yet?'

'Yes, sir. As soon as I found out his details, I drove to Beeston and took him to the City Hospital. He made a formal identification of the four victims to me at two o'clock this afternoon. He told me that his sister and her family should have been on holiday this week. They always took the kids away for ten days at this time of year, as it was cheaper.'

'Did he know where?'

'They went to the same place every year: Golden Sands Caravan Park in Mablethorpe.'

'Have you confirmed this?'

'As soon as I got back here, I telephoned the caravan site. They confirmed that they had a booking for the Rawlings family and that they hadn't turned up on the twenty-seventh as expected.'

'Good work, Jeff. Come and see me afterwards. I want you to fully brief the family liaison officer on what you've learned about the brother and any other family members so far. How did David Mackintosh take the news?'

'He was devastated. He couldn't take in what had happened. According to him, his sister and brother-in-law were just an ordinary family going about their daily lives. He doesn't know of anybody who would want to harm them.'

Danny looked for DC Helen Bailey. When he saw her, he

said, 'Helen, I want you to undertake the role of family liaison officer and stay with the families of Robert and Kate. Speak to Jeff immediately after this briefing. I want you to locate as many relatives of our deceased family as you can. Speak to them all. I want to know if the rest of the family share the same opinion as Mr Mackintosh.'

'Will do, sir.'

Danny turned to Rob. 'Can you brief the team on what was discovered at 23 Parkdale Road, please?'

Rob said, 'Twenty-three Parkdale Road is a three-bedroom terraced house in Bakersfield. The family of four were all found dead in the living room of their home at nine o'clock this morning. They were discovered by a postman who was trying to deliver a parcel. He looked through the front room window and saw the family sitting down, as though they were watching the television together. There was no sign of any forced entry into the property. The front and back doors were both locked when the police arrived. No windows had been forced. There were no signs of a struggle anywhere inside the property. We haven't carried out a full search of the property yet. Scenes of Crime are still working in the house. As soon as they have completed their tests and photographs, we'll go back in and undertake a thorough search.'

Danny made eye contact with Detective Inspector Tina Cartwright and said, 'Tina, I want you to supervise the search of the property.'

'Yes, sir.'

Danny asked Tim Donnelly, 'How much longer do you think your team will need?'

Tim replied, 'We're working through the last of the bedrooms now, so we should be finished in another hour or two.'

'As soon as you're finished, let Tina know. I want that property gone through with a fine-tooth comb.'

'Will do.'

'Have you found anything of importance yet?'

'Nothing yet, sir. It's a very unusual scene. Unlike most murder scenes, there doesn't appear to be anything of obvious evidential value. There are no blood splashes, no discarded weapons, nothing on the victims. We're taking samples of all the opened food and drink in the house, as well as swabs of the food and drink left on the unwashed pots in the sink.'

'Thanks, Tim. Let's have another conversation when you've completed your work.'

Danny said to Rob, 'Seamus Carter was the pathologist attending the scene. Can you brief us all on his observations?'

'The pathologist believed the victims had all been dead for approximately three to seven days. He could find no marks of violence on any of the victims, at least, not at the scene. This will be confirmed at the post-mortem this afternoon, when he can properly examine the bodies. He will also be able to tell us then if they died where they were found. He believes that a poison or toxin of some kind is the most probable cause of death. There was a white residue found around the mouths of each of the victims that supports this theory.'

Danny turned to Tim and said, 'I take it we got swabs of that substance from the victims?'

'Yes, we have. They were taken under the direction of the pathologist.'

'Good.'

Danny paused and then said, 'So that's what we're investigating. We may know more after the post-mortems. In the meantime, I want you all to treat this enquiry in the same way as if those four people had been shot or stabbed to death. We cannot afford to think that this may not be a murder enquiry. We will treat it as such until we know different. Understood?'

There were general murmurings of agreement amongst the gathered detectives.

Danny said, 'Who started mastering the surrounding streets earlier?'

DC Simon Paine and DC Phil Baxter both stood up. Simon said, 'I've made a start on that, and Phil did the scoping for any CCTV.'

'Good, after the briefing, I want you to liaise with DS Wills and hand over to him everything you've done so far.'

Danny then looked for Andy Wills. When he saw him, he said, 'Andy, I want you to take charge of the house-to-house enquiry. It's going to be a huge undertaking. There's a lot of houses in that area of Bakersfield. See if the Special Operations Unit can assist us with some manpower.'

'Will do, sir.'

Danny asked, 'How did you get on with the CCTV, Phil?'

'I've made a list of all the cameras I've found so far. To be honest, there aren't that many.'

'I want you to stick with that enquiry. Start gathering any CCTV evidence you can find, please. DS Wills will give you the parameters to work to, okay?'

'Yes, sir.'

Danny began allocating tasks to the remaining detectives. Enquiries would be carried out at the workplaces and schools of the victims. The final role he allocated was a dedicated exhibits officer for the enquiry, assigning that to DC Nigel Singleton.

'No problem,' Nigel said. 'I'll start getting the bags and labels together that I'll need for the post-mortem examinations.'

'Come and see me as soon as you've got what you need.

The post-mortems are due to start at four o'clock this afternoon.'

'Yes, sir.'

'Okay, everyone. You all have your tasks. Anyone who hasn't personally been allocated a task, liaise with DI Cartwright. You will be carrying out the search of 23 Parkdale Road. We'll debrief again tonight at nine o'clock. I know it's going to be a long day for all of you, but let's get cracking and start making some progress.'

4

5.45pm, 29 April 1988
City Hospital Mortuary, Nottingham

Danny and Rob stood together in the examination room at the City Hospital mortuary. To the left of them stood DC Singleton, who was carrying out the task of exhibits officer. A Scenes of Crime officer was also present. Her role was to take photographs of each stage of the examination. She was guided in her task by the pathologist.

The three detectives stood in reverent silence, heads bowed, as they watched the pathologist complete the last of four post-mortems. This time, he was examining the body of the young girl, Susan Rawlings.

There was something devastating about witnessing the post-mortem of a child. All three detectives had been to many such examinations. It was something none of them would ever get used to.

The mood in the room was sombre and dark. The silence weighed heavily.

Seamus Carter and his assistant, Brigitte O'Hara, worked methodically, carrying out the same examination on the young girl as they had on the three previous bodies. He took the same samples for toxicology as he had from the other victims. Only when he had finished the examination did he finally break the silence.

He looked at Danny and said, 'There were no marks of violence on any of the bodies. The lividity present suggests to me that they died in the same seated position they were found. None of them have been moved after death. They weren't staged in the armchairs and on the settee. That's where they died.'

With his mouth feeling dry and his throat constricted, Danny croaked, 'Have you established the cause of their deaths?'

'Yes. All four died of heart failure. What the exact cause of that heart failure was still needs to be established.'

'What's your best guess?'

'I'm still of the same opinion as I was at the scene. I think all four ingested a poison, which caused immediate paralysis and, subsequently, death. It's the only scenario that explains why they were found in the positions they were. Normally, if we start to feel unwell, we move to try to remedy the situation. These people literally died where they were sitting.'

'Is there anything else you've found that supports your theory?'

'Yes, there is. When I examined the eyes of each of the victims, there's evidence of rapid onset cycloplegia.'

Rob asked bluntly, 'And what's that?'

'It's something that we often see in drug addicts when they've overdosed on certain illegal street drugs. The pupils of the eyes become distorted and out of shape due to the lack of muscle control brought about by the toxicity of whatever drug they've taken.'

Danny said, 'Do you think they took controlled drugs?'

'There's no evidence to suggest that. There are no needle marks on any of the bodies. No, I still think it will be an ingested poison of some description. I'm confident that the samples I've taken from the stomach contents and the livers of each of the victims will identify any toxin or poison present.'

'How soon will you have the results from toxicology?'

'I can fast-track them, so you should have them in the next twenty-four hours.'

'That would be brilliant. It's imperative I understand what killed this family. Until I know that, I don't really know where to start looking.'

'I understand, Danny. I'll call you as soon as I get the results.'

'Thanks. Anytime, day or night. Call me at home if you need to. You've got my number.'

'Will do.'

'One last question. Do you think this is murder or misadventure?'

The big pathologist shrugged. 'Let's wait and see what the toxicology report says. I'll have a much better idea then.'

Danny nodded, turned to Nigel Singleton and said, 'Have you got everything you need, exhibit-wise?'

'Yes, sir.'

'Right, let's get the exhibits back to Carlton. There's a lot of bags with all the victims' clothes. We'll give you a hand to carry them down to the car.'

Danny took one last look over his shoulder at the dead family. Their bodies, now devastated by the post-mortem examination, all lying in a neat row on the stainless steel benches.

It was a vision he knew would haunt him.

5

9.30pm, 29 April 1988
Carlton Police Station, Nottingham

Danny was alone in the small, windowless room, next to the main incident room, that he would be using as his office for the duration. He had just finished the debrief for the first day's enquiries and was feeling satisfied with the progress that had been made. The house-to-house enquiries had been planned out and would start in earnest tomorrow morning. Andy Wills had managed to acquire the services of the Special Operations Unit to assist for the first week.

Enquiries into the friends and relatives of the Rawlings family were progressing nicely. Arrangements had been made to start interviewing the workmates of Robert Rawlings at the Marden Brothers factory and the colleagues of Kate Rawlings at Parkdale primary school.

DC Baxter had found several possibilities for CCTV and

would begin collecting the tapes tomorrow morning, ready to start the painstaking process of long hours of viewing their contents. The only enquiry that hadn't been completed was the full search of 23 Parkdale Road. DI Cartwright and her team of detectives were still engaged in searching the property. It would be a late finish for them.

Danny grabbed his jacket and was about to leave when he heard a gentle knock on the door.

He shouted, 'Come in!'

The door opened, and Detective Sergeant Lynn Harris walked in. 'Have you got a minute, boss?'

'Of course. You look worried. Is there a problem?'

'It's not a problem, sir. I've just got something important to tell you.'

'Go on.'

'I know that now's not the best time to spring this on you, but I'm handing my resignation in tomorrow. I wanted to tell you first.'

Danny was shocked and sat back down. He gestured for Lynn to take a seat and said, 'I'm not going to lie, Lynn; that's come as a massive shock. I always thought you enjoyed your work on the MCIU.'

Lynn smiled. 'It's not like that. I love my job. My circumstances have changed, that's all. As you know, I already have two kids who are both under seven. Well, last week I found out that I'm expecting my third child.'

'Congratulations. You and Phil must be overjoyed with that news. I still don't understand why you want to resign from the force, though. You know I'll always support you with any time-off request, and there'll be additional maternity leave available to you.'

'Thank you, sir. I understand all that. Ever since we received the news from the doctor confirming my pregnancy, my husband and I have done nothing but discuss my options.

My decision to resign hasn't been an easy one. After a lot of soul searching, the conclusion I reached was that I'm now at the stage in my life where I want to devote my time to being a mother to my children. It was hard enough trying to juggle my duties as a detective sergeant with being a mum when I just had the two little ones. I think with a new baby to take care of as well, it would just be too much.'

Danny said nothing for a while. Then he said, 'Will you be okay financially?'

'Phil's business is doing well, so there's no need for me to earn a wage. I've always wanted to be a full-time mother, and now I have the chance to do just that. I've enjoyed every minute of this job, and working on the MCIU has been the highlight of my career.'

'I can see that you and your husband have given this a lot of thought, and I'm not going to try to change your mind. I genuinely wish you and your family all the very best in the future. I will say one thing, Lynn, you'll be sorely missed by myself and everyone else around here. How much notice will you work?'

'I'm owed three weeks' leave, so I'll only be here for a week after I hand in my resignation.'

Danny stood up and offered the sergeant his hand. They shook hands, and Danny said, 'Do you want me to tell everyone? Or would you prefer to do that yourself?'

'I really don't want any fuss. I'll tell people nearer the time if that's okay with you?'

'That's fine by me. Thanks for letting me know, Lynn, and I really do wish you, Phil, and your ever-growing family all the very best for the future.'

A beaming Lynn Harris said, 'Thanks, boss.'

As soon as she had left the office, Danny grabbed his car keys, slipped his jacket on and made his way to the car park. He was thoughtful as he walked outside into the cold night air. It was a bombshell he could have done without after what had been a very long day.

Lynn Harris was an intelligent, conscientious and extremely capable detective. She'd be difficult to replace.

As his thoughts turned to replacements, he recalled that Rachel Moore had recently passed her promotion board and was expecting a promotion to the rank of sergeant at any time. Maybe he could arrange for Rachel to be promoted to detective sergeant and remain in post on the MCIU.

It would be a much easier task to find a new detective constable to join the unit than a new sergeant who had no idea how the tight-knit group of detectives operated.

With those thoughts in his mind, he started the long drive home to Mansfield. This commute was going to be a real pain and would impact greatly on the amount of time he would be able to spend with his wife and daughter.

Suddenly, he had every sympathy for Lynn Harris and totally understood why she wanted to be a full-time parent to her children.

6

1.30am, 4 June 1982
Port Arthur Road, Sneinton, Nottingham

Nabin Panchal couldn't sleep. He sat up in bed and looked across the small room to the bed occupied by his father. He could hear his slow, rhythmic breathing in the dark. He could tell his father was also awake.

He didn't want to wake his mother or sister, who were sleeping in the room next door, so he whispered, 'Father, are you still awake?'

The older man grumbled softly, 'Go to sleep, Nabin.'

The younger man persisted. 'I want to talk.'

'Well, I don't. Go to sleep.'

'How much longer are we going to live like this? Renting these two rooms in Uncle's house. Don't you miss sharing a bed with your wife?'

'What do you want me to say? You know we must stay with

your mother's uncle. We've no money for anything else. I cannot get the job I should have, because I'm a foreigner here.'

'It's been almost ten years now. You've given up, haven't you? When was the last time you actually applied for a proper job?'

Aadesh was becoming angry. He growled, 'Yes, I've stopped bloody looking. What's the point? Nobody wants to know about my qualifications. In this country, I'm deemed worthless. I'm only good for sweeping up and cleaning at the cycle factory. At least I get paid a small wage. What do you do?'

'Without the food I grow at my allotment, we would all starve on the pittance you earn. And I have a job as well.'

'Oh yes, the big man has a job. Washing dishes at the restaurant. At your age, I was doing important work as a biochemist, not washing dishes.'

A bitter silence filled the room.

After five minutes, Nabin said, 'Let's not argue, Father. I just want a better future for us all. Why can't we use the money and the jewellery we brought with us to get our own house? You've seen the looks we get from auntie. Aren't you sick of her looking down her nose at us?'

'You don't understand. We can't spend that money. We may need it to get back to Uganda.'

'No, you don't understand, baabujii. *We can never go back there. We must try to make a life here.'*

'Among the bigots and racists who don't want our kind here?'

'They let us come here to live when Amin exiled us. They brought us to safety when we were in danger.'

'You don't know what you're talking about. They didn't do us any favours. We were all British passport holders. It was our right to live here, but they all hate us being here.'

'Not everyone thinks like that. I have good friends at the allotments. You should come with me one day and meet them.'

'I'm not a botanist like you, son. I have no interest in plants and the soil.'

'You must know that none of us are happy in this house. Please think about spending that money, baabujii.*'*

'I'll think about it. Now go to sleep, Nabi.'

7

10.00am, 30 April 1988
Nottingham Police Headquarters

Danny had just finished briefing Detective Chief Superintendent Adrian Potter about the investigation into the deaths at Bakersfield. He had painstakingly explained the enquiries he had already commenced.

Potter looked troubled and leaned back in his chair. He twirled a pencil between his fingers and said, 'You've set all that in motion already. Good God, man. You don't even know if you're investigating a murder yet.'

'I can't afford to run the risk of losing any possible evidence, so I need to treat these suspicious deaths exactly as if I'm investigating four murders. If it all turns out to be a tragic accident, I'll be the first to close everything down.'

'And I understand you've commandeered the briefing room at Carlton police station to use as the incident room.'

'Yes, sir. I cleared it with the divisional commander there. It makes sense to parade on and off duty at Carlton rather than traipsing back and forth to Mansfield every day.'

'Good decision. One that should save you a lot of time. How soon will you have the toxicology reports?'

'I'm hoping to get them later today. Those reports will give us a better indication of whether we're looking at foul play or not.'

'Okay. Well, keep me informed, one way or the other.'

'Will do, sir," He paused and then continued, 'There's something else I need to speak to you about.'

Potter looked over the top of his glasses. 'What's that, Chief Inspector?'

'Detective Sergeant Lynn Harris is handing in her resignation this week. She's expecting her third child and wants to concentrate on raising her family.'

'That's going to leave you short of a supervisor. Couldn't she delay her decision for a few months?'

'She's pregnant and has made her choice, so I don't see her wanting to delay that decision.'

Potter grunted disapprovingly.

'It will leave me short-staffed, but it wouldn't be fair to ask her to wait. I'll be sorry to lose Lynn. She's a bloody good detective.'

'Are you going to advertise the post?'

'I think that whole process will take too long. I really need somebody to fill the void quickly.' Danny again paused, 'I did have one thought on the matter. DC Rachel Moore has recently passed her promotion board. I was hoping the chief constable might consider promoting her to detective sergeant and allowing her to remain on the MCIU. She's well respected by all her colleagues, is an extremely capable detective, and has been with the MCIU since its inception.'

Potter was thoughtful for a few seconds and then nodded.

'I'll speak to the chief constable today and recommend her promotion immediately. I know he thinks very highly of DC Moore, so it shouldn't be a problem.'

'It will be much easier for me to fill the vacancy for a detective constable post than it would be for the detective sergeant one. We already have a list of applicants, who only just missed out on the last intake. They were told at the time that should a vacancy arise in the near future, they would be offered the post.'

'That's excellent. I'll let you know Jack Renshaw's decision as soon as possible.'

Danny stood to leave and said, 'Thank you, sir.'

As he reached the office door, Potter said, 'Chief Inspector, I want to know what those toxicology reports say as soon as you get them.'

'Understood, sir.'

8

3.00pm, 30 April 1988
Incident Room, Carlton Police Station, Nottingham

Tim Donnelly walked into the incident room and said, 'Has anybody seen DCI Flint?'

Fran Jefferies replied, 'He'll be in the room next door. He's using that as his office while we're all here.'

'Okay, thanks.'

Tim walked along the corridor, tapped lightly on the door and walked in. Danny had his head down, reading the statements obtained the day before.

Tim said, 'You wanted to see me, boss.'

Danny looked up. 'Grab a seat and tell me how you and your team got on at Parkdale Road yesterday. I know it was a late finish for you all. That's why I asked to see you this afternoon.'

'It *was* a late one. It was almost two in the morning by the time we secured the place and left.'

'Tell me about the forensic side of things first, and then we'll have a chat about the actual physical search of the property.'

Tim opened the folder he had brought with him and handed Danny a typed list. 'This is a list of every sample of food and drink we took. It covers what it is, where it was found, and has a cross reference to the photograph album we're preparing.'

Danny looked at the list. It was extremely comprehensive and easy to follow. As he read, he said, 'This is good work, Tim. Have you submitted all these samples to the Forensic Science Service?'

'They've all been sent today.'

'How soon will we have a result?'

'It's hard to say. Because of the volume of samples, I couldn't fast-track them all. I've asked for the samples we took from the unwashed dishes found in the sink to be fast-tracked. I'm hoping we'll have some answers within a week.'

'If Seamus Carter can identify the type of toxin used, from the samples he took from the victims, could that speed up the FSS testing?'

'It could do. If that's the case, and Seamus does identify the poison ingested, I'll certainly ask the question.'

'Did you find anything useful, forensically?'

'As you can imagine, there were fingerprints everywhere. The fingerprints of all four deceased were obtained at the post-mortems. I have three people in the fingerprint identification bureau who are comparing those four sets of prints with all the fingerprints we lifted at the scene. As you can appreciate, that's going to be a time-consuming job.'

'I know, but I'm worried that time is the one thing we may not have. Keep checking how they're progressing, Tim.'

'Will do. I checked before I came over to see you. So far, all the prints we lifted have matched those of the deceased.'

'Anything else?'

'Albums of all the photographs taken at the scene and the four post-mortems are being prepared. You should have those by tomorrow.'

'Good. What about the physical search? Did that turn up anything?'

'DI Cartwright has the log of all the items seized. There was nothing startling. I know she seized anything connected with the deceased's work, school, family or finances. There was no "smoking gun" found, if that's what you're asking.'

'Okay. I want you to stay on top of the Forensic Science Service. We can't afford for them to drag their feet. I'll let you know if Seamus has had any joy, once I've seen the toxicology reports. I know you and your staff all had a long day yesterday, so don't be late off today. There's no need for you to stay for tonight's debrief.'

'No problem, sir. Talk to you soon.'

As the Scenes of Crime supervisor was going out the door, Danny shouted after him, 'Don't forget to keep chasing the FSS!'

'Will do, sir.'

9

8.30pm, 30 April 1988
Incident Room, Carlton Police Station, Nottingham

Danny sat down heavily in his office chair. He had just finished debriefing the day's enquiries. A start had been made, but he was feeling disappointed at the progress. It seemed that most of the day had been spent researching the various enquiries to be done.

He knew his staff had all worked hard, and that it was necessary for them to establish exactly what was needed. Tomorrow would be much more productive. The detectives tasked with investigating the co-workers of Robert and Kate Rawlings now had a definitive list of the names and addresses of the people they needed to speak to. Arrangements had been made to interview the school friends of Timothy and Susan Rawlings. This had been a particularly delicate thing to organise, as all the children would need to be spoken to in the presence of their parents.

DC Baxter had made good progress seizing CCTV tapes from various businesses and private houses in the vicinity of Parkdale Road. He would start the long process of viewing the tapes in the morning.

DC Moore had been tasked with investigating the Rawlings family finances. She had been held up getting the court order that would allow her to view the family's bank details.

DC Bailey had worked flat out all day, identifying names and addresses of all the dead family's relatives. Her task was going to be monumental, so Danny had now assigned DC Sam Blake to assist her.

The house-to-house enquiries were progressing steadily with the assistance of the Special Operations Unit. Danny was satisfied that it would be completed within a week.

What he really needed was that telephone call from Seamus Carter. Until that came, he still had no idea what it was they were investigating. Were the deaths of this ordinary family of four all just an avoidable, tragic accident, or something far more sinister?

10

10.00pm, 30 April 1988
Mansfield, Nottinghamshire

Danny was at home, watching television. He was trying hard to concentrate on the late night news and failing miserably. His mind kept wandering away from the news reports to the deaths of the Rawlings family. He hated this feeling of limbo he was experiencing. The sooner he knew the cause of their deaths, the happier he would feel about trying to determine what had happened to them.

Sue had picked up on her husband's distracted mood and moved from the armchair to sit at his side on the settee.

She said, 'Is everything okay?'

'I'm fine. Just a bit preoccupied with work.'

'Anything you want to talk about?'

'I just feel stuck. I'm investigating the deaths of four people, two of them young children, and I still don't know if they died because of some tragic accident, or if they were killed.'

Sue knew there was nothing she could say to alter her husband's mood, so she just snuggled in next to him and whispered, 'I'm sure things will become clearer soon.'

The telephone in the hallway began to ring. Danny leapt from the settee to answer it before it woke his sleeping daughter. On the third ring, he snatched up the telephone and said, 'Danny Flint.'

Seamus Carter said, 'Sorry to ring you so late at home, but you did say to contact you at any time.'

'It's no problem, Seamus.'

'I tried to phone the incident room at Carlton about an hour ago, but nobody picked up.'

'Like I said, no problem. How come you're working so late?'

'I finally received the Rawlings toxicology reports this evening. I've been reading through them, and I think I've found something significant.'

This was what Danny had been waiting for all day. He had been bracing himself for the possibility of the tests being inconclusive. This sounded encouraging.

With just a hint of excitement in his voice, he asked, 'What do the tests show?'

'The samples taken all show abnormally high levels of a toxin called scopolamine.'

'Even the children?'

'Yes. The stomach contents and livers of each of the victims all showed these extreme levels of scopolamine.'

'What would the effects be?'

'In such high levels, this toxin would cause tachycardia, leading to heart failure.'

'How would that manifest itself?'

'In layman's terms, the amount of toxin they had all

ingested would have caused rapid onset paralysis, alongside a massively increased heart rate. This is known as acute tachycardia. They would have been unable to move as the major muscles in their bodies became paralysed. Eventually, the increased heart rate would have led to heart failure and then death. This is also backed up by the rapid onset cycloplegia I pointed out to you at the post-mortems.'

'That's horrendous. Would they have known they were dying?'

'It's possible. Certainly, the adults would have understood something was seriously wrong.'

Danny was silent as the enormity and horror of what he was hearing sank in.

After a long pause, he said, 'And this toxin was found in their stomach contents. Does this mean it was definitely something they all ate or drank?'

'Yes.'

'How long between eating or drinking whatever it was before the paralysis set in?'

'Hard to be precise, but certainly long enough for the family to have cleared the table and settled down in front of the television to watch their programme.'

'What can you tell me about scopolamine?'

'I know it can be found in some street drugs, but it's usually associated with plant-based alkaloid poisons. I'll do some research and get back to you tomorrow.'

'Thanks.'

Danny was thoughtful for a few seconds and then said, 'Are you free to join me at Carlton Police Station tomorrow morning, around ten o'clock, so you can brief the team on what we should be looking for?'

'I'll just check my diary.'

Danny heard a thud as Seamus put his phone down onto something hard. There was a brief pause before the pathologist said, 'That's fine. I'll see you at Carlton at ten o'clock. I should have some answers for you by then. I'll try to establish the most common substances that contain abnormally high levels of scopolamine. It could help you with tracing the same toxin in the food and drink seized from the house.'

'That would be good, if you can. It could speed things up with the Forensic Science Service.'

There was a brief silence, and then Danny continued, 'Do you think I'm investigating a murder or an accident?'

'That's the million-dollar question. Right now, looking at the high levels of toxin found in these toxicology tests, I would lean towards foul play. I can't think of anything sold as food or drink that would have that concentration of this particular toxin in.'

'Thanks, Seamus. See you in the morning.'

Danny replaced the telephone and walked back into the lounge.

Sue looked up and said, 'Who was that calling at this time of night?'

'Seamus Carter, the pathologist.'

'Has he managed to set your mind at rest?'

'Not really. He's identified the toxin that killed the family. All I need to do now is find the source of that toxin.'

'What is it?'

'Scopolamine, whatever that is.'

'Oh, deadly nightshade contains that. When I worked on the casualty department at the hospital, I dealt with a few cases of scopolamine poisoning in toddlers who had eaten deadly nightshade berries. They were very sick, but it was never fatal. It must have been extremely concentrated to cause the deaths of these people.'

'It leaves me with more questions than answers, as usual. I'm going to turn in now. I'm bushed.'

'Me too. I've got a long shift at the hospital tomorrow. I

know you're going to be working long hours on this enquiry, and I don't want you to worry about Hayley. I've spoken to the childminder, and she's happy to have her for the duration of my shifts.'

'That's good to know. I've no idea what time I'll be getting finished. This bloody commute to Carlton every day isn't helping.'

11

6.00pm, 15 January 1986
Hungerhill Road, St Ann's, Nottingham

Nabin Panchal hated his life.

He was now thirty-two years old. He felt that his life was slipping by without him being able to achieve any of his dreams. He had been stuck in dead-end jobs ever since he and his family had arrived in Nottingham.

As a skilled botanist who had studied at the Kyambogo University and the National Agricultural Research Laboratories in Kampala, he had always envisaged his life would be spent doing important work with plants.

Now he was reduced to washing mountains of dirty dishes every night at a local Indian restaurant.

As he traipsed through the cold, dark streets of Nottingham, heading for the Taj Mahal Tandoori Palace at Sneinton, he felt ready to give up. The thin coat he wore barely kept out the cold, and he shivered as he walked.

Nothing he said to his father ever seemed to get through. The old man had lost all his drive and ambition. He had been reduced to a bitter shell of a man, who blamed everyone else for his shortcomings.

As he reached the corner of Hungerhill Road with Aster Road, something caught his eye.

There was a garishly coloured 'For Sale' board displayed on the wall outside the small grocery shop situated on the corner.

Nabin saw that the lights inside the shop were still on, so he stepped inside and spoke to the man behind the counter: 'Are you selling your shop?'

Bill Strathdon was a terse man at the best of times. After yet another long day on his feet in the shop, the old man was feeling particularly tetchy. His sarcastic reply reflected his mood. 'Is that what the sign says on the wall outside?'

Nabin didn't recognise the sarcasm and replied, 'Yes, it does. How much do you want?'

Bill Strathdon's attention levels suddenly shot up. 'Are you interested in being a shopkeeper, son?'

'It depends how much you want for it, but I think my family might be interested.'

Strathdon reached below the counter, grabbed one of the brochures prepared by the estate agent and said, 'Take this home with you. Everything you need to know is in there. If you're still interested after you've spoken to your family, come back and see me. I'm warning you, though, there's been a lot of interest in the business already.'

A beaming Nabin took the brochure and said, 'Thank you, thank you. I'll speak with my father. We'll both come and see you tomorrow.'

Nabin left the shop and carried on walking to work. He had a huge smile on his face as he read the contents of the brochure. The shop also had a self-contained, three-bedroom flat upstairs. Not only was this a great chance to have their own business and earn some real money, but it would also give them the chance to escape the house owned by his great-uncle.

For the first time in years, Nabin felt there was hope. All he had to do now was convince his father.

12

11.00pm, 15 January 1986
Port Arthur Road, Sneinton, Nottingham

It had been another long night bent over the sink, washing endless piles of dirty dishes, at the restaurant. Nabin was exhausted. He poured himself a glass of water and walked, heavy-footed, up the stairs to his family's rooms. As he passed his great-uncle's bedroom, on the first-floor landing, the door opened, and his great-aunt stepped outside. 'I don't appreciate being woken up at this time of night. You sound like a herd of elephants coming up the stairs. Why can't you have some consideration for others, you ignorant man.'

Nabin bit his lip and just said, 'I'm sorry, Auntie. I've just got in from work. I didn't mean to wake you.'

The old woman tutted loudly and flounced back inside her bedroom.

Nabin climbed the final flight of stairs and walked into the room his family used as a sitting room. It also doubled as the men's bedroom. The light was still on, meaning his father was still awake.

When Nabin walked in, his father was sitting at the small table. He was bent over, with his head in his hands. His mother and sister were nowhere to be seen.

Nabin said, ‘Have Mum and Padama gone to bed?’

Aadesh nodded. ‘How was work?’

Nabin shrugged. ‘The same as always.’

There was a tension in the air that was palpable. Nabin got the duvets from the cupboard and began preparing the pull-out bed and the settee into their beds. He looked across at his father, who was still holding his head in his hands, and asked, ‘Is everything okay, baabujii*?’*

His father shook his head. With his voice cracking with emotion, he said, ‘Not really. There’s been an enormous row tonight. Your great-aunt wants us to leave. She told your mother that we’ve lived off their charity for too long, and she wants us all out.’

Nabin knew the old lady resented their presence in her house, but he never thought she would ask them to leave. They were family, after all.

He said, ‘What did Uncle say?’

‘He told the old woman to be quiet, and that it was his house. He said we were welcome to stay as long as we needed to.’

Nabin could see genuine rage in his father’s eyes when he said, ‘Your mother was so upset; it made me so angry.’

He tentatively took the brochure from his coat pocket and said, ‘Look at this, baabujii*. We should buy it.’*

The old man began reading the estate agents brochure. When he got to the price, he said, ‘It’s way too much money. We could never afford that.’

‘Yes, we can. We would only need to raise enough money for a deposit. We could get a mortgage for the rest. We would have our own business, where we could earn some real money. There’s also a

three-bedroom flat above the shop. We could have a real future there.'

Aadesh was hesitant. 'I don't know. It would mean we had a lot of debt. What if the business failed? We'd be left with nothing.'

'We're all hard workers; we wouldn't allow it to fail. Trust me, I pass this little shop every night on my way to work, it's always full of customers. It's a gold mine.'

'If it's so bloody good, why is it up for sale?'

'Because the man who owns it is old. He looked totally fed up with his life. I think he wants to retire, but to do that, he needs to sell the shop. I'm telling you, baabujii; *we could make a real future for ourselves there. Why don't you come and see it with me tomorrow morning?'*

The old man climbed into the uncomfortable pull-out bed and said, 'I'll think about it in the morning.'

'No. Think about it now. Instead of trying to sleep in that uncomfortable pull-out bed every night, you would be able to get into a soft comfortable bed, next to Mother. Me and Padama would have our own rooms, and the best thing of all, you would never have to look at auntie's poisonous face again. We would have money to spend on whatever we wanted. Who knows, with a real future, I might even be able to get a wife.'

The old man suddenly sat up in bed and hissed, 'Okay, Nabi. We'll go and see the bloody shop tomorrow. Now can we go to sleep?'

Nabin was beaming from ear to ear. He knew that as soon as his father saw the shop and the flat, Nabin would be able to convince him to sell the family gold and jewellery to raise the deposit for a mortgage. He turned out the light and settled down on the settee, slowly getting warm beneath the thick duvet. He knew the excitement he was feeling wouldn't allow him to get any sleep.

13

10.00am, 1 May 1988
Incident Room, Carlton Police Station, Nottingham

It was standing room only in the small room Danny was using as his office. He had called a meeting to discuss the toxicology reports from the Rawlings family post-mortems.

Crammed into the office with him were Seamus Carter, DI Buxton, DI Cartwright, and Tim Donnelly.

Danny said, 'Seamus, thanks for coming over this morning. Can you explain to everyone what was found in the toxicology tests, please?'

'Sure. Each of the victims was found to have high levels of a toxin called scopolamine in their livers and in the contents of their stomachs.'

Tim Donnelly scribbled down the name of the toxin and said, 'Do you think the Forensic Science Service would be able to find scopolamine in the food and drink samples we sent to them for analysis?'

'I don't see why not. The levels were extremely high, so I would expect there to be traces in the food and drink samples.'

Danny said, 'Get straight onto them after this briefing, Tim. We need to know exactly what it was they all ingested that poisoned them.'

'Will do.'

Danny looked at his two detective inspectors and said, 'We have to treat this as a murder enquiry. I know we have no suspects and no obvious motive, but I don't think these are accidental deaths.'

Seamus said, 'I totally agree. I can't think of anything innocent that would produce the high levels of scopolamine we found in the toxicology tests. Something had been deliberately added to whatever it was these people ate or drank.'

Tina said, 'Where is scopolamine usually found?'

The burly pathologist said, 'As soon as I got the results yesterday, I started doing some research. Scopolamine is an alkaloid, naturally found in certain plants, with varying levels of toxicity. There's a species found in the tropics called *Brugmansia*. These are the only plants that generate toxicity levels like the ones we found in the toxicology reports.'

Rob said, 'Can these plants be grown here?'

'*Brugmansia* is usually found in much hotter climates. It was used as a decorative houseplant in Victorian times but isn't popular now.'

Danny asked, 'What else can you tell us about *Brugmansia*?'

'It has the common name of Angel's Trumpets because of the long, pendulous flowers produced by the mature plant. It grows naturally in all hotter climates, from South America through Africa to the jungles of the far east. A lot of those countries have now banned its propagation because of its toxic nature.'

He paused before continuing, 'It has been used widely by shamans in South America and witch doctors in Africa to produce a powerful hallucinogen. Unfortunately, a lot of the people who ingested the liquid, which is made from boiling the leaves and seeds of these plants, subsequently died.'

Rob looked at Tim and said, 'Did you find any house-plants at the scene? I can't recall seeing any.'

Tim said, 'There were no houseplants anywhere.'

Danny said, 'Okay. As a top priority, we need to establish what it was this family ate or drank that contained this poison. Once we do that, we can try to ascertain how it got there, and who would have the access and opportunity to put it there. Tim, get onto the Forensic Science Service straight away. This must be treated as a top priority.'

He paused, then said, 'My biggest fear is that this family were targeted at random. If that's the case, then other lives could be in danger.'

14

11.00am, 1 May 1988
Misterton Lodge, Cragmoor Road, Burton Joyce, Nottingham

Fred Turner had enjoyed his morning labours. For the retired miner, being a self-employed gardener was so much more satisfying than working underground.

Part of him had been overjoyed when he had been made redundant from Gedling Colliery. That was over two years ago. He now had a thriving gardening business that paid all his bills and left him plenty of spare cash to buy a little of what he fancied, every now and then.

Life was good.

He enjoyed the simple pleasures of breathing in fresh air and toiling away with the sky above his head.

As well as the better working conditions, Fred also got to meet some lovely people. Today was no different. He had been busy getting the garden of Derek and Sheila Judd ready for the summer. The spring flowers had been magnificent, but he had spent the morning clearing all the beds of the daffodil and crocus tops, ready to plant the annuals. He had just finished cutting the vast lawn and was now ready for his morning cup of tea.

Sheila always made him a hot drink around eleven o'clock, and there was usually a plate of biscuits or home-made cake to go with it. She had always said if she wasn't around at eleven o'clock, to just knock on the back door and remind her.

He had knocked on the back door a few times, but there was no answer. He knew the couple were at home because their Jaguar was still parked on the driveway.

It was puzzling why nobody had answered his knocking. He began to forget about his cup of tea and started to feel a little anxious.

There must be something wrong.

With a real sense of trepidation, the ex-collier made his way to the front of the house. He knocked loudly on the front door, glancing up at the bedroom windows as he did so. The curtains had all been opened, so the couple weren't still in bed.

There was no answer to his loud knocking, so he began to look in the downstairs windows. The first window he looked in, at the front of the house, was the lounge. The room was as big as his tiny, terraced house in Netherfield. He peered inside, but could see no sign of the elderly couple.

He made his way to the side of the house, where the French doors led into the dining room, and looked inside. The sight that greeted him made him gasp out loud. He staggered back away from the glass.

Plucking up all his courage, he tried the handle on the French doors, but they were locked. He stared through the glass at the horrific sight inside.

The couple had obviously been having their breakfast at the long dining table. He could see Derek Judd lying on the floor at the side of the table. His chair had been tipped up, and he had fallen face first onto the carpet. He wasn't moving and was a deathly colour.

Sheila Judd was a petite woman, and she had remained seated on a dining room chair. She had slumped forward and was now lying face-first on the table. Her face was resting on the remnants of her breakfast, her hair mixed in with leftover bacon and eggs.

He could see that the table had been laid for breakfast. There were sauce bottles and salt and pepper pots, as well as coffee cups. A fancy French coffee-making contraption and half-empty glasses of fruit juice were also on the table. There were slices of toast in the rack that had remained untouched.

There was a newspaper lying on the floor next to Derek Judd.

Fred Turner had seen dead bodies before, both at the mine where he had previously worked, and with members of his own family. He knew that the delightful old couple were both dead.

He raced around to the front of the house and jumped in his Ford Escort van. Without putting on his seat belt, he accelerated down the driveway and out onto the street. He had driven down three streets before he saw a public telephone box.

He braked hard, and the van screeched to a halt. He leapt from the van and ran inside the telephone kiosk.

He was breathless when he spoke to the operator. 'You need to send the police to Misterton Lodge, Cragmoor Road, Burton Joyce, as quick as you can. I've found Mr and Mrs Judd in their dining room. I think they're both dead.'

15

11.50am, 1 May 1988
Misterton Lodge, Cragmoor Road, Burton Joyce, Nottingham

Danny was standing just outside the front door of Misterton Lodge, getting some fresh air. The stench of death seemed to be everywhere in the house. It was extremely warm inside the house, as the central heating radiators were all on full blast.

The attending detectives and Scenes of Crime personnel had opened several windows to try to alleviate the smell, but to no avail.

Danny saw Seamus Carter's battered Volvo pull up at the end of the driveway next to all the other police vehicles.

Seamus and Brigitte O'Hara donned forensic suits and walked towards the house. Seamus was carrying his small black case.

The constable on the front door, who was keeping the

scene log, asked, 'Do you know who they are, sir?'

'That's Seamus Carter, the home office pathologist, and his assistant, Brigitte O'Hara.'

The constable wrote their names into the log. 'Thanks, sir.'

Seamus walked directly up to Danny and said, 'Your control room told me it's identical to the Parkdale Road scene. Is that right?'

Danny shook his head. 'The scenes are as different as chalk and cheese. The dead families couldn't be further apart on the social scale. You saw Parkdale Road, a small terrace house. This is like a bloody mansion inside.'

'So why did they say they were identical?'

'Whatever killed the Rawlings family at Parkdale Road, looks as though it's been used again to kill Derek and Sheila Judd here.'

'You think they've been poisoned?'

'It certainly looks that way to me. Let's go inside, and you can see for yourself.'

The pathologist and his assistant followed Danny through the beautiful house to the dining room. Inside the large room, Scenes of Crime technicians were busily getting samples of all the food and drink on the table.

Danny said, 'Don't forget to get samples from the two sauce bottles.'

One of the white-suited technicians nodded and carefully began to brush powder onto one of the sauce bottles. She said, 'We just need to check the bottles for fingerprints first, sir. Then we'll be obtaining samples of the contents.'

Cameras flashed and film whirred softly as the Scenes of Crime staff made a photographic record of everything in the room.

Seamus stepped forward and squatted down next to the body of Derek Judd.

He turned to Tim Donnelly and said, 'Have you got all the photographs you need? Are we okay to move them?'

'We've got everything we need. They're all yours.'

Very carefully, Seamus rolled the dead man onto his back and examined his eyes.

He said, 'There's evidence of rapid onset cycloplegia again. There's also a white residue around his mouth that looks identical to what we saw on the Parkdale Road victims.'

He stood up and walked to the body of Sheila Judd.

He turned to Brigitte and said, 'Brig, can you stand that side of her, please? I want to try to sit her up. You'll need to support her head while I examine her eyes and mouth.'

The two pathologists then lifted Sheila Judd until she was back in a seated position. While Brigitte supported the dead woman, Seamus examined the tiny woman's eyes.

He said, 'Look at this, Danny. It's identical to all the other victims. This woman's pupils are massively distorted and enlarged. Cycloplegia again.'

Danny stepped forward and looked for himself. The distortion was plain to see. 'How long do you think they've been dead?'

'I know the decomposition looks bad, but it's so bloody hot in this house, I'm a little surprised it's not worse than it is. I'm not the detective here, Danny, but seeing as they were eating what looks like a full English breakfast, and the newspaper he was reading is the *Sunday Times*, I think it's fair to say this occurred on Sunday morning. Which was four days ago.'

Danny gave Seamus a dryly humorous look and said, 'I had noticed the newspaper was one of the *Sundays*, but thanks for pointing it out.'

Seamus winked at the senior detective, who was also a good friend, and said, 'I knew you would have, Danny. How soon before we can get the bodies to the mortuary?'

Danny glanced at his watch. 'The undertakers should be here in half an hour. Are you happy for us to move them?'

'More than happy. The sooner we can get started on the post-mortem examinations, the better. I'm pretty sure the examination and the toxicology results will be the same as for the Rawlings family. Massive heart failure caused by rapid onset tachycardia as a result of ingesting high levels of scopolamine.'

'Can I leave you and Tina to arrange the transportation to the mortuary?'

'Of course. The post-mortems will be at the City Hospital at two o'clock this afternoon.'

'Thanks, Seamus. I'll see you there.'

Danny walked out of the dining room and shouted to Rob Buxton, who was upstairs.

Rob walked downstairs and said, 'Did you want me, boss?'

'How's the search progressing?'

'No sign of any forced entry anywhere, no signs of a struggle. It's like a carbon copy of the Parkdale Road scene.'

'I know. That's what's worrying me. What have you organised so far?'

'DC Blake is obtaining a witness statement from the gardener, Fred Turner. I've got the remainder of available staff carrying out a search of the property and the grounds. It's going to be a long job.'

Danny looked around the vast hallway. 'There's a lot of houseplants here. Make sure we arrange for a plant expert to have a look at them. We need to make sure we haven't got any samples of that plant Seamus was on about.'

'*Brugmansia*.'

'That's it. Who do we have left at Carlton?'

'There's only Fran and Rachel left at the incident room.

When the call first came in, I scrambled everyone to travel straight here.'

'That's okay. I would have done the same thing if I'd been in the office instead of being stuck in that meeting with the divisional chief superintendent. I can't believe he was already wanting to know how long we would need the incident room for. Christ! We've only been in there a few days.' Danny got his annoyance under control and went on. 'I want you to stay here and supervise the search. Tina's going to remain with Seamus and meet me at the City Hospital for the post-mortems later. I'll need you to release Nigel Singleton from the search. I want him to attend the post-mortems as exhibits officer again. There's no doubt in my mind that these deaths are linked. I need to get back to Carlton and speak to Fran and Rachel. I need to establish if there's any connection between the Rawlings family and the Judds.'

Danny paused to allow Rob to take note of his instructions, and then said, 'As you complete areas of the search and people become free, task them to scope the area for any CCTV opportunities. I'll also need somebody to master the local streets. We need to be ready to start any house-to-house enquiries I decide to do later.'

'Will do, boss. I'll go and find Nigel now and tell him to get back to the incident room.'

Danny signed himself out of the crime scene and took off his forensic suit, overshoes and gloves. He walked slowly along the gravel driveway and made his way back to his car parked on Cragmoor Road.

He was deep in thought as he drove back to Carlton. What he had feared from the outset of the Rawlings enquiry had just happened. It now appeared that he was dealing with multiple random victims who had all died in the same way.

How on earth am I going to find the warped individual who poisoned all these people?

16

11.00am, 12 March 1986
The Ropewalk, Nottingham

Bill Strathdon walked out of his solicitor's office, feeling a mixture of elation and relief. He never thought the sale of the property would go through, but today it had all been finalised. He was no longer the owner of the Aster Road corner shop.

He had been desperately trying to sell the shop and the stock inside it ever since his friend on the county council planning department had told him of Valumart's intention to develop land close to the shop. He knew that development, when it came, would sound the death knell for the little shop that had provided him a living nearly all his working life.

He had known that he would only have until that planning application was made public to sell the property. Nobody in their right mind would purchase it once the giant supermarket chain's intentions were revealed.

He had played things very craftily when he had been approached by the two Asian men. Pretending that there was overwhelming interest in the shop, as it was so profitable. He would have gladly accepted whatever they offered him. In the end, they had agreed to pay the full asking price.

As he walked through the city centre, Bill Strathdon contemplated his retirement. A lovely little bungalow, near the east coast somewhere, would suit him down to the ground. No more early morning starts and late night finishes. No more trips to the cash and carry. No more loading and unloading his small van, with heavy, backbreaking boxes of groceries.

The truth was that he should have sold the shop ten years ago, but the profits were so good, greed kept him working.

He was now sixty-eight and not in the best of health. It was time for him to retire and put his feet up.

He spared no thoughts for the unfortunate Asian family who had bought the shop, though he knew it would soon become a millstone around their necks.

He was just glad it was now their problem and not his anymore.

17

8.00pm, 15 July 1986
Hungerhill Road, St Ann's, Nottingham

It had been three months since the Panchal family had taken ownership of the corner shop at the junction of Hungerhill Road and Aster Road.

Aadesh had sold all the gold and jewellery the family had managed to smuggle out of Uganda. It had raised just enough money for the deposit on the very large mortgage required to complete the purchase at the vendor's asking price.

He had been overjoyed when the vendor, Bill Strathdon, had told him that all the stock within the shop and the furniture inside the flat were all included in the price. The relief he had felt hearing that had been enormous. He had no money left over to buy new stock, nor furniture, for the flat.

He still felt nervous that he had allowed his son to talk him into buying the shop. The debt they now had was enormous, and he knew it would take them a long time to clear the mortgage.

True to his word, his son had worked like a man possessed. Nabin seemed to be able to exist on very little sleep. He spent hours either serving in the shop alongside his mother and sister, or driving backwards and forwards to the cash and carry to replenish stock they had sold. Nabin had even found time to carry on working at the allotment he loved. He had struck a deal with other allotment holders, to buy their surplus fresh produce, so he could sell it at an increased price at the shop. It would be another good way to increase the shop's profits, as customers always seemed to want fresh fruit and vegetables.

The early signs were good. The little corner shop had a large customer base, as there were no other similar shops in the area. It was busy throughout the day, every day, and the profits were good. The shop was turning over enough profit to easily pay the mortgage, buy more stock, and save for a rainy day.

Aadesh smiled to himself as he locked the door of the shop and made his way upstairs to the flat. Maybe his son had saved them all, with his vision for a better future.

18

3.00pm, 1 May 1988
City Hospital Mortuary, Nottingham

The two bodies, lying naked on the stainless steel benches of the mortuary examination room, could not have looked any different.

Derek Judd was a big man, in every sense of the word. Now in his late sixties, he was six feet five and weighed close to nineteen stone. His wife, Sheila, was a similar age, but was barely five feet tall and weighed less than seven stone.

Seamus Carter had already completed the post-mortem examination of Sheila Judd and was now working on the body of her husband.

Danny was standing next to Tina Cartwright, quite a way back from the examination tables. There was no need to stand closer, as they were only there to observe. DC Singleton was standing a little nearer, as he was accepting exhibits from the pathologist.

As Seamus carried out a thorough examination of the man's heart, he spoke into his Dictaphone: 'There's overwhelming evidence of heart failure again.'

He switched off the recording device and said, 'Danny, let me show you something.'

Danny stepped forward, and as Seamus pointed out all the heavy scar tissue running around the heart muscles, he said, 'Can you see all this scarring around the heart?'

Danny nodded.

Seamus continued, 'This man was already suffering from severe heart disease. His heart wouldn't have been able to withstand any rapid onset tachycardia. Once it started, he would have died quickly.'

'Are you convinced that the cause of their deaths is the same as the Parkdale Road victims?'

'Well, there are no external marks of violence on either body. The cause of death was heart failure. Whether the cause of that heart failure was rapid onset tachycardia, caused by scopolamine poisoning, remains to be seen. I'm not a gambling man, but on this occasion, I'd happily stake my house on it. Only the results of the toxicology tests will confirm it once and for all.'

Danny stepped back away from the bench. 'How soon can you let me have those test results?'

'Don't worry, it will be my top priority. I know how important it is for you to be able to link these deaths.'

'In my mind, these deaths are already linked. The first deaths could have been caused by some tragic accident, but now this ...' He gestured at the bodies. 'It's vitally important that I'm able to link them officially. If someone has deliberately poisoned all these people, I need to find out why and stop them. My biggest fear is that if I can't do that, then more people are going to die.'

19

6.00pm, 1 May 1988
Incident Room, Carlton Police Station, Nottingham

The incident room was crowded, and detectives jostled to find a space where they could sit and take notes. There was a constant hum of noise as they all discussed the latest developments in the cases they were investigating.

Danny walked in, followed by Tina, Rob and Tim Donnelly. The room fell silent, and Danny said, 'It's yet to be confirmed, but I think the deaths of the Rawlings family at Bakersfield and the Judd couple at Burton Joyce are connected.'

He allowed a pause so everybody grasped the importance of what he had said.

He continued, 'I want Detective Inspector Buxton's team to concentrate on the deaths of the Rawlings family, and Detective Inspector Cartwright's team to concentrate on the deaths of Mr and Mrs Judd. I realise that this is going to cause a little upheaval, as some of you will have done considerable work on the Rawlings case already. Use your common sense and hand over everything you've already done to a colleague on the other team. You all know what's expected of you.'

Again, he allowed that message to sink in.

Then he turned to Tim Donnelly and said, 'I want you to go over the lists of property seized at both scenes. All the items of food and drink that you obtained samples from are a priority. I want to know if there were any types of food and drink that were found at both scenes. If you find any common items, I want those samples fast-tracked with the Forensic Science Service to establish if they can find traces of scopolamine.'

Tim quickly made notes and said, 'Will do.'

Danny then spoke to the gathered detectives. 'I've already briefed your DI's. They'll now speak to you individually and give you specific tasks to move the two enquiries forward. I've already obtained a commitment from the Special Operations Unit. Chief Inspector Chambers has made one of his sections available to undertake any house-to-house enquiries we need completing.'

Danny looked at DS Wills. 'Andy, I'd like you to liaise with the chief inspector and oversee that. Come and see me after the briefing so we can set the parameters.'

Andy nodded. 'Will do, boss.'

Danny ended the briefing by saying, 'As I said at the start of this short briefing, I believe these six deaths are all linked. As a top priority, we need to establish something that links the two families. The enquiries your DI's will be giving you are geared up to try to find that link. We must all be aware that if we can't find the twisted individual responsible, we could well be looking at more deaths. There will be some long days and nights ahead, so let your families know to expect you when they see you. I want you back here at eight o'clock tomorrow morning, ready to get cracking. We'll debrief again at eight o'clock tomorrow night. That's all.'

Danny stood up and walked back to the side room he was using as his office. He closed the door, sat down and picked up the telephone.

The telephone went directly to the answerphone service. Danny said, 'Hi, Sue, it's me.'

He paused before saying, 'I hope you and Hayley are both okay.'

He allowed a shorter pause and said, 'There have been two more unexplained deaths today. As you can imagine, it's hectic here. I don't think I'll be home for hours, so don't wait up. I love you, sweetheart.'

He put the phone down and massaged his temples with the tips of his fingers.

His head was pounding.

20

6.00pm, 3 May 1987
St Ann's Well Road, St Ann's, Nottingham

Aadesh and Nabin Panchal stood side by side on St Ann's Well Road. The two men stood in silence, staring up at the huge Valumart superstore that had opened its doors four months ago. It was quite late, but the huge shop was still incredibly busy, and the car park was full.

Ever since the Nottingham Evening Post *had covered the story of the giant supermarket chain opening a new store in the city, the two men had felt a sense of foreboding. Looking at the huge building in front of them now, that feeling of dread was confirmed.*

Aadesh said quietly, 'It's no wonder we've lost all our customers. Look at the size of this place.'

Nabin said, 'I know, it's bloody massive. It sells everything you could ever want.'

Aadesh shrugged. 'Does it sell what we sell? Can we undercut them for price?'

'They sell everything we sell. There's no chance of us being able to undercut them. I checked the prices of some of their own-brand stuff yesterday. They're selling it cheaper than I can buy it at the cash and carry.'

'What?'

'It's true. We can't compete with them. They're too big. They buy everything in such huge amounts, they get it at a knockdown price. That means they can then sell it cheaper than we ever could, and still make huge profits.'

'What are we going to do, Nabi?'

'I don't know, baabujii. *The shop was doing so well. The profits we made this year will keep us going for a while. After that, I don't know.'*

'What about the mortgage repayments? If we can't pay them, we'll lose everything.'

'Try not to panic. I'll think of something.'

Nabin could see the look of fear on his father's face, and he was suddenly filled with rage. Angry questions raced around inside his head. Why did Valumart have to build their monstrous shop here? Why develop a site just three streets away from their little shop? Did Bill Strathdon know it was going to be built when he sold them the shop?

He watched as the stooped figure of his father shuffled away. The enormity of their dire situation seemed to have destroyed his father before his very eyes.

A steely resolve descended upon Nabin. He vowed to make the massive supermarket chain pay for their greed. He just didn't know how he was going to do it.

Yet.

21

4.00pm, 2 May 1988
Incident Room, Carlton Police Station, Nottingham

The knock on his office door broke Danny's concentration.

He'd been reading the statement made by the Judd family's gardener, Fred Turner, checking for any discrepancies or possible leads the detective who took it might have missed.

There were none.

He put down the statement and shouted, 'Come in.'

The door opened. He was surprised to see Seamus Carter walk in.

The big Irishman said, 'Good afternoon, Danny. I was in Nottingham, and I thought you'd want to hear this news in person.'

'Grab a seat. What news?'

'I've just received the toxicology results from the post-mortem examinations of Derek and Sheila Judd.'

'Go on.'

'It was scopolamine again. They had both ingested huge amounts. The results from the stomach contents were startling. Sheila Judd had almost double the levels of her husband.'

'Is that significant?'

'It suggests to me that whatever food or drink it was that contained the poison, she had consumed more of it than her husband.'

'Well, you saw her, Seamus. There was nothing to the woman. I can't see her having a massive appetite.'

'Appearances can be deceptive, but I tend to agree. I think it could mean that the toxin was more likely to be in whatever they drank rather than what they ate.'

'You said the levels they had ingested were huge. Does that mean the toxin was deliberately put into whatever it was that killed them?'

The pathologist stroked his bushy beard thoughtfully before saying, 'I don't see how that much toxin could have found its way into our food supply chain without it being put there deliberately. I genuinely believe that somehow, the food or drink these people consumed had been tampered with.'

'A deliberate act would make this a murder investigation.'

'I appreciate that, but I just don't see any other scenario. Once the lab rats at the Forensic Science Service have discovered exactly what food contained the toxin, we'll know for sure.'

'I've just been on the phone to the supervisor at the FSS. Their workload's horrendous. I stressed to her the importance of determining which item it was that contained the toxin.'

'And?'

'She told me that the fastest they could work their way through all the samples would be fourteen days.'

'That's way too long.'

'I know,' Danny said. 'I've got Tim Donnelly comparing all the foodstuffs seized from both addresses, trying to find something both families had consumed. He's in constant touch with the FSS and is trying everything to speed up the process. I'm having a meeting with him later today to see if he's found any common ground.'

'I'm not presumptuous enough to ever tell you your job, my friend, but I think you need to establish what's carrying this toxin, and fast. There could well be other contaminated food or drink out there.'

'That's what scares me the most. I've been unable to find any motive, any reason why these two families should have been targeted. That's screaming to me that they weren't selected at all, that this was a random act by some lunatic.'

Seamus stood up. 'And if that's the case, there'll definitely be other victims turning up, sooner or later. I'll let you have the full written report in the morning. Good luck, Danny.'

'Thanks. Hopefully, I won't see you anytime soon.'

Seamus smiled and closed the door behind him.

22

8.00pm, 2 May 1988
Scenes of Crime, Nottinghamshire Police Headquarters

Danny parked his car in the main car park at police headquarters.

He had called in to see the Scenes of Crime supervisor, Tim Donnelly, on his way home to Mansfield.

He took the stairs to the Scenes of Crime department and walked through the large room that housed the Scenes of Crime technicians. He made his way along the corridor, knocked politely on the supervisor's office door and walked in.

Tim Donnelly was seated behind his desk, which was covered in a mass of papers.

Danny looked down at the mess and said, 'I take it you know where everything is in amongst that lot?'

Tim chuckled. 'I do. It's an ordered chaos.'

'How did you get on comparing the samples recovered from the two scenes?'

Tim moved a couple of sheets of paper before picking one up and saying, 'Here we are. I've finished going through everything now, and these are the common samples we took.'

Danny took the paper from Tim and began reading. He was disappointed to see such a long list of food and drink samples.

He said, 'There's over thirty items on this list. How come there's so many?'

'I'll be honest with you, boss. I thought there'd be a lot more than that. If you think about it, there are so many things that we all consume every day.'

'Will narrowing the search like this speed things up with the Forensic Science Service?'

'I've already spoken to Fay Weaver, the supervising scientist, and she says they'll do their utmost to expedite the results, but it will still be around seven days.'

'Bloody hell!'

'It can't be rushed, boss. I know Fay. She won't be dragging her heels.'

'I want you to speak to her every day. Chase her until we have those results. I can't move this enquiry forward until I have that information. Stress to her that other people's lives could be in danger.'

Danny's face must have portrayed the level of anxiety he was feeling, because Tim said, 'She understands, boss. We all do.'

'I know you do.'

'I take it you've had the toxicology reports for Derek and Sheila Judd by now?'

'Yes, Seamus contacted me earlier today. High levels of scopolamine found in both victims. He thinks the poison was deliberately put in whatever it was they ate or drank. That's why it's so important we get that information.'

'I'll keep chasing her.'

'Thanks.'

23

1.00pm, 7 June 1987
Royal Botanic Gardens, Kew, London

It was somewhere Nabin Panchal had always wanted to visit.

As he stood outside the Elizabeth Gate, the main entrance into the Royal Botanic Gardens at Kew, he couldn't quite believe he was finally here.

He had caught the nine o'clock train from Nottingham Midland railway station to London, St Pancras. Walking out of the bustling station, he had hailed one of the famous black cabs to make the journey across London, travelling through Paddington and Hammersmith.

It was the first time he had ever been to the capital, and he felt a little overawed as he saw some of the city's famous landmarks. He couldn't quite believe how busy it was. There were people and traffic everywhere.

Prior to making the journey, Nabin had spent hours in his shed at the allotment, poring over botanical reference books he had taken out from the library.

He had finally identified the plant that would be suitable for his needs. Because of its potentially lethal properties, the only specimen available in the entire country was to be found at this unique horticultural place.

Before going through the gates, he took the rucksack from his back and made sure he had the secateurs and the clear plastic bags he would need.

Having carried out the last-minute check, he took out his wallet and walked in through the Elizabeth Gate, purchasing an 'access all areas' day ticket. This ticket would allow him to go into the different glasshouses and conservatories, as well as the herbarium and library.

It was before the school holidays, so the number of visitors inside the majestic gardens was still quite low. In a few weeks' time, when the schools were off, the place would be packed, making his task impossible.

He passed the huge sign that laid out the rules of the gardens. At the very top, in large red letters, it stated that no plants were to be touched, and it was forbidden to take cuttings.

He looked at the map of the gardens just inside the gate and saw that the herbarium and the library were just a short walk to his right.

After five minutes, he walked into the library, where a record was kept of every plant to be found at the gardens. It listed the Latin name as well as the common name of all the plants, where they were to be found, and a brief description of what they looked like.

He quickly found the entry for the plant he was searching for. The Brugmansia, *or Angel's Trumpet, was to be found inside the Palm House Conservatory.*

Having found what he was looking for, he went back outside and studied the map again. He quickly located the Palm House on the map. There was an arrow leading from the picture of the Palm House to the side of the noticeboard. At the end of the arrow was a printed note stating that the Palm House was currently undergoing an extensive refurbishment, and only two-thirds of the building were currently open to the public.

Feeling a sense of anxiety, Nabin walked briskly along Broad Walk, following the signposts for the Palm House.

When he first saw the conservatory, which was in reality a huge greenhouse, with its curved iron girders and glass panes, it took his breath away. It was such a beautiful building. He could see the small section of the greenhouse that was still undergoing the renovation work. He walked to the other end of the ornate building and made his way in through the main entrance. There was only one elderly man at the door, inspecting the tickets.

Nabin showed him his ticket and made his way inside. There were very few visitors inside, and he only saw a couple of gardeners tending to the plants. He wandered slowly around, getting his bearings. He had made a mental note of where the Brugmansia *plant was to be found, and after fifteen minutes or so, he had located the huge plant, with its emerald green leaves and white pendulous flowers hanging down. It was these long white blooms that afforded the plant its common name of Angel's Trumpet.*

He looked around and saw a gardener working a few yards away, stripping the dead leaves from an olive palm. Nabin continued walking and returned ten minutes later. This time, there was nobody in sight. He took the secateurs from his rucksack and deftly took several six-inch cuttings from the very ends of the plant's branches. He knew he would be able to propagate healthy plants by rooting these cuttings and raising them carefully in his greenhouse at the allotment.

He secreted the cuttings inside the individual plastic bags he had brought with him. The bags would keep the plants moist and protect them until he could dip the ends of the cuttings in a rooting hormone, then plant them in the correct compost.

The plants, once they had flourished, would give him the materials to carry out his plan.

He placed everything back in his rucksack, then made his way out of the hot and humid greenhouse.

Once outside and in the fresh air, he realised how hungry he was. He saw a sign giving directions to the Victoria Gate café. He made his way towards the buff-coloured brick building, which stood in the shadow of the huge water tower.

He ordered a cheese salad sandwich and a large coffee. After hungrily devouring the sandwich, he slowly sipped his scalding hot coffee and started thinking about his plans for the plants secreted in his rucksack.

He knew that once the plants had grown to maturity, he would be able to extract the toxin contained in the seed heads and leaves. He could still vividly remember the lectures from his professor at the agricultural college in Uganda. The man's description of the deadly poison used by shamans and witch doctors, for their potions and spells, had stuck in his mind. How the natives of some of those countries had their own name for the liquid extracted from the plant. They called it 'the Devil's Breath'.

Nabin was fully aware how strong the poison produced from the plant could be. The only gap in his knowledge was how much of the extracted toxin to use. He knew that it always made people extremely sick, but in the wrong dosage, it could easily kill.

That was something he could worry about after the plants had grown. He finished his coffee and made his way to the nearby Victoria Gate, intending to leave the gardens. He needed to get back to Nottingham as quickly as he could. The sooner the cuttings were rooted and planted in compost in his greenhouse, the more chance he would have of cultivating them successfully.

As he walked towards the ornate black and gold gate, he could see rows of black cabs on the other side.

He hailed one of the cabs, climbed in the back and said, 'St Pancras railway station, please. My train leaves in thirty minutes.'

The cabbie replied cheerily, 'No problem, guv'nor. I'll have you there in fifteen.'

Nabin opened the rucksack and smiled down at the woody cuttings inside their plastic bags.

He would soon be able to provide for his family and make Valumart suffer for their greed.

24

10.00am, 3 May 1988
Nottingham Police Headquarters

The corridor outside Chief Superintendent Adrian Potter's office was unusually quiet. There was no sign of his secretary. Her desk, stationed immediately outside his office door, was neat and tidy, as though nobody had been working there today.

Danny glanced at his watch; he was still ten minutes early for his appointment to brief the head of CID. He sat down opposite the secretary's desk and waited.

At exactly ten o'clock, the door to Potter's office opened, and the diminutive chief superintendent stepped outside. He saw Danny waiting and said, 'Come in, Chief Inspector.'

Danny walked in and was surprised to see the chief constable, Jack Renshaw, sitting at the side of Potter's desk.

Danny remained standing and said, 'Good morning, sir.'

Renshaw said, 'Sit down, Danny. How are your enquiries

into these deaths at Bakersfield and Burton Joyce progressing?'

'I can tell you that the deaths are no accident and are all linked. All six victims were killed after ingesting large amounts of a toxin called scopolamine. We're currently working alongside the Forensic Science Service to establish the vector of that poison. We're concentrating on the food and drink found at both scenes, as the pathologist believes the poison was ingested, not inhaled. If we can establish exactly what food or drink that was, we can then take steps to hopefully prevent further deaths.'

Potter said, 'Why do you think it's murder and not simple food poisoning?'

'The toxin, scopolamine, is not a substance usually found in our food supply. Also, the levels found in the toxicology tests carried out on the victims are so concentrated.'

Renshaw said, 'So you think somebody has deliberately tampered with something these people have either eaten or drank, intending to kill them?'

'I can't talk about the offender's intent yet, but he or she must have known that the levels placed in the food would have the potential to be lethal.'

'So why these families?'

'At the moment, we can find no motive as to why these two families were targeted. It's possible they're all random victims and haven't been targeted at all.'

A worried expression descended over Renshaw's face. 'If that's the case, there could be more victims.'

'Exactly. That's why I'm throwing resources at the enquiry to find any links between the two families and to establish exactly what has been used as the vector to deliver the poison.'

Potter said, 'How soon will you know what's been used to poison them?'

'The FSS have promised me they will have determined that within the next week.'

Renshaw said tersely, 'Too slow. Are you meeting any resistance at the FSS?'

'Not at all, sir. They're working flat out, it's just the weight of work they have to deal with from other forces, as well as ours.'

'Chase them, Danny. I don't want any more deaths. Understood?'

'None of us want that, sir.'

'Of course. You must keep me informed on all developments.'

There was a brief pause, and then Renshaw continued, 'I do have some other news for you. Adrian told me about your upcoming staff vacancy, following the impending retirement of Detective Sergeant Harris. I've decided to listen to your idea. I'll be promoting Detective Constable Moore to sergeant, and she can remain in post on the MCIU.'

'That's great news, sir. Thank you. I'll arrange for a detective to join us from division to replace DC Moore and bring us back up to strength. We've a waiting list of suitable candidates who are on the reserve list after the last round of interviews.'

'That's fine, Danny. Just make sure that when you have selected the replacement, their transfer is included on Weekly Orders. Speaking of which, you can inform Rachel Moore of her promotion, but it's not to be made common knowledge until after it's appeared on Weekly Orders. Understood?'

'Yes, sir.'

'On these suspicious deaths, let me know as soon as the FSS have got back to you with a result. I want to be kept informed.'

Potter said, 'That will be all, Chief Inspector.'

Danny stood and said, 'Will do, sir.'

As he walked back to his car, his emotions were conflicted. He was overjoyed that his colleague, Rachel, was going to be promoted to sergeant, in post.

At the same time, he could feel the enormous pressure of responsibility weighing heavily upon his shoulders.

All he could hear inside his head was Chief Constable Jack Renshaw's voice saying, '*I don't want any more deaths. Understood?*'

25

2.00pm, 3 May 1988
Incident Room, Carlton Police Station, Nottingham

Danny walked into the incident room and saw Rachel Moore at her desk, studying intelligence reports. She had been tasked with establishing if there had been any sightings of people going door-to-door selling items in the Bakersfield and Burton Joyce areas, leading up to the deaths.

As he walked past, he said, 'Rachel, I need to see you in my office.'

The detective stood up and followed Danny along the corridor.

Danny said, 'Close the door and grab a seat.'

Rachel sat down and said, 'Is something wrong?'

Danny allowed a smile to form on his lips and said, 'Just the opposite. I've got some very good news.' He paused and then continued, 'I saw the chief constable earlier today, and he's informed me that he's promoting you to the rank of sergeant. Congratulations.'

Rachel let out a whoop of delight, overjoyed at the news. But almost as quickly, a worried frown replaced the excited expression.

Danny saw the change and said, 'It's great news, isn't it?'

Finally finding her voice, Rachel said, 'It's brilliant news, but where will I be posted? I haven't worn a uniform for so long, it will all feel very weird.'

'That's the best bit. You're staying here. He's going to promote you in post. You'll be a detective sergeant here on the MCIU.'

The smile immediately returned to Rachels face. 'How's that even possible?'

'It isn't common knowledge yet, but Lynn Harris has handed in her resignation so she can be a full-time mum. I know she won't mind me telling you she's expecting her third child and feels the time's right to spend more time with her family. It's a decision I applaud her for, and one I wish I had the opportunity to make myself. I'd love to spend more time with my own daughter.'

'I don't know what to say. When's this all happening?'

'Weekly Orders are next published in three days' time, so it will be official from then. You mustn't tell anybody about it until then, okay? I expect the chief constable will want to see you in his office the day before, to inform you personally. Congratulations, Rachel. It's very well deserved.'

'Thank you.'

She started to get up to leave, but Danny said, 'Before you go. How are you getting on with the intelligence reports?'

'I'm almost finished. There are no reports of anybody selling anything door-to-door.'

'Good. There's something else I want you to look at. It occurred to me that we still haven't completed a full financial investigation into the two families yet. I know you've got contacts on the Fraud Squad; I want you to use those contacts and gain access to the financial records of the two families. We may find a link within their spending patterns that could help us.'

'That shouldn't be a problem. I would think their finances are going to be very different, but I'll check them out.'

'Thanks.'

Just as Rachel reached the door, Danny said, 'Congratulations, Sarge.'

Rachel chuckled. 'I suppose I'll have to get used to people calling me that.'

'Only until they have to call you "ma'am". Very well done, Rachel. Let me know how you get on with those financial records.'

26

2.00pm, 21 September 1987
St Ann's Allotments, Ransom Road, Nottingham

Nabin had left his mother and sister in charge of the corner shop and had spent the day working on his allotment. It was his personal sanctuary, away from all the stress and worry of the family's failing business. Ever since the Valumart supermarket had opened, the tiny corner shop they owned had been running at a loss.

His father, Aadesh, was now a broken man. Unable to cope with the stress of the situation, he now spent his days in bed. His wife, Eashwari, doted on her ailing husband's every need.

Nabin knew that the savings they had would only be enough to pay the mortgage for another four months. He hoped the mortgage company would offer them an extension plan to help with the repayments, but if they didn't, he knew the family would lose both the business and their home.

Try as he might, he could only see one way out of their

predicament. It was to go through with the plan he had set in motion three and a half months ago, when he stole the cuttings of the plant at Kew Gardens.

Thanks to his expertise and knowledge of horticulture, the Brugmansia cuttings he had stolen back then had flourished in his warm greenhouse. Grown in perfect conditions and fed every day, the plants now stood well over five feet in height and were resplendent with white flowers that were rapidly turning to seed heads.

He had harvested some of the older leaves and the seed heads that had developed already. After filling a bucket with the vegetation, he was now in the process of simmering it slowly in a large saucepan of boiling water. The small camping stove he kept in his garden shed, to make himself a cup of tea on cold mornings, was perfect for the job of slowly cooking down the vegetation until it was little more than pulp.

Satisfied that it had been simmering for long enough, he used an old potato masher to further pulp the leaves and seeds, to extract the potent juices from the plants. He then poured the contents of the saucepan through a strainer to catch the juice from the pulped-down vegetation. At the end of the process, he was left with a container full of warm liquid. He had hoped the resulting liquid would be clearer. At the end of the long process, the juice appeared the colour of brackish water. It wouldn't be a problem. It just meant he would need to be extra careful when selecting which products to deposit the juice into.

As he poured the now-cooled, dirty-looking liquid from the saucepan into a discarded lemonade bottle, a look of concern came over his face. The one thing he had been unable to establish was the strength of the liquor he had brewed.

From his extensive studies, he knew that each strain of the Brugmansia family of plants had differing levels of the toxin scopolamine in the leaves and seeds. There was no way he could know exactly what the toxicity of the liquid was that he had extracted.

He placed the now-full lemonade bottle onto the top shelf and pondered his next move.

Feeling hungry, he washed his hands thoroughly under the tap outside before returning to the shed to eat his cheese roll.

He made himself a mug of tea to have with his meagre lunch. It was as he stirred sugar into his mug that an idea came to him. He suddenly knew how he could test the potency of his liquid.

He would carry out an experiment before he put his main plan into operation. If everything went to plan during the experiment, he would soon be able to relieve his family's torment, and their money troubles would all be over.

With a broad smile on his face, he raised his mug of tea towards the bottle of brown liquid and said, 'Cheers, Valumart. Thanks for nothing.'

27

11.00am, 22 September 1987
Silver Teapot Tea Room, St James's Street, Nottingham

Nabin ordered a milky coffee and sat at the table nearest to the door.

He had chosen this café to hold his little experiment because of the layout inside and its quieter location. St James's Street was just off the main town centre, so the Silver Teapot tea room was never as busy as some of the other town centre cafés.

He could feel the small plastic bottle in his jacket pocket. He had filled it half full of the brackish liquid he had prepared yesterday. Prior to pouring the liquid into the bottle, he had put it through a strainer three more times. Now it had settled, the liquid was slightly less brackish to look at.

It was almost odourless, and he felt confident that he could carry out his experiment this morning without being discovered. The only thing he didn't know, for obvious reasons, was what the liquid tasted like.

As he had expected, now the breakfast rush had finished, the small tea room wasn't too busy. It was a cold, blustery day outside, so the city centre was quiet anyway. It wasn't really a day to be mooching around the shops.

An elderly woman walked into the café and plonked her bags down on the table next to his. She took out her purse and walked to the counter to order food. She returned a few minutes later, carrying a large cup of tea. After carefully putting her purse back in her handbag, the woman took off her coat, hat and scarf before sitting down wearily.

She had placed her teacup and saucer near the edge of her table. It was within arm's reach of Nabin. He watched the woman closely, biding his time.

Ignoring her tea, the woman started to look through the bags she had with her, inspecting the items she had recently purchased.

She turned her back towards Nabin and removed a lemon-coloured cardigan from a Debenhams carrier bag.

As the woman carefully checked the garment, Nabin seized his opportunity. He took one last quick glance around him to check nobody was watching him. Then he took the small plastic bottle from his jacket pocket and flipped open the lid. He reached over and poured the light brown liquid into the old woman's teacup.

It was all done in a flash. He placed the empty bottle back inside his jacket pocket and took another sip of his coffee.

After checking and replacing all her purchased items back into their respective bags, the old woman turned around in her seat and took a sip of the hot tea. She screwed her face up at the bitter taste and tutted loudly.

Nabin was about to stand up and bolt out of the café, fearing his actions were about to be exposed. Before he could move, the woman grabbed the teaspoon from the saucer and heaped three large spoonfuls of sugar into her tea before stirring vigorously. She took another sip and said aloud, 'Ah, that's better.'

Nabin relaxed and began to drink his own coffee, carefully observing the old lady. The girl who worked behind the counter approached the woman and said, 'Toasted teacake?'

The old lady smiled and said, 'That's mine, love, thanks.'

The girl placed the teacake on the table in front of the woman and returned to the counter. The old lady used the knife provided to scoop out butter from the punnet. She spread the creamy butter in thick layers on the hot teacakes.

Nabin looked on as she took a bite of the teacake and washed it down with gulps of warm sweet tea. She repeated this process until the teacake and the tea were all gone.

Five minutes later, Nabin had finished his own coffee. Just as he thought his experiment had failed, he saw the old lady start to sway in her seat, rocking back and forth. She rubbed her eyes furiously and began to splutter, as though she had swallowed something that had got lodged in her windpipe.

Suddenly, her eyes rolled back in their sockets. Nabin could now only see the whites of the woman's eyes. She toppled forward slowly, landing face first on the table. There was a loud crash as the teacup and saucer were sent flying to the floor.

Two young women, who were sitting at the table nearest the counter, shouted in alarm at the sudden noise and turned to see the collapsed woman. One of them rushed over and checked on the woman. She immediately turned to her friend, shouting, 'Get them to call an ambulance! She's passed out.'

As the tea room staff and other customers began to mill around the old lady, Nabin stood up quietly. In all the panic and confusion, he was able to slip out of the door, unnoticed.

As he walked along St James's Street, towards the Old Market Square, he had a huge smile on his face. He was overjoyed at the power of the liquid. It had only taken just over five minutes for it to have an effect.

He had no thoughts or concerns for the old lady, who had

slipped into unconsciousness after swallowing his poison. He was already totally focussed on how he was about to make the supermarket giant, Valumart, pay for its greed and selfishness.

28

11.00am, 6 May 1988
Incident Room, Carlton Police Station, Nottingham

It had been a strange few days for Rachel Moore.

Strange, but exciting in equal measure. Weekly Orders had been published that morning, informing everybody on the force of any changes in the law, operating procedures, or changes of personnel. It was where all promotions, resignations, or transfers were listed.

It had felt surreal seeing her name on the list of promotions. It would take a while before she got used to the fact that she was now Detective Sergeant Rachel Moore.

She had driven over to headquarters the previous day, to keep an appointment with Chief Constable Jack Renshaw. He had informed her personally of her promotion before offering his congratulations and telling her to keep up her good work on the MCIU.

It had been difficult not to tell everyone her good news when she had returned from headquarters.

This morning had been totally different.

As individual colleagues read Weekly Orders, they approached and offered her their warmest congratulations. She had felt slightly embarrassed, but also overjoyed to witness the overwhelming support for her promotion.

The constant interruptions throughout the morning had made it difficult for her to concentrate on her current enquiry. Danny had tasked her with obtaining all the financial records of the Rawlings family and the Judd's.

He specifically wanted her to make a comparison of the two, to establish any similarities.

As she had suspected, the two families were at completely different ends of the social scale. It was obvious that the Rawlings family had little disposable income, whereas the Judd family were very wealthy in their retirement.

She had only found one thing that the two families had in common.

As she studied their recent bank transactions, she had noticed they both did their weekly food shop at the recently opened Valumart superstore located on St Ann's Well Road. The amount spent by each family was vastly different, but they both shopped there every week. It was something, and it was nothing. After all, thousands of families did their weekly shop at the huge Valumart superstore.

She had arranged to have a celebratory drink after work, at the Railway Inn in Mansfield. She knew that Danny was out of the office for most of the day, so she would wait and speak to him at the pub about the one financial similarity she had found.

It was probably just a coincidence.

She had been in the superstore herself, on several occasions. It never ceased to amaze her how many things there were available to purchase. It was like a visit to the High Street of a small town, but all under one roof.

29

9.00pm, 6 May 1988
The Railway Inn, Mansfield, Nottinghamshire

The four detectives all sat in the small lounge bar of the Railway Inn. They had all been home first, to get changed and have something to eat. The four had then been dropped off at the pub to have that celebratory drink. It would mean getting taxis home later. Better to do that than to think about driving after having a few beers.

Danny was happy to celebrate Rachel's promotion, but he didn't want that celebration to turn into a heavy drinking session. He was conscious that they all had to be on duty again in the morning.

Seeing his colleagues, Rob Buxton, Andy Wills and Rachel Moore all sitting there, chatting away and laughing as they had a drink, he was suddenly reminded of the time that same small team of detectives were investigating the murders committed by Jimmy Wade and Michael Reynolds during the miners' strike.

They had been dark, stressful days.

Tonight was totally different.

It was a time for celebration. He leaned over to Rachel and said, 'Tina sends her apologies. She couldn't make it tonight, as she has a prior engagement she couldn't get out of. She told me to pass on her sincere congratulations, and to say it couldn't have happened to a more deserving person. She also said you two would go out for a "proper" drink another time. Whatever that means.'

Rachel laughed and said, 'That means it had better be on a night that's followed by a rest day.'

'I'm so pleased for you, Rachel. You've been through so much over the years. This is a justified reward for all your hard work, bravery, and skill as a detective.'

'Thanks, boss. When I was at headquarters yesterday, Chief Superintendent Potter told me that it was your idea to promote me in post, so thank you.'

'That's true; it was my idea. But you would have been promoted soon, anyway. It just made perfect sense when I learned that Lynn was leaving, to have you promoted in post, on the MCIU. You are that square peg in a square hole. You know the MCIU and how it operates, inside and out. You also know the strengths and weaknesses of all your colleagues. It was the right thing to do. I'm just pleased Jack Renshaw saw it that way too. Anyway, that's enough about work. It's my turn to get the drinks in.'

Danny asked everyone what they wanted, and then made his way to the bar. The cosy lounge bar was empty; the detectives were the only people in there. Rachel followed Danny to the bar and said, 'I'll give you a hand to carry the drinks back.'

The landlord started to pull a pint of Guinness, then

stopped and said, 'Sorry, folks. I need to nip down and change the barrel. I won't be a minute.'

Danny looked over the counter as the landlord disappeared down the cellar. Rachel said quietly, 'There was something I found in the financial records of the families. It's probably nothing, though.'

Danny waited for her to elaborate.

'Both families did their weekly grocery shop at the Valumart superstore, on St Ann's Well Road.'

'The new one?'

'Yes.'

'I think half of Nottingham do their weekly grocery shop in that store. Whenever I've driven by, the car park's always full.'

'Like I said, it's probably nothing.'

'And it might be something. Make a note of it, and let's see what the Forensic Science Service come back with. Good work.'

30

6.00pm, 3 March 1988
Hungerhill Road, St Ann's, Nottingham

Nabin Panchal had spent another long and lonely day working on his allotment. Nothing was growing. It was still too early to plant out, as there was still a risk of frost. He had spent the day tending to the Brugmansia plants in his greenhouse and drinking tea in the shed.

There were now three lemonade bottles full of the light brown liquid he had obtained from boiling down the leaves and seed heads of the toxic plant.

Looking at the bottles always sent a chill through his body. He had seen the devastating effect just a small amount of the liquid had on the old lady at the café. Although he desperately wanted Valumart to pay for what they had done to his family, he was also frightened what the liquid might do.

He had seen no news reports about the old lady's collapse in the café, and he now regretted not waiting there at the time to see whether she had survived or not. Even after the little experiment, he still had no way of knowing how much to use, and that terrified him.

He had temporarily put his potentially lethal plan to the back of his mind. Instead, he had spent his time concentrating on coming up with ways to generate more income for the family and their ailing business.

He was pondering whether to get another job. At least that would bring a wage in and hopefully earn enough to continue paying the mortgage on the shop.

As he got nearer to home, he suddenly realised that an ambulance was parked right outside the corner shop. The back doors of the emergency vehicle were wide open.

Any thoughts of a job, the plan, the liquid, disappeared in that instant, and he sprinted the remaining fifty yards to the shop.

As he burst through the shop door, he was greeted by the sight of his sister crying.

He said, 'What's happened?'

'Baabujii opened this letter. Maamii tried to hide it from him, but he saw it and snatched it from her. He read it and collapsed, shaking and howling. I didn't know what to do, so I called for an ambulance.'

Nabin took the letter from his sister and read it.

It was from the building society. It informed his father that he was now in arrears with the mortgage on the shop. It also said that the building society were prepared to give the family until November to clear the arrears and get back on track with the monthly payments. If they failed to do so, the society would have no choice but to repossess the shop and the flat above.

Nabin was shocked at the coldness of its content.

He said quietly, 'Where's baabujii?'

'He's upstairs with the doctor and the ambulance people. Maamii's with him.'

Nabin raced upstairs and saw his father strapped into the chair stretcher the ambulance crew had brought in with them. It was the only way they would be able to get him back down the steep flight of stairs.

He turned to his tearful mother and said, 'What's happened?'

'When your dad read that letter, he just collapsed. I think the stress of everything has finally taken its toll.'

Nabin looked at his father. His head was lolling to one side, and there was spittle hanging from his lips. His nose was running. His eyes were glazed over, and his tongue protruded ever so slightly from his mouth.

Bending down in front of his father was an elderly man, wearing a suit, shining a penlight into his father's dead-fish eyes.

The man in the suit turned round and looked at Nabin. He stood upright and said, 'Are you his son?'

Nabin nodded, still in shock at what he was seeing.

The man said, 'I'm Dr Nicholson, from the on-call Mental Health Team. The ambulance crew called me out to make an assessment on your father, as they couldn't find anything physically wrong with him. I've just finished my examination. I'm sorry, but I believe your father's suffered a complete nervous breakdown. I've arranged for him to be taken to Mapperley Hospital for more tests so I can evaluate the extent of the breakdown. Come and see me at the hospital tomorrow morning. I should be able to tell you more then.'

Nabin nodded and whispered, 'Thank you.'

The ambulance crew picked up the chair and carried his father down the stairs and outside to the waiting ambulance. Several people were now standing on the corner, gawping as the shopkeeper was carried out.

The sight of the rubberneckers pointing and saying things about his father, along with sound of his mother and sister crying inside the shop, turned Nabin's feelings of helplessness and desperation into rage.

As the ambulance slowly drove away along Hungerhill Road,

he rounded on the crowd that had gathered, and shouted angrily, 'What are you all staring at? Why don't you just fuck off and leave us alone!'

Nabin walked back inside the shop, slammed the door and flipped the 'Closed' sign around. He locked and bolted the door before trudging slowly up the stairs to the flat.

He found his mother and sister holding each other and crying. As he tried to comfort them, he said, 'Don't worry. Everything's going to be fine. I'll soon have enough money to clear all our debts and settle the mortgage. Then we can get rid of this business and move away.'

His mother said, between sobs, 'I know you mean well, Nabi. But how on earth are you going to do that?'

'Don't worry. Everything's already in place. I've just been waiting for the right time to act. That time has now come.'

31

9.30am, 9 May 1988
Incident Room, Carlton Police Station, Nottingham

Just over a week had passed since the bodies of Derek and Sheila Judd had been discovered at their Burton Joyce home. Danny was thankful that there had been no other victims of poisoning since then, but he was fearful that his enquiries were now stalling.

There were still numerous leads and enquiries for his staff to follow, but nothing that realistically looked as if it would provide him with the breakthrough he needed.

The telephone on his desk began to ring. He quickly snatched it up, saying, 'DCI Flint.'

'Boss, it's Tim Donnelly. I've just had a phone call from Fay Weaver, the supervising scientist at the Forensic Science Service.'

'I hope it's good news.'

'It's great news. They've identified the vector of the poison, at both scenes.'

'At both scenes?'

'Yes. Tests done on two bottles of Sunvit fresh orange juice have both shown extremely high levels of scopolamine.'

'So, the same brand of orange juice was found at both scenes?'

'Yes. The bottle at the Rawlings scene was a quarter full and found in the fridge. The bottle at the Judd scene was half full and found on the dining table, next to the condiments.'

'Did you manage to lift any fingerprints off either bottle?'

'That's the first thing I checked when I got the news this morning. Fingerprints were found on both bottles, but they matched those of the deceased.'

Danny was thoughtful for a moment. Then he said, 'Have the FSS completed all their tests now?'

'Yes. They wanted to complete all the other checks before they contacted us, to make sure there were no other vectors.'

Danny suddenly felt annoyed. 'Oh, great. So how long have they known this bloody poison was in the orange juice?'

'She didn't say. It's just the way they work, boss. They must exhaust all other possibilities before they will give a definitive answer. She did say that they had purchased a bottle of Sunvit orange juice to use as a control sample, and there were no traces of scopolamine found in it.'

'Does that mean the scopolamine had been deliberately put in the juice found at the scenes by an outside agency?'

'Yes.'

'Thanks, Tim. How soon can you let me have the written report from the FSS?'

'As soon as it lands on my desk, I'll bring it over to the incident room at Carlton.'

'Thanks. And thanks for letting me know so quickly. Talk to you later.'

Danny put the telephone down and stared at the words he had scribbled down in his notepad, *Sunvit orange juice.*

Now that he finally had this information, he needed to decide what was the best way to use it.

He walked into the main office and saw that Fran Jefferies was the only detective in the incident room.

He walked over to her and said, 'Fran, I want you to telephone the force control room and tell them to contact DI Buxton and DI Cartwright. I want them both back here at ten thirty. I'd do it myself, but I've got to nip out for something.'

'No problem, sir.'

32

10.30am, 9 May 1988
Incident Room, Carlton Police Station, Nottingham

Danny pointed at the bottle of Sunvit orange juice on his desk. He had purchased it twenty minutes ago at the local Co-op supermarket on Carlton Road.

He looked at Tina and Rob and said, 'This is the vector of the poison used to kill the Rawlings and Judd families.'

He paused, then said, 'Tina, I want you to take two detectives from each side of the enquiry and start finding out which shops stock this particular brand of orange juice.'

Tina nodded. 'Will do.'

Danny turned to Rob. 'It says on the label that it's produced in Spain. So there must be a distribution centre here. I want you to establish where the distribution centre for this product is here in the UK.'

'Right.'

'I'll need that information as quick as you can, Rob. I want to put out a press release first thing tomorrow morning about the deaths. I think it would be prudent to be able to reassure the public, at that time, that this brand of orange juice is to be withdrawn immediately from all supermarkets. We can then add that if they have any unopened bottles at home, to return them to the store they purchased them from, and that if they have any opened bottles, the contents should be tipped away.'

'I'll get straight on it. We'll need to know if the product is shipped here in bulk and then bottled in the UK? Or if it's exported in the bottles? If it's bottled here, we'll need to examine the bottling plant, to see if it's possible it could be tampered with at that stage.'

'Good point. Let me know what the situation is, as soon as you've established that. You'll also need to contact the Sunvit production plant in Spain.' Then Danny said, 'This is the break we've been waiting for. Let's get cracking. Keep me informed of progress. I'm going to headquarters to set up the press release for tomorrow morning.'

33

6.00pm, 10 April 1988
Hungerhill Road, St Ann's, Nottingham

Nabin Panchal sat alone in his bedroom in the flat above the corner shop.

In front of him was a portable Olivetti typewriter. He wore canary yellow Marigold gloves as he typed out yet another letter to the manager of the Valumart Superstore on St Ann's Well Road.

The previous two letters he had sent had been ignored. He knew he had to say something different this time. He needed to make the store manager take him seriously.

A month had passed since his father had been sectioned at Mapperley Hospital. The old man showed no signs of making a recovery. He looked a broken man, crumbling before his family's eyes.

Every time Nabin visited him at the hospital, he came away with a renewed conviction that he was taking the right path. He was the man of the family now. It was down to him to provide for them all and to save the family home.

He read the content of the letter again.

It contained the same instruction to the store manager as the previous two. The manager was instructed to place a cryptic message in the personal ads column of the Nottingham Evening Post *newspaper. This message would confirm that Valumart had agreed to pay the half a million pounds demanded, to prevent goods in the store being contaminated with a potentially lethal toxin.*

The message the store manager was to place in the personal ads had to read:

> Thanks for getting in touch, Baby Doll.
> I'm looking forward to hearing from you again, with details of our hot date.
> Happy Chap.

He looked at the letter and then added a chilling final paragraph that hadn't been on the previous letters.

He slowly typed.

> If no such personal advertisement has been placed in the newspaper within the next seven days, poison will be administered to products within your store. This could result in serious injury, or death, to your customers. This is your last chance. You have been warned.

He slowly read the letter a final time. Satisfied with its contents, he took the sheet of paper from the typewriter and replaced it with a plain white envelope. He addressed the letter to the Store Manager, Valumart Superstore, St Ann's Well Road, Nottingham.

With a flourish, he ripped the envelope from the typewriter and placed the letter inside. He sealed the letter using Sellotape and placed a self-adhesive, first-class stamp on the top corner of the envelope.

He would post the letter first thing in the morning, on his way to the allotment. It meant the letter would arrive at the store on the twelfth, at the latest. If no personal ad had been placed by the nineteenth, he would act.

Everything was now in place.

It was almost time to carry through his threats.

34

10.00am, 12 April 1988
Valumart Superstore, St Ann's Well Road, St Ann's, Nottingham

Owen Bradley was feeling stressed.

Ever since he had arrived at work at seven thirty that morning, it had been problem after problem for him to deal with. The forty-minute commute from his Loughborough home to the superstore in the middle of Nottingham had once again been a nightmare.

It was the one downside to the fantastic job he now had.

At forty-two years of age, Owen Bradley was the youngest store manager employed by the Valumart supermarket chain. He was already tipped for a role at head office in the future, and for him to have been given the post of store manager at their latest flagship superstore was a real feather in his cap. It was a highly paid, responsible job. But with the big money came a lot of stress.

The daily commute wasn't helping those stress levels. He knew that he seriously had to think about relocating his wife and two young daughters closer to Nottingham. It would make his life so much easier.

He sat down heavily in his office chair and stared at the pile of mail on the desk in front of him. He would have to clear it before he could even think about doing anything else.

He methodically worked his way through the pile of correspondence until he was left with one unopened letter. There was something about this last letter that he recognised.

He opened the bottom drawer of his desk and took out two similar letters.

He compared the typed address on each of the three envelopes. The final unopened letter left on his desk appeared identical.

He carefully opened the letter and read the contents.

This letter had also been typed, and it contained a message that was identical to the previous ones. The only difference being there was an additional threat in this last letter. That additional threat made it clear that this was his last chance.

He was convinced the letters were the work of some deranged crank. He was satisfied that it would be virtually impossible for somebody to tamper with goods in his store in the way the letter writer described. The CCTV cameras were part of a state-of-the-art security system that covered every area of the huge store.

He was troubled by the persistent nature of the threatening letters, though, and decided to contact Valumart head office, in Stevenage, for advice. He was just about to pick up the phone when his office door burst open. It was the store's head of security, who said breathlessly, 'You'd better come downstairs, Mr Bradley. My staff have detained a shoplifter in the wines and spirits area. He had a knife and has assaulted a couple of staff members. They're quite badly injured.'

Bradley instantly snatched up the three threatening letters, stuffed them back into the bottom drawer of his desk and stood up.

As he followed his head of security out of the office, he said, 'Have the police been called?'

'The police are on the way. I've also requested an ambulance for the injured staff members.'

Owen Bradley muttered under his breath, 'For Christ's sake!'

All thoughts of contacting the head office about the threatening letters were forgotten as he walked downstairs to deal with this latest crisis.

35

7.00am, 10 May 1988
Incident Room, Carlton Police Station, Nottingham

Danny said, 'Come in and close the door.'

Tina and Rob walked into Danny's office and sat down. Danny could see they were both exhausted after working all the previous day and most of the night.

It was Tina who spoke first. 'It's a nightmare, boss. Sunvit orange juice is sold literally everywhere. Supermarkets, cash and carry warehouses, corner shops ... like I said, everywhere.'

Danny said, 'Did you locate the main distribution centre in the UK?'

Rob replied, 'I'm working that side of the enquiry. The only distribution plant for this product is just outside the town of Felixstowe, in Suffolk. All the shipments arrive in the port on container ships. It's exported already in the bottles, so there's no bottling plant here in the UK.'

'I know it's imported from Spain, but where's the main bottling plant?'

'Sunvit fruit juices are all bottled in a huge plant near a town called Roquetas de Mar, in Almeria, southern Spain.'

'Bloody hell, is there any good news?'

Tina shook her head. 'Not that I can see, boss. It really is like looking for a needle in a haystack.'

Danny was worried. He was silent for a minute; then he said, 'We can't just give up because it's a huge task. Tina, I want you to get a comprehensive list from the distribution centre in Felixstowe. I want to know every location they deliver this orange juice to.'

'I can do that. But the problem will be what happens on the next leg of the distribution chain. If it was just supermarkets, it would be okay, because they keep full records. The problem's going to be the cash and carry outlets. There's no way of us establishing who purchases the product from them. It could be small corner shops, even members of the public. There will be no record.'

'I understand all that, but we've got to try.'

Danny turned to Rob and said, 'Have you spoken to anybody at the bottling plant in Spain?'

'I spoke to the Guardia Civil yesterday morning and explained the situation we have here. I told them six people had died after consuming the product. They were extremely cooperative and immediately sent investigators to the plant to see if there was any possibility the fruit juice had been contaminated at the source. Their investigators spent hours yesterday going through the entire production process with the plant's managers. At five o'clock this morning, I received a telephone call from the Guardia Civil Comandante for the Roquetas area. After their investigation, he was satisfied there's no way the fruit juice could have been contaminated inside the plant. The process is almost entirely automated. The only human involvement is right at the beginning, when the oranges are loaded into a huge hopper at the very start of the process.'

'Could the toxin have been added at that stage?'

'If that was the case, it would have been quickly detected, as the product is constantly tested throughout the production and bottling process.'

'So we can rule out the fruit juice being contaminated in Spain.'

'Yes, boss.'

'Which means it's contaminated somewhere between the Felixstowe distribution centre and the consumer. Bloody hell, this is a nightmare.'

He paused, then looked at Tina. 'I've got a meeting scheduled with Potter at ten o'clock this morning. I want that list of shops, supermarkets, and cash and carry outlets on my desk before then.'

'I'll get straight on it, boss.'

Tina stood up and left the room, leaving Danny and Rob alone.

'Rob, I want you to speak with the top management at the Felixstowe distribution centre. I want them to place a temporary hold on all future deliveries of Sunvit orange juice.'

'Do you think they'll agree to that?'

'Don't give them a choice. Until we can determine exactly where this product is being contaminated, we must try to stop it at the source. I'm going to use the media and push for a national recall of this product. I want it off the shelves, or other people could die.'

36

10.00am, 10 May 1988
Nottingham Police Headquarters

Detective Chief Superintendent Adrian Potter peered over his rimless glasses at Danny and gestured for him to sit down.

In his high-pitched, reedy voice, he said, 'I understand there's been a significant development, courtesy of the Forensic Science Service?'

As Danny sat down, he wondered how Potter managed to keep himself so well informed when he hardly ever set foot outside his office.

He replied, 'Yes, sir. We now know that the vector for the poison, in both cases, was orange juice. More specifically, Sunvit orange juice.'

'What do we know about that product?'

'I've had detectives working on that ever since we got the report from the FSS. Sunvit is a Spanish company that supplies fruit juices across Europe. They are based in Almeria, Spain.'

'What about the imports into this country?'

'All their products arrive in the UK by container vessel. They are then delivered by several haulage companies across the country, from a distribution centre located on the outskirts of Felixstowe Port.'

'Are Sunvit products widely sold in this country?'

'Unfortunately, yes.' Danny handed Potter several sheets of A4 paper. 'This is a list of every outlet the Felixstowe distribution centre delivers to. As you can see, it's very extensive.'

'What about outlets in the Nottingham area?'

'They are shown separately, on the last two pages of that document. Outlets in the Nottingham area are also extensive.'

Potter perused the contents of the list.

Danny continued, 'The problem is, we can't afford to limit our thinking to just this city. We still don't know the motive for these apparently random attacks. For all we know, it could be something political.'

Potter was thoughtful. 'Terrorism? Do you really think that's likely, Chief Inspector?'

'Right now, I just don't know. I think I should hold a press conference and call for a national withdrawal of the product from all retail outlets.'

'Do you think that's necessary at this stage?'

Danny couldn't quite believe what he was hearing, so he took a moment and then chose his words carefully, 'We have to assume there are other contaminated bottles of Sunvit orange juice still out there. Until we go national, we'll never know. We could just be the tip of a very nasty iceberg. For all we know, there may have been other deaths already.'

'I very much doubt that. I'm sure we would have heard about it if there had been.'

Danny said, through gritted teeth, 'How many other forces have you notified about our six deaths in Nottingham?'

The point was made. Potter knew he had contacted nobody about the deaths in the city.

He nervously chewed the tip of the pencil he was holding, and said, 'And how do you suggest we make this national news?'

'After this meeting, I'll talk to the press liaison officer and arrange for the national television companies, BBC and ITV, to cover the story.'

'Very well. Have you spoken to the company that distributes Sunvit orange juice?'

'Detective Inspector Buxton has been on the telephone to the senior management at the distribution centre all morning. Just before I left to come here, he informed me they had reluctantly agreed to suspend all deliveries of Sunvit orange juice until further notice.'

'Well, at least that's something, I suppose.'

'They've also agreed to send a standard letter to all their customers, informing them that any Sunvit orange juice currently on the shelves should be removed. The press conference will just reinforce that message. It will also let members of the public know of the possible danger.'

Potter nodded in agreement. 'Chief Inspector, I know you said earlier that the motive for these poisonings could be anything, including terrorism. What exactly are you doing to establish the actual motive?'

'My staff are working around the clock to try to establish just that. We've carried out numerous enquiries with the friends and family of the deceased. We've interviewed all their work colleagues. Investigated their finances. We have literally delved into every aspect of each of their private lives, trying to find something that could push this enquiry forward. So far, we've drawn a total blank. It's looking more and more likely that all these people were randomly selected. They weren't chosen for any specific reason. Which makes me think the person responsible has no thought for who the victims turn out to be. I think he, or she, is driven by something else. It's that something else we need to establish.'

'Find it, Chief Inspector, and quickly. After you carry out this press conference today, the pressure on you, me, and the force generally is going to be enormous. I hope you're ready for the shitstorm that's coming our way.'

As Danny left the office, he thought about Potter's final words. Right now, pressure from the media was the least of his worries.

37

6.00pm, 25 April 1988
Hungerhill Road, St Ann's, Nottingham

For the fifth time that evening, Nabin Panchal picked up the Nottingham Evening Post. *He turned the pages quickly until he found the personal ads column.*

Once again, he scanned the newspaper for messages left by anonymous lonely hearts. He somehow hoped he had missed the message from 'Happy Chap' the first four times he had read the column.

There was no message.

Two weeks had passed since he had walked to the post box on the corner of Cromer Road and Ransom Road and posted the letter to the store manager at the Valumart Superstore. Even allowing for a delay in the postal service, the letter he had posted on the tenth should have been received by now.

On the outside he appeared calm, but inside he was raging at being ignored for a third time.

He had purchased the newspaper from the newsagents on Porchester Road as he walked home from Mapperley Hospital. The regular visits he made to the hospital to see his father were always depressing, but today had been particularly distressing. His once vibrant, intelligent father, his beloved baabujii, had been reduced to a pathetic, vacant shell.

When Nabin had first walked onto the ward and seen the old man shuffling towards him, he had barely recognised him. His father's hair was lank and unkempt, he had three or four days' growth of stubble on his chin, and there were food stains down the front of his jumper. He was bent over, like a man twice his age, and could barely string a sentence together. There was no sign of the brilliant biochemist he had once been.

The tears that had welled in Nabin's eyes stung sharply before they tumbled down his cheeks. He had dried his eyes and spent half an hour with the old man, trying his best to communicate. After thirty minutes, he had made his excuses and left. He just couldn't bear to see his father that way any longer.

He blamed himself for his father's severe decline. If Nabin hadn't talked him into purchasing the corner shop, he would still be well. He would still be his baabujii.

He screwed up the newspaper and hurled it across his bedroom. Enough was enough.

He stormed downstairs, grabbed his coat and the keys for the Ford Escort van. It was the first time he had driven the van for weeks. There was no need to drive to the cash and carry to replenish stock these days.

In less than five minutes, he drove onto the car park of the Valumart superstore. He put the hood of his coat up and walked into the store. He grabbed a wire handbasket and stalked up and down the aisles.

He kept his head down, aware of all the security cameras above. He selected a loaf of bread, a bag of basmati rice and a hand of bananas before making his way to the aisle that had the vast selection of fresh fruit juices.

He grabbed two bottles of Sunvit fresh orange juice, placed them in the basket and made his way towards the checkout. Once again, he kept his hood up and his head down as he used cash to pay for the few items he had chosen. He stuffed his shopping into one of the free plastic carrier bags and walked back to his van.

He had given the manager at Valumart more than enough chances.

It was time to follow through with his threats and put his plan into action.

38

11.30am, 26 April 1988
St Ann's Allotments, Ransom Road, Nottingham

The shed at his allotment felt cold and damp.

Ever since he arrived, Nabin had sat there, unmoving, for the best part of an hour. In front of him, on the small table, sat the two bottles of Sunvit orange juice. Behind the bottles, in the background high on the shelf, he could see the three lemonade bottles. The plastic bottles were all filled with the light brown liquid he had extracted from the leaves and seed heads of the Brugmansia plants.

He felt conflicted.

Part of him was worried about the potency of the liquid he had made.

His head was filled with unanswered questions. How strong was the poison? Would it make people very ill? Or would it prove too much and be fatal? How much should he use?

Then pictures of his desperately ill father would flood his brain.

Those images turned the worry he had been feeling into an all-consuming rage.

Suddenly, it became clear to him what he needed to do. The people who had caused his family such grief and hardship had to pay the price.

He reached forward and removed the lids from both bottles of orange juice. He drank a third of the juice and placed the bottles back on the table.

He stood up and grabbed one of the lemonade bottles containing the toxic potion. Very carefully, he undid the screw cap and poured the brackish liquid into the bottles of orange juice. He poured in just enough to top up the bottles, replacing what he had consumed.

He returned the plastic bottle back to the top shelf, then carefully resealed the glass Sunvit bottles. He gave the fruit juice bottles a good shake and was pleased to see there was no discernible change of colour.

He secreted the two glass bottles in his baggy parka and walked out of the shed, padlocking the door as he left.

It took him ten minutes to walk from the allotment to the Valumart superstore. He stood on the pavement of the busy road, just staring at the huge superstore. For Nabin, it was the point of no return.

An image of his father in the hospital, then one of his mother and sister being evicted from the shop and their home burst into his brain.

Suddenly, his legs were moving. He put the hood of the parka coat up and walked confidently into the store. He made his way to the fruit juice aisle and walked up and down it a few times, making sure the coast was clear.

Satisfied he wasn't being observed, he surreptitiously removed the two bottles from his baggy coat, placing them on the shelf next to all the other bottles of Sunvit orange juice.

The entire act had taken just a few seconds.

He walked to the checkout and picked up a bar of chocolate at the side of the cash register. He paid cash for the chocolate and walked out.

As he made his way back to the allotments, he allowed a smile to form on his lips. Any worrying thoughts about the lethal nature of the contents of the fruit juice bottles had long gone.

All he could think about now was his next move.

He decided that it had been a huge waste of time trying to connect with the lowly store manager. In a few days' time, he would write to the head office of the Valumart organisation and make his demands directly to them.

As he walked, he began to compose the contents of that letter in his head. He would coldly inform them that somewhere in their store, there was a deadly poison on the shelves. The only way they would find it in time would be for them to co-operate and pay him what he demanded. If they failed to agree to his demands, then they would risk their customers becoming seriously ill or worse.

Surely, head office would take his letter seriously.

39

2.30pm, 26 April 1988
Valumart Superstore, St Ann's Well Road, St Ann's, Nottingham

Kate Rawlings was feeling harassed. She only had thirty minutes to grab some shopping and get home before her two children would be coming home from school.

As she walked into the brand new superstore, she opened her purse and checked the contents. She already knew exactly how much money she had to spend. The budget for food was always tight, but she wanted to get the kids a little surprise. They had been so well behaved all week, even though they were getting excited about their holiday. She wanted to reward them.

Tonight's evening meal would need to be something quick and easy, as she still had to pack for the caravan tonight.

She selected a pack of budget frozen fish fingers and a bag of oven chips from the chest freezers, then a tin of Heinz baked beans from one of the shelves.

As she walked to the checkout, she was pondering what special little something she could get that they didn't usually have. She saw that the Sunvit fresh orange juice was on special offer. All the family enjoyed a glass of fresh orange, and as it was on offer, it was something she could afford today. She picked up the nearest bottle and placed it in the basket.

As she walked home, she thought about how she would surprise the kids and her husband with the orange juice. Then, after their meal, they could have an hour in the lounge watching TV with the kids before she started packing for their holiday.

The kids would think the holiday had started a day early. They would love it.

40

5.00pm, 26 April 1988
Valumart Superstore, St Ann's Well Road, St Ann's, Nottingham

Derek and Sheila Judd were slowly meandering their way around the new Valumart superstore. The weekly food shop was something they both enjoyed doing. Money was no object to the elderly, retired couple. They liked to take their time and browse, walking up and down the well-stocked aisles. The new store had so much more choice than what they were used to.

Derek was half pushing and half leaning on the shopping trolley, while his energetic wife flitted between the aisles, selecting various items.

They had almost finished their shopping and were making their way towards the checkouts. They walked along the refrigerated aisle, which contained a vast selection of fresh fruit juices.

Derek said, 'How about a bottle of fresh orange juice? We can have it with a cooked breakfast at the weekend?'

Sheila said, 'That would be lovely.'

She picked up the nearest bottle. Derek said, 'Don't get that one; it's got bits in. Get the Sunvit one. It's much nicer.'

Sheila replaced the first bottle and, as she picked up a bottle of the Sunvit brand, frowned at her husband and said, 'Goodness me, Derek. You're such a fussy so-and-so.'

Her husband laughed, 'Not at all. I just know what we both like.'

The old lady placed the bottle in the trolley, and the couple made their way to the checkouts.

41

10.00am, 11 May 1988
Nottingham Police Headquarters

Danny was feeling nervous as he looked out across the room full of reporters. He had previously held news conferences that had gone disastrously wrong. Right in front of him were two television cameras on tripods. Bright white lights at the back of the small room blinded him, and he blinked hard, trying not to look directly into them.

The press liaison officer, Julie Matthews, was sitting to the left of Danny.

She whispered, 'Are you ready, sir?'

Danny nodded.

She stood up and said, 'Ladies and gentlemen, Detective Chief Inspector Flint will make a statement first and then take a few questions. Please wait until he has finished his statement before asking your questions. Thank you.'

Danny saw small red lights on top of the two television cameras come on. He said, 'Over the last two weeks, there have been six unexplained deaths in the city of Nottingham. These deaths all appear to be linked to the consumption of a certain brand of fresh orange juice. My message to the public is this: If you have recently purchased a family-size bottle of Sunvit fresh orange juice, please do not drink it and dispose of it carefully. If you've recently consumed some and are feeling unwell, please seek medical assistance immediately. I can assure the public that we've already taken steps to ensure this product will be removed from all shops. Thank you.'

As soon as Danny stopped talking, the room erupted into a crescendo of noise. All he could see was a sea of raised arms as the gathered reporters clamoured to ask the first question.

Julie Matthews remained calm and pointed to one of the reporters. The room fell silent, and the reporter asked, 'Chief Inspector Flint, do you know what's wrong with the product? What it is that's caused the deaths of these people?'

Like all good reporters, the *Daily Mirror* man had managed to ask two questions.

Danny said, 'At the moment, we're keeping an open mind as to exactly what the toxin is that's in the orange juice.'

The reporter pressed ahead: 'So at this time, you haven't identified the toxin?'

Danny had known this would be one of the questions. It wasn't important what the toxin was, and he knew it would be necessary to keep that information out of the public domain for the time being.

He said, 'We haven't managed to identify the toxin at this time, but we're working hard, along with our colleagues at the Forensic Science Service, to do so. What the public needs to know is that whatever the toxin is, it's extremely potent and can be fatal, as we have unfortunately already seen.'

Julie Matthews pointed to another reporter. The young

woman stood up and said, 'Hilary Jackson, BBC news. Are you treating these deaths as murder? If so, what's the motive behind the killings?'

'We haven't determined any clear motive for the deaths. So currently we are not treating the deaths as murder. Right now, they are suspicious deaths, and we are investigating them all thoroughly.'

'How do you think the toxin came to be in the orange juice?'

'Again, it's too early to answer that question. What I can tell you is that the manufacturing plant in Spain has been thoroughly examined and found not to be the source of the toxin.'

Hilary Jackson continued, 'If that's the case, where do you think the toxin was put into the product?'

'We believe the Sunvit orange juice was contaminated somewhere between the distribution centre in Felixstowe and the point of sale. We're working around the clock to try to locate exactly where that occurred.'

The room once again erupted into a cacophony of sound.

Julie Matthews stood up and said, 'No more questions at this time. I'll be providing regular updates. In the meantime, let's concentrate on getting the message out to the public not to purchase or consume any Sunvit fresh orange juice. Thank you.'

She grabbed Danny's arm and physically led him from the room.

Once they were both out of earshot of the reporters, she said, 'Well done, Chief Inspector. I didn't want to subject you to any more awkward questioning this morning. The important message had already been delivered.'

'Thanks, Julie. I don't know how you cope, dealing with them all the time.'

'It's like everything else: You get used to it. Keep me

posted with regular updates on your enquiries, please. Now we've involved the press, we'll have to keep feeding them regular updates, or they'll get bored and start speculating with their own wild theories.'

'I will do, and thanks again.'

42

10.00am, 2 May 1988
St Ann's allotments, Ransom Road, Nottingham

Nabin sat in his shed at the allotment. The gardens were busy this morning. Other allotment holders were planting seeds for the new season and tending to the seedlings that had already sprouted.

He sat nursing a mug of hot coffee. As he sipped the hot drink, he studied the typed letter on the table in front of him. He had typed it out the previous night, in his bedroom.

This letter was intended for the top bosses of the Valumart supermarket chain. He had carried out some research at the local library and established that the head office for the company was located at a place called Stevenage, in Hertfordshire. He had made a note of the postal address.

The letter was almost identical to the ones he had previously sent to the store manager on three separate occasions.

There was one significant difference.

This letter informed top management that he had been previously ignored by the manager at the St Ann's Well Road store, and that he had now placed contaminated articles in the store.

It contained the same demand for half a million pounds, but this time, the money was to prevent him contaminating further items. He'd included the same instruction to acknowledge receipt of his demands as in the first three letters.

It was a simple instruction. Valumart were to place a specific message in the personal ads column of the Nottingham Evening Post *within one month of receipt of the letter. He had decided to give head office more time to respond to the threat.*

That message was to read:

Thanks for getting in touch, Baby Doll.
I'm looking forward to hearing from you again, with details of our hot date.
Happy Chap.

He had finished the letter with a chilling instruction to the recipient not to make the same mistake the store manager had.

If he was ignored, he would place further contaminated items in the superstore, putting the lives of their customers at risk.

Satisfied with the contents of the letter, he placed it inside the typed envelope. He slipped off his gloves and dipped his finger in the coffee mug, then ran it along the glue of the envelope, to stick it down. The envelope already had a self-adhesive first-class stamp on it.

He slipped his glove back on and finished his coffee before stepping outside his shed. A neighbour on the adjoining allotment was bent over, erecting a split cane frame for the row of sweet peas she had planted that morning.

He shouted over, 'Hi, Steph! Would you mind keeping an eye on my shed, please? I've got to nip out and post this letter. The post box is on Cromer Road, so I'll only be gone a few minutes.'

The woman stood up from her labours, stretched her back and said, 'No problem, Nabi. Who's the lucky lady?'

He laughed. 'Now that would be telling. And you know a gentleman never tells.'

43

10.00am, 3 May 1988
Valumart Head Office, Delaney House, Stevenage, Hertfordshire

Steve Dawson emerged from the lift on the top floor of Delaney House. It was the first time he had been summoned to see Chief Executive Sir Donald Waring, the man responsible for running the Valumart supermarket empire.

Even when he had been employed as head of security for the company, he hadn't been interviewed by the chief executive.

His mouth was dry and his palms sweating as he walked across the reception area to the secretary's desk. He was totally out of his comfort zone in these corridors of power.

He coughed politely and said, 'Steve Dawson. I'm here to see the CEO.'

The young woman said, 'Just a second, Mr Dawson.'

The secretary picked up the telephone on her desk and punched a button. There was a brief pause; then she said, 'Mr Dawson is here, sir.'

Almost immediately, she put the telephone down and said, 'Go straight in, sir.'

Steve knocked once on the twin oak doors, then walked into the spacious office.

Sir Donald was sitting behind the large mahogany desk that dominated the room. There was another man sitting to one side of the desk, whom he instantly recognised. Theodore Scott was an American, from San Francisco. He had made his name developing shopping malls across the United States. He had been headhunted by Valumart to oversee the development of the chain of brand new superstores the company were now intent on building across the United Kingdom.

Steve was now even more intrigued as to why he had been summoned to see the men who were, in effect, the two most powerful people in the company.

Sir Donald pointed to a leather chair in front of his desk. 'Take a seat, Mr Dawson. We appear to have a problem in Nottingham. Read this. It arrived this morning.'

Steve took the offered envelope and removed the typed letter. He began to read it and was shocked at the contents.

Once he had finished, he said, 'It could be just a crank, but I think we need to take the threat seriously. Has anybody spoken to the store manager at Nottingham?'

'We haven't spoken to anybody yet. As head of security, what would you advise?'

'Like I said, this threat needs to be taken seriously. I think we should contact the police and inform them of this possible danger to the public.'

Theo Scott stood up and began to pace around the office. He clicked his fingers as he walked.

Eventually, he stopped pacing and stared out of the large plate-glass window that overlooked the sailing lake at Fairlands Valley

Park. Without averting his gaze from the window, in his strong West Coast accent, he said, 'I'm not sure involving the police at this stage would be such a great idea. That new superstore in Nottingham has done superbly well ever since it opened. Profits are up every week, and we are attracting more and more customers. The police would want to flood this problem with publicity, doing their best to warn the public of the possible danger.'

As he said the word 'warn', he used his fingers to make imaginary speech marks in the air. It was an annoying habit and something he did a lot.

Steve said, 'The police would definitely want to do that. The safety of the public is always paramount for them.'

Theo Scott turned, glared directly at Dawson and growled, 'Safety from what, Dawson? This threat is so goddamn vague. Have you any idea how many products we sell from that store?'

Steve Dawson had spent fifteen years as a captain in the Royal Military Police and wasn't easily intimidated. He said, 'Vague or not, a threat is a threat, sir.'

'So the police say, "Don't shop at the Valumart superstore because something – one item in all the items we sell – has been tampered with. It could make you very ill or possibly even kill you." Can you imagine that? It would be a fucking disaster. Nobody would ever want to shop there again.'

'And if the author of this letter is some deranged individual who's done what he's stated and contaminated food? And a customer becomes sick or even dies ... what about the publicity from that?'

'Come off it, Dawson. People die all the time, and for a thousand different reasons.'

Steve Dawson was shocked at the coldness of the American's remark. He looked to Sir Donald for support.

Sir Donald remained silent, deep in thought.

Theo Scott returned to his seat and whispered something into the CEO's ear.

Sir Donald said, 'It seems to me that we have at least a month to respond, so I don't want any police involvement at this time. Dawson, I want you to drive to Nottingham and assess the situation on the ground. Talk to the store manager –'

Scott interjected, 'It's Owen Bradley, sir. One of our brightest talents. He's doing a brilliant job.'

'Talk to Owen Bradley and see what he has to say,' Sir Donald continued. 'See if there's any truth in this maniac's claim that the store manager has ignored him previously. When you've done that, I want you to report back here in no later than one week's time, and we'll reassess the situation. Ask my secretary to photocopy the letter and the envelope so you can take them both with you.'

Steve Dawson stood up and said, 'Yes, sir.'

As he reached the door, Theo Scott said, 'And Dawson, show some damn discretion, okay? If a single word of this was to reach the press, the damage to the reputation of that individual store, and to the entire Valumart brand, could be catastrophic. Do you understand?'

Dawson nodded. 'Understood, sir.'

44

9.00am, 4 May 1988
Valumart Superstore, St Ann's Well Road, St Ann's, Nottingham

Owen Bradley had just taken his first break from work.

Ever since the new superstore had opened, he had thrown himself into his role as store manager. He was making a huge success of the store, and profits continued to rise. He knew that head office was impressed with the performance of the store. More importantly, he knew the top bosses were pleased with his personal performance.

He had hoped to come back, after spending three days in the Lake District with his wife and two young children, feeling relaxed and refreshed.

Any relaxation he felt had quickly disappeared, though, when he returned home and heard the message left on his answerphone.

A visit from security was all he needed.

He had no idea what the security issue that had been discov-

ered could be. But for the head of security to be travelling all the way from Stevenage, to interview him, spelt trouble with a capital T.

Owen had only met Steve Dawson once. That had been at a meeting in Birmingham attended by all the new superstore managers. It was to introduce the brand new, high-tech CCTV system that was being installed in all of Valumart's new stores.

Dawson had a fearsome reputation. The ex-military policeman had an intimidating physical presence, and his short, crew-cut hairstyle and once-broken nose only added to his menacing aura.

When Owen had engaged the head of security in conversation at that meeting, he had been surprised at just how acutely intelligent and astute the former soldier was.

Steve Dawson was obviously not a man to cross.

Owen had spent the morning going over the figures of the recent profits, trying to establish if there was money leaking from any departments. He could find nothing. His anxiety levels had continued to rise throughout the morning. The last two hours, waiting for the head of security to arrive, had been horrendous.

Suddenly, a sharp knock on his office door meant the time had come.

He stood up and shouted, 'Come in.'

The door opened, and Steve Dawson walked in.

Owen said, 'Good morning, Mr Dawson. Can I get you a tea or coffee?'

Steve Dawson put his briefcase on the floor, slipped off his overcoat, smiled and said, 'No, thanks, Owen. While it's just the two of us here, why don't you call me Steve?'

'Very well.'

The two men sat down, and Owen waited for Steve Dawson to speak first.

Dawson said, 'I expect you've been racking your brains all morning, trying to find the hole where money's leaking from the store's profits, haven't you?'

'I can't lie. That's exactly what I've been doing, and I can't find a bloody thing.'

'No, you won't. That's not why I'm here.'

'Why, then? It's got to be something serious to make you drive all the way from Hertfordshire to Nottingham.'

'I don't know if it's serious or not. Head office are flapping though; that's why I'm here – to see if you can shed any light on this.'

Dawson reached down and picked up his briefcase. He opened it and took out the photocopies of the envelope and the letter received at head office.

'Read this and tell me your thoughts.'

Owen took the letter and began to read. As he scanned the contents, he instantly remembered the three letters stuffed in the bottom drawer of his desk. Why hadn't he contacted head office straight away? He was now in deep shit and knew he had to try to bluff his way out of it.

Having read the contents, Owen handed the letter back to Dawson.

The head of security said, 'Well, what do you think?'

'Hard to say, really. A crank possibly?'

'That was my first impression, but then I read the part where he states he had previously sent letters here that had been ignored. Is that what's happened? Have you had similar letters delivered here?'

The lie slipped out easily: 'No. There's been nothing like that sent here.'

Dawson persisted, 'It's strange that he should claim that if it's not true. He must know that the first thing we would do is check.'

'He sounds like a proper nutjob to me. Do people like that ever think rationally?'

'So no other letters, then?'

Owen shook his head. 'If I'd received something like that, the first thing I would have done would be to contact head office for some advice.'

'Okay. Have you had any problems dismissing staff lately?'

'I haven't had to dismiss anybody for three months. The ship, as they say, is running smoothly.'

'That's good to hear, Owen.' Then Dawson said, 'Have there been any disgruntled customers making threats to your staff?'

'There have been sporadic incidents where members of staff have been threatened with physical violence by complaining customers. There was one very serious incident, when two security staff received minor injuries from a detained shoplifter who was armed with a knife. But there's been nothing like the threats made in that letter.'

'Okay, Owen. Thanks. If you do receive any threats through the post like this or otherwise, I want you to contact me immediately. Do you understand?'

'Yes, of course.'

Dawson returned the photocopied letter and envelope to his briefcase, retrieved his coat and said, 'That's it. I bet you're relieved to know that you're not losing money from the store?'

Owen let out a nervous laugh. 'That's always good to know.'

As Dawson reached the door, he turned, made eye contact with Bradley and said, 'Don't forget. Any threats, and I want to know about them. If this is genuine, it could have serious consequences for all of us.'

'No problem.'

As soon as Dawson had left, Owen snatched open the bottom drawer of his desk and stared at the three letters. For a second, he considered taking them out, destroying them and maintaining he had never received them. In the end, he just slammed the drawer shut, leaving the letters where they were.

Hopefully, they were the work of a deluded crank, and nothing would ever come of them.

45

8.00am, 5 May 1988
Delaney House, Stevenage, Hertfordshire

Steve Dawson was surprised when Theodore Scott walked into his office. He had been expecting to brief Scott and Sir Donald later that morning about the result of his enquiries at the Nottingham store.

Scott said, 'Sir Donald's in London all day today. He's asked me to see you first thing this morning to sort this letter business out once and for all.'

'Okay, sir.'

Scott sat down and said, 'How did you get on in Nottingham?'

'I spent the day talking to the staff and the various managers of departments before I spoke to the manager, Owen Bradley.'

'Anything at all from the staff?'

'Nothing. They've experienced the same issues all new stores do, with disgruntled customers and violent shoplifters. There was nothing to suggest anything like what's spoken about in the letter.'

'I take it you didn't discuss the contents of the letter with the staff?'

'Of course not. I spoke to them in general terms about threats and violence reduction, that sort of thing.'

'And what did Owen Bradley have to say?'

'He assured me there had been no similar letters received at the store.'

'That's good news.'

'I pressed him quite hard about it. I felt he wasn't being totally honest with me at the time, and I'm still not sure now. But he maintained that no such letters had been received.'

'So this letter is a one-off. Undoubtedly the work of a crank.'

'It would seem so, sir.'

'Good work, Dawson. A threat of this nature would be a nightmare to try to contain.'

46

9.00am, 12 May 1988
Valumart Superstore, St Ann's Well Road, St Ann's, Nottingham

Owen Bradley was a worried man.

The previous night he had been at home with his wife, watching the ten o'clock news. There had been a story that concentrated on six unexplained deaths in the city of Nottingham. The detective giving the news conference had explained how the deaths could be linked to the consumption of a particular brand of fresh orange juice.

As soon as he arrived at work at seven thirty that morning, the first thing he had done was to check the stock list. To his horror, he saw that Sunvit fresh orange juice was indeed stocked on his supermarket shelves.

He had tried to ignore the problem and carry on with his normal duties as store manager, but now, as he sat down to open the day's mail, everything was suddenly brought back into sharp focus. The first letter he opened was from the Sunvit distribution centre at Felixstowe. It was a strongly worded letter that advised the immediate removal from sale of all family-size Sunvit fresh orange juice products.

He pressed the button for the tannoy and said, 'Mrs Wardle, to the store manager's office immediately, please.'

The first thing he needed to do was get those bloody bottles removed from the shelves. Gwen Wardle, the wines and spirits manager, would see to that. She was responsible for ordering and stocking the shelves with all the drinks sold in the store.

His thoughts then turned to the more pressing problem he had. What to do about the previous threatening letters he had received? He cursed himself for not talking to Steve Dawson about them when he had the chance.

As he mulled over what to do, there was a knock on his office door that broke his chain of thought.

He shouted, 'Come in.'

Gwen Wardle walked in. 'You wanted to see me, Mr Bradley?'

'Yes. Apparently, we stock a product called Sunvit fresh orange juice.'

'Yes, we do. It's one of our most popular sellers.'

'This letter arrived today, advising us to remove all the family-size bottles of Sunvit orange juice from the shelves. Can you organise that straight away, please?'

'Of course. Is it to do with what was on the news last night? All those deaths. Those poor people; a couple of young kids as well. It was horrible.'

'I would think so. Make sure your staff know not to restock the shelves with that product until I inform you personally that it's safe to do so. Understood?'

'Yes, sir.'

'Right, let's get them removed as soon as possible.'

Gwen Wardle knew when she was being dismissed. 'Yes, sir. I'll get straight on it.'

As soon as his office door closed, Owen opened the bottom drawer of his desk. He took out the three letters and sighed heavily. There was only one thing he could do. He picked up the telephone and dialled a number from memory. It was answered on the second ring. 'Hello, this is Delaney House. Can I help you?'

Owen bit his bottom lip to try to stop it trembling, and said, 'I'd like to speak to Steve Dawson, please.'

'Can I ask who's calling?'

'Owen Bradley. Store manager at the Nottingham City superstore.'

'Just a moment, sir. I'll put you through.'

There was a brief pause, and then he heard Steve Dawson say, 'Owen, this is an early call. Is everything okay?'

'I've just been made aware of something that's quite disturbing.'

'Go on.'

'I've recently employed a new secretary. She has just brought three letters to my attention that had been filed under complaints before being shown to me.'

'And these three letters ... they just *happen* to contain threats to contaminate food in your store, do they?'

Owen Bradley wasn't a stupid man. He could hear the heavy sarcasm and disbelief in the voice of the head of security. He was feeling fraught, but had to maintain the lie, or he would risk facing disciplinary action or even dismissal.

He said quietly, 'Yes, they do. I can't believe the stupid woman, my previous secretary, just filed them without mentioning them to me. She must have assumed they were from a crank.'

'I can't believe it either. It sounds like a good thing she was dismissed.'

There was that heavy sarcasm again.

Owen paused and then said, 'What do we do now?'

'I'll speak to senior management, but considering the news reports last night, I think the police will have to be informed. I want you to send copies of those letters to my personal fax machine, here at head office, and then place the originals in the safe. Nobody in the store must see those letters. Understood?'

'Yes, sir. I'll ensure that doesn't happen.'

'What about your secretary?'

'Excuse me?'

'Your secretary? She must have read the letters, to bring them to your attention.'

Trying not to allow his voice to betray the panic he was feeling, Owen spluttered, 'She'll be fine. I told her they were unimportant and that I would deal with them.'

'She's new. Can you trust her not to gossip?'

'Yes, sir. She's not the gossiping type.'

'That's okay, then. If you're sure. Try not to worry, Owen. You've done the right thing. You can leave this with me now.'

Owen put the phone down and let out a huge sigh of relief.

He removed a Filofax from his desk that contained all the numbers for the various departments of the Valumart empire. He found the number for the personal fax machine in Steve Dawson's office. He took the letters to his own fax machine, dialled the number and sent copies to Dawson. Then he returned the letters to their respective envelopes and placed them all in the safe in his office.

He felt physically and mentally drained with the stress of it all. He didn't dare to wonder what would happen next.

47

10.00am, 12 May 1988
Delaney House, Stevenage, Hertfordshire

Steve Dawson knocked on Theo Scott's office door and waited. After a few seconds, he heard Scott's distinct American accent: 'Come in.'

Steve walked in, and Scott looked up from the paperwork he was reading. 'What is it, Dawson? I've got a mountain of work to get through here.'

'We have a serious problem, sir.'

Scott knew this wasn't going to be something quickly sorted out, so he removed his glasses and sat back in his chair. 'Don't tell me: It's to do with that fucking letter again, isn't it?'

Steve handed him the faxed copies of the three letters from the Nottingham store and said, 'It's four letters now, sir.'

As he read the three letters, Scott's lips were clenched together as he fought to suppress his anger.

When he had finished reading the last one, he said through gritted teeth, 'Where the hell did you get these?'

'They were just faxed to me by Owen Bradley, the store manager at Nottingham. He claims that his previous secretary had filed them without letting him see them first.'

'Do you believe that?'

'Not for a second, but right now, that's not the issue. Considering the news reports last night, about the unexplained deaths in Nottingham, I think we must inform the police about these letters immediately.'

Scott was silent. He closed his eyes and massaged his temples, as though trying to physically extract an answer from his brain.

Eventually, he said, 'Very well. But this must be handled extremely carefully. We cannot afford to allow the police, or the public, to think that we have in any way dragged our feet over this matter. We must be shown to be co-operating every step of the way. That's the only way we'll be able to achieve a positive spin on this shitty situation.'

Dawson was beginning to understand Theodore Scott's callous nature. The only thing that mattered to him was profit. The loss of life involved had barely registered with the hard-faced American.

Dawson said, 'I'll speak with the head of the CID for the Hertfordshire force. I'm sure he'll know the best way to handle this matter.'

'Don't forget, Dawson ... discretion's the key. I'm relying on you to get this sorted in the correct way. We cannot afford for the Valumart brand to be damaged by this lunatic's actions. Understood?'

'Yes, sir.'

48

10.00am, 13 May 1988
Incident Room, Carlton Police Station, Nottingham

Danny was slumped in his chair. He felt mentally drained and physically exhausted. It had been two days since he had appeared before the nation's press and television cameras.

The response to the television appearance from the public had been pathetic. There had been no new leads to follow up. The only thing the appeal had achieved was to convey a sense of panic to the public. There was now a tangible feeling of fear spreading throughout the city.

Every morning, he had to field a few telephone calls from eager news reporters, all vying to be the first to hear of a breakthrough. He had got used to the personal abuse he received as he forwarded all their enquiries on to the press liaison officer.

Today had seen the first negative press report. There was

an editorial piece in today's copy of the *Daily Mail*. Danny had frowned when he read the report that had proclaimed the Nottinghamshire force was too small and inadequate to be left to investigate such a massive task, and that the enquiry should be handed over to New Scotland Yard.

He had been expecting a telephone call from the chief constable all morning.

The telephone on his desk started ringing.

He took a deep breath and picked up the telephone. 'DCI Flint, can I help you?'

'Good morning, Chief Inspector. My name's Detective Chief Inspector Jacquie Wallace, from the Hertfordshire CID.'

Danny was surprised. 'What can I do for you, Jacquie?'

'I need to speak to you about the press conference you held two days ago, about the six suspicious deaths you're investigating in Nottingham.'

Of course you do, thought Danny. 'What about the press conference?'

'There's been a development down here that you need to be aware of.'

The blood in Danny's veins suddenly ran cold. 'Don't tell me you've got similar victims?'

'Thankfully not. What I do have is a threatening letter to the senior management of the Valumart chain of supermarkets. Their head office is in Stevenage, which is in this county.'

'What does the letter say?'

'It basically states that unless a large sum of money – five hundred thousand pounds, to be exact – is paid out to the author of the letter, they'll go on to contaminate further goods in one of their stores.'

'How were you informed of the letter?'

'The head of Valumart's security, Steve Dawson, contacted

the head of our CID and informed him that they had received it. I was then despatched to Delaney House in Stevenage to speak to Dawson and commence enquiries into the blackmail.'

'Was there anything else in the letter?'

'Yes. Valumart are to acknowledge receipt of the letter within one month.'

'At least that gives us some time.'

'Not really. The letter was postmarked the second of May.'

'That's over two weeks ago. Why has it taken them so long to contact the police?'

'When I went to see Dawson yesterday, he informed me that they initially thought the letter was from a crank. But that they had just been made aware of three other letters all of a similar nature that had previously been sent to the store manager at the new Valumart superstore in Nottingham.'

'Have you seen those letters?'

'Only fax copies. The store manager, Owen Bradley, still has the originals at the superstore in Nottingham.'

Danny recalled Rachel informing him that both the dead families had done their weekly food shop at the new Valumart superstore. He picked up the list of stores supplied by the Sunvit distribution centre and quickly saw that the new superstore at St Ann's was on the list.

'Jacquie, I'm going to need the original letter that was sent to head office. I'll arrange for the three letters sent to the Nottingham store to be picked up. I need to get them all submitted for forensic analysis as soon as possible.'

'Do you think the threats in the letters are connected to your unexplained deaths?'

'They've got to be. The one thing we've always lacked throughout this investigation was a motive for the poisonings. I think these letters provide us with that motive. It's a plain and simple blackmail, for money.'

'I'll arrange for the original letter and envelope to be brought up to you by police motorcyclist. It will be with you this afternoon.'

'Thanks. You mentioned that Valumart had to respond within one month. Does it say in the letters how that response is to be made?'

'Yes. Bizarrely, it's all to be done through the personal ads column of a newspaper called the *Nottingham Evening Post*. I take it that's one of your local rags?'

'It is. Does the letter state how the response is to be worded?'

'Just a minute, and I'll tell you exactly.'

There was a brief pause as Jacquie Wallace examined the letter in the exhibit bag; then she said, 'The message in the personal ads has to read, "Thanks for getting in touch, Baby Doll. I'm looking forward to hearing from you again, with details of our hot date. Happy Chap." '

Danny was deep in thought for a few moments; then he said, 'I'll need to meet with you and Steve Dawson as soon as possible. We only have a limited time left to respond. I'd like to discuss how we're going to move forward after we've placed the ad. I'll need input from you and Dawson on exactly how best to do that.'

'Leave that with me. I'll get back in touch with Dawson and arrange to come up to Nottingham as soon as we can.'

'If any other letters arrive, let me know straightaway.'

'Of course.'

'Thanks, Jacquie.'

Danny put the telephone down and walked into the main incident room. He saw Rachel was busy at one of the desks.

He said, 'Rachel, have you got any car keys?'

'Yes, boss. Why?'

'Get your coat. We're going to see the manager of the Valumart superstore at St Ann's.'

49

11.30am, 13 May 1988
Valumart Superstore, St Ann's Well Road, St Ann's, Nottingham

Danny thanked the shopworker who had shown him and Rachel to the manager's office. He waited for her to start walking away before knocking loudly on the manager's door.

Owen Bradley shouted, 'Come in.'

Danny opened the door, and he and Rachel walked in. He took his identification card from his jacket pocket, held it out towards the store manager and said, 'Owen Bradley?'

'Yes. Who are you?'

'Detective Chief Inspector Flint, and this is Detective Sergeant Moore. I understand you're in possession of three threatening letters that were sent to this store last month?'

'That's correct. Have you been speaking to head office?'

'That's where we got our information. I'd like to see the letters, please.'

'Of course. Just a minute.'

Bradley stood up and walked to the large Chubb safe positioned in the corner of the room. He dialled in the combination and opened the heavy door, taking out a manilla-coloured folder.

He handed the folder to Danny and said, 'They're all in there. I've put them into see-through folders, so they haven't been handled too much.'

Danny opened the folder and saw the three letters and the three envelopes all in separate plastic pockets.

He examined the dates on the postmarks and said, 'The first of these letters was posted in March, and the other two in April. Why didn't you inform the police or your head office about them until yesterday?'

For a split second, Owen Bradley thought about continuing with the fabrication of events he'd invented for Steve Dawson. There was something about the experienced detective's steely-eyed gaze that made him change his mind.

He sat down heavily in his chair. 'I thought they were the work of some nutter, so I disregarded them.'

'Did you tell your head office that?'

'No. I told them my secretary had filed them without showing me. I could lose my job over this; I had to say something. I realise now that was a mistake. I'm sorry.'

Rachel said, 'As I walked through the store, I noticed lots of new-looking CCTV cameras all over the place. Is it a good system?'

Bradley half-smiled. 'It's the best system money can buy.'

'What exactly do the cameras cover?'

'All the aisles and every single cash register in the store are covered.'

She turned to Danny and said, 'I know the exact dates the

victims did their shopping here. If I could find them on the system, it would confirm once and for all that they purchased the Sunvit from this store. If I then backtrack through the stored images, I might be able to find the person who placed the contaminated bottles on the shelf.'

'It's worth a try.'

Danny looked at Bradley and said, 'How long do you store the images captured on your system?'

'They are deleted after three months.'

'Who's the best person to help DS Moore view the stored images?'

'That would be Josh. He's one of the younger members of our security team, but he's really switched on when it comes to the camera system. I'll get him up here.'

Bradley pressed the button on the intercom. 'Josh Booth, to the store manager's office immediately, please.'

Danny winked at Rachel and whispered, 'I could do with one of those for our office.'

She half-grinned and whispered back, 'Yeah, right.'

Bradley hadn't heard the whispered conversation between the detectives and said, 'Booth won't be long.'

Danny said, 'Can you think of anyone who may hold a grudge against the store or against you personally?'

Bradley was about to answer when there was a knock on the door, and a slim young man, with long, greasy, dark hair and a severe case of acne, walked in. He was wearing the navy blue NATO-style jumper worn by all the security staff.

Glancing nervously at the two detectives, Josh Booth said, 'You wanted to see me, sir?'

'Yes, Booth. These people are detectives, who need your assistance to interrogate our CCTV system.'

Breathing an audible sigh of relief, Booth looked at the detectives and said, 'What do you want to know?'

Rachel said, 'I want to try to pick up several specific

people as they carried out their shopping. Will that be possible?'

'Of course, if you know what they look like, or if you have a very good description. It will save a lot of time if you have some idea when they did their shopping.'

'I know exactly what the people looked like, and I know the date they did their shopping.'

'In that case, we should be able to find them. Can I ask what this is all about?'

'I tell you what, Josh. Let's see if we can find these people first; then I'll let you know.'

'Is that okay with you, Mr Bradley?'

Bradley waved his hand at the young security guard. 'Yes, yes. Just do whatever the detectives want, Booth.'

Booth said, 'This way, Detective. All the monitors are locked in the back room of the security office, so we'll need to go down there. There are a lot of cameras to check, so it could take a while.'

Rachel handed the car keys to Danny and said, 'I'll call the office for a lift back when I'm done.'

'Okay.'

Once Rachel and Booth had left the office, Danny said to Bradley, 'You were just about to tell me about people who may hold a grudge against either the store or you.'

'I have had to sack quite a few people since the store opened. It's always the same when you're employing staff for a brand new store. You take on a lot of people without any previous experience. Some of them are just useless at the job and need to be dismissed. Some of the ones I sacked left without any fuss, as they appreciated the job wasn't really for them. On the other hand, there were quite a few others who really kicked up a fuss and made threats against me and against Valumart in general.'

'I want a list of the names and addresses of all those ex-employees.'

'No problem. It will take me a few minutes to get their details from records. Is there anything else you need?'

'I'll need to seize these letters, and I want to know immediately if you receive any more. Understood?'

'I understand. Will you have to inform head office what I've told you today?'

'I'm not obliged to divulge anything we've discussed to your head office. My own advice would be for you to be honest with them. In my experience, these things always have a habit of eventually coming out.'

'Thanks. I'll get those ex-employee details you need.'

'One last thing: Have you withdrawn all the Sunvit products from your store's shelves?'

'Good God, yes.'

50

6.00pm, 13 May 1988
Incident Room, Carlton Police Station, Nottingham

Danny walked into the incident room and waited for the noise of murmuring amongst the gathered detectives to stop. The room fell silent, and he said, 'We now appear to have a motive for both the deaths of the Rawlings family and those of Derek and Sheila Judd.'

He allowed a pause to let that important information register before continuing. 'A person or persons unknown are attempting to extort a large sum of money from the Valumart organisation. The method they're using is to contaminate foodstuffs on the shelves of Valumart supermarkets. For some reason, the new superstore in the St Ann's district of Nottingham has been chosen. We now know that three letters were sent to the store manager at that location, demanding cash. These letters were ignored as the work of a crank. I strongly suspect that the contaminated goods, namely the bottles of Sunvit fresh orange juice, were placed in that store as a direct result of the store manager's inaction.' He paused. 'Are there any questions so far?'

Andy Wills asked, 'How did the letters finally come to light?'

'A further letter was sent to the Valumart head offices in Stevenage, Hertfordshire, and subsequently the previous letters were discovered.'

The room remained silent, so Danny pressed on. 'All four letters and the envelopes they came in have now been sent for forensic analysis. They are being fast-tracked through the system, so I'll hopefully have the results in the next couple of days. There are photocopies of all the envelopes and the four letters available for you to see. These are for your eyes only. I want you all to familiarise yourself with the contents, but under no circumstances are you to take them out of this incident room. The public are agitated and worried enough without this news being made readily available.'

DC Glen Lorimar stood up. Danny said, 'Do you have something to ask, Glen?'

'Yes, boss. How do we go about finding this person? It's one thing knowing the reason why somebody's doing something; it's something else catching them.'

'It's a good point. As always, we'll start with the basics. DI Cartwright has a list of disgruntled ex-employees, all of whom were recently sacked from that store. Once that list is exhausted, we will widen it to incorporate all such Valumart stores in the county. Fortunately for us, the store at St Ann's has a state-of-the-art CCTV system. The in-store cameras cover all the aisles, as well as all the cash registers. DS Moore is currently viewing the stored images on that system. I spoke to her prior to this briefing, and she informed me that she has spotted Kate Rawlings selecting a bottle of Sunvit orange juice from the store, at 2:35 on the twenty-sixth of April. She has also managed to find Derek and Sheila Judd picking up a bottle of the Sunvit juice at five o'clock on the same afternoon. She's now working with Valumart security staff and backtracking through the stored images, trying to find anything suspicious. The only problem she has found so far is that the camera only faces one way down the aisle. Therefore, a lot of the time, she is only able to see the backs of customers.'

DC Baxter asked, 'Is she looking at staff working in that aisle, as well as customers?'

'I'm sure DS Moore will be checking everyone.'

But the detective's question troubled Danny. What if the disgruntled person placing the poison was still an employee at the store? They would have the perfect opportunity to place contaminated goods on the shelves without falling under suspicion.

He turned to Rob and said, 'I need to talk to you straight after this briefing.'

Rob nodded, and Danny addressed the room again. 'There's a meeting scheduled for ten o'clock tomorrow morning at headquarters. I'll be meeting with the DCI from Hertfordshire who started the blackmail enquiries in Stevenage, and the head of security for Valumart. I will be deciding on our next course of action at that meeting. Are there any further questions?'

The room remained silent, so Danny said, 'See DI Cartwright after this briefing. She'll allocate one sacked employee to each pair of you. I want you to use what remains of this shift to research these ex-employees. I want them all interviewed at their home addresses tomorrow. I want statements obtained from them, outlining the circumstances under which they left the organisation, and what they have been doing since. I want their houses searched as you talk to them. Use your discretion and your instincts as seasoned detectives. If you're not happy with someone, don't be afraid to bite the bullet and fetch them into the station. This is not an enquiry we can afford to go "softly-softly" on; other lives could still be at risk. I will always support you in your actions if you can justify your suspicions. Is everybody clear on that?'

There was general nodding and answers of, 'Yes, boss,' from the gathered detectives.

Danny walked back into his office, followed by Rob.

He said, 'Close the door.'

Rob closed the door and said, 'What is it?'

'It's that question Phil Baxter asked, about the staff being seen on the CCTV.'

'I'm sure Rachel will be looking at everybody.'

'That's not the point. It's all very well us investigating a list of ex-employees; what if the person bearing the grudge is still employed at the store? They would have the perfect opportunity to place contaminated goods on the shelves, and nobody would suspect a thing.'

'We could start by having a close look at the staff involved on the drinks aisle, I suppose.'

'I think we should. Get in touch with the store manager, Owen Bradley, and obtain a list of all the staff involved with wines, spirits and other drinks sold in the store.'

'Will do, boss. It will stretch our resources, though.'

'We may have to consider splitting the teams up and not working in pairs. I know it's not ideal; we should always work in pairs where we can. But I think time is of the essence here. For all we know, there could already be other poisoned items on the shelves of that supermarket.'

'Will do.'

Just as Rob was about to leave, Danny said, 'Don't make any plans for tomorrow morning. I want you with me for the meeting at headquarters.'

'Okay, boss.'

51

10.00am, 14 May 1988
Nottingham Police Headquarters

Danny and Rob walked into the conference room at police headquarters. Already waiting in the room was Detective Chief Superintendent Potter. He was sitting next to a slim woman dressed in a smart, navy blue pinstripe business suit. She looked to be in her early forties, with short blonde hair and piercing blue eyes.

Sitting next to the woman was a man who had short crew-cut hair and a nose that had once been badly broken. The man was also in his early forties and looked slightly uncomfortable, wearing a suit and tie.

Potter said, 'Chief Inspector Flint, this is Detective Chief Inspector Jacquie Wallace and Steve Dawson, the head of Valumart's security.'

Danny introduced Rob Buxton to the two guests and said, 'Thank you for coming here so promptly. I wanted you both to attend so we could organise our response to this very real threat. Shall we get straight down to business?'

He paused before continuing, 'Jacquie, I know all the offences so far have occurred in Nottinghamshire, but given the location of the Valumart organisation's headquarters, I would very much like you to remain involved. I would like you to act as liaison between ourselves and Valumart's head office. Is that a role you would be comfortable in undertaking?'

'No problem at all. It makes sense. My boss has told me to remain on this enquiry for the duration, anyway. I've also worked with Mr Dawson on quite a few occasions in the past, as well.'

'Thanks. I'm going to need you two to work closely together on this. I'm aware that the company may want things done in a certain way, to avoid adverse publicity, while we may want something done differently, to ensure the public's safety.'

Steve Dawson spoke for the first time. 'Chief Inspector Flint, I know our organisation was slow to appreciate the level of threat we were facing. But that was solely down to one man's poor judgement. Let me reassure you that Valumart will do anything, and everything, to ensure the safety of the public. Whatever it takes. Our customers' safety is and always has been of the utmost importance.'

'Have you spoken to your senior management about the amount of money demanded? Are they prepared to pay that money to prevent further deaths?'

'Like I said, whatever it takes. Since this all came to light, I've been involved in several lengthy meetings with senior management. They are quite prepared to pay the amount the blackmailer is demanding, to alleviate any immediate threat and in the hope that the police can apprehend the perpetrator. We're prepared to work closely with the police in order to make that happen.'

'That's reassuring to hear, Steve. Are you prepared to personally play an active part in this?'

'In what way?'

'I anticipate that as the time gets closer for any money to be handed over to the extortionist, he or she will demand that there's no police involvement. We could well face the scenario where you or a member of your security team will have to deliver the cash. There's always an inherent risk involved to the person making the cash drop. It would mean you or your representative could be facing an extreme level of danger.'

'I would never ask anybody else on my team to carry out such a task. If and when that scenario happens, I'll be the person making the cash drop. I spent fifteen years as an officer in the military police, so risk and danger are things I've faced on many occasions.'

'I appreciate that. Thank you.'

Potter said, 'How do you intend to try to flush this person out?'

Danny replied, 'First and foremost, we must reply to the blackmailer by placing the message requested into the personal ads column of the *Nottingham Evening Post*. It's imperative that's done today, as we are rapidly running out of time. Only when the blackmailer has seen that will he or she respond with new demands that we can act upon.'

Jacquie Wallace said, 'I agree. The quicker that's placed, the sooner we'll know how they want us to deliver the cash. The more time we have to prepare for that cash drop, the better.'

'I'll speak with the editor of the *Evening Post* immediately after this meeting. I'm going to instruct him to run the ad indefinitely. Or at least until we've seen a response from this character calling themselves Baby Doll.'

Jacquie asked, 'Baby Doll? Do you think it's possible the blackmailer is a woman?'

'I'm not ruling anything out.'

Dawson asked, 'Are you doing anything else to catch this person, or are we totally reliant on further instructions from the blackmailer?'

'I have officers investigating all the recently dismissed employees from that store. I also have officers investigating all current staff who have any involvement with the wines and spirits distribution in store. They have the perfect opportunity to carry out this act. I also have an officer working alongside one of the security team at the store, checking all the images on the CCTV system.'

Dawson nodded. 'Anything from CCTV so far?'

'The officer has identified all our victims as they selected the Sunvit orange juice from the shelves. She's currently trying to find anything suspicious in the hours and days prior to the victims taking the poisoned product from the shelves.'

'I may be able to assist you with your investigation of staff still working in the store. I have access to a lot of their background information, which you'll need. I'm going to be staying at the Savoy Hotel in Nottingham for the duration, so if I can be of any assistance, just ask.'

'Thanks. Speak to Rob after this meeting. He'll go through the list of names we have. Anything you can add would be very welcome. Does anyone have any other questions or anything to add?'

Potter said, 'What do we tell the press?'

'It's imperative that we tell them nothing about the messages in the newspaper. That's probably going to be our only real chance to catch this killer. I'll keep the press apprised of our general enquiries, and I'll stress to the editor of the *Evening Post* that there's a news blackout in force on the personal ads.'

Potter nodded. 'Make sure you advise Julie Matthews accordingly.'

'Will do, sir.'

Jacquie Wallace said, 'I'll return to Hertfordshire so I'm near to Valumart's head office, as and when things develop. Good luck.'

Danny said, 'Thanks. Okay, that's it for now. I'll go and speak to the editor of the *Evening Post*. Steve, do you want to come with me and Rob to the incident room? That way you'll be able to see for yourself what's been done so far.'

Potter stood up and said, 'Thank you, everyone. Chief Inspector Flint, I want to be kept informed of any future developments immediately. I'm reporting directly to the chief constable on this, so keep me informed.'

'No problem, sir. I'll make sure you're kept up to date.'

'See that you do.'

52

9.30pm, 15 May 1988
Hungerhill Road, St Ann's, Nottingham

Nabin rubbed his eyes. He couldn't quite believe what he was seeing. He looked again, and there it was, in black and white.

Thanks for getting in touch, Baby Doll.
I'm looking forward to hearing from you again, with details of our hot date.
Happy Chap.

He put the newspaper down on his bed and said in a croaky, emotion-filled whisper, 'Finally, I have your attention.'

From the bedroom next door, he could hear his mother, Eashwari, crying. It was all she seemed to do these days. Ever since his father had been sectioned and put into the care of the Mapperley Hospital, his mother had found it difficult to cope.

It had been left to Nabin and his sister to run the family business, such as it was. If they had more than a dozen customers in the shop throughout opening hours, it was deemed to have been a good day. The corner shop that his father had purchased was now dying a slow death. Most of the stock on the shelves was rapidly becoming past its sell-by date, and there was no money left to restock. They could no longer afford to pay the hefty mortgage on the property. They only remained in the property under the terms of a six-month grace period afforded by the building society. That would soon expire, and the family would lose everything. They would be homeless and on the streets.

The message in the small ads was now his family's only hope.

He had thought long and hard about this moment, but now that it had finally arrived, he felt hesitant about taking the next step. It was one thing to demand the money, but getting your hands on the cash and managing to evade the clutches of the police was something else entirely.

Nabin knew this would be the most dangerous part of the whole plan.

He closed his eyes and listened to his mother crying next door. As he concentrated on the sounds in the flat, he could now also hear the quieter sobbing of his younger sister. He thought about his once-proud father rocking back and forth on a chair in the ward of the mental hospital. An image of his father's tortured face burst into his brain. He could see the anxiety behind his brown eyes, the deep furrows on his brow and the spittle running down his unshaven, unwashed chin.

He opened his eyes; he knew what he had to do.

He put on a pair of latex gloves and placed a sheet of A4 paper into the portable Olivetti typewriter. Using his two index fingers, he began to type another letter to the Valumart head office.

Within the letter, he gave details of the way the money was to be delivered to the drop. He maintained his demand of half a million pounds, stating the money was to be made up of unmarked twenty-pound notes. The cash was to be packed carefully into a very specific type of bag.

He typed in the details of the location for the drop and insisted the money was to be delivered to that location by Owen Bradley, the manager of the Valumart superstore who had caused his family such grief. He had seen a photograph in the *Nottingham Evening Post* of Bradley, standing next to his wife and two young children, as the huge superstore was officially opened by the sheriff of Nottingham. He knew exactly what Bradley looked like, so he would know if the police or anybody else had taken his place.

He made it clear that if he suspected the police were involved at any point, he would abort the collection of the cash and place further contaminated goods within another Valumart supermarket somewhere in the UK. If he was detained during the collection, then his accomplices would ensure the terror continued by placing contaminated goods in other stores on his behalf.

Finally, he stated that a further message to 'Baby Doll' must be placed in the same personal ads column within the next forty-eight hours. This message would be confirmation that 'Happy Chap' agreed to all the details of their upcoming date.

To add more menace to his demands, he stated that any failure to place the message within the next forty-eight hours would have dire consequences, and further deaths might occur.

He read back the typed letter.

Satisfied with the contents, he removed the paper from

the typewriter and replaced it with a small white envelope. He typed the address for Valumart's head office on the envelope.

He checked the letter one last time, folded it and placed it inside the envelope. He used Sellotape to seal the envelope before placing it into a plastic bag.

He walked out of his room, closed the door and tapped lightly on his mother's bedroom door. He leaned forward until his mouth was less than an inch from the door and said, 'I've got to go out, *maamii*. I'll lock the door behind me so you and Padama will be safe. I won't be long.'

There was no reply.

He walked downstairs, grabbed his parka coat and stepped out into the darkness. There was a clear sky with a bright moon, and after the warmth of the flat, it felt extremely cold outside. He was glad he still wore the latex gloves on both hands. He gripped the plastic bag containing the letter in one hand and thrust his other hand deep inside one of his coat pockets.

He saw a gang of youths standing on the street ahead of him. He was wary of their intentions, so he averted his eyes to prevent making any eye contact, before crossing over to the other side of the road to avoid them.

He walked briskly to the post box on the corner of Cromer Road and Ransom Road. He took one last glance all around him before removing the letter from the plastic bag and slipping it inside the post box.

Having posted the letter, he screwed up the bag and tossed it over a fence.

Thrusting both gloved hands in his coat pockets, he turned and started for home. As he made the short walk back to his family's corner shop, he began to have serious doubts about the letter. What if the police were called? He had thought it through a hundred times, but now was racked with an illogical uncertainty. Had he provided too much detail about the method and location of the drop? Would it give them too much time to prepare a trap?

He became overwhelmingly concerned about the content of the letter, so he turned and made his way back to the post box. He tried to squeeze his hand inside the slot to retrieve the letter. It was hopeless. He couldn't reach any of the letters inside the box, and it was pitch black, so he couldn't see what he was doing.

He thrust his cold hands back inside his coat and felt a box of Swan Vesta matches. He slid open the matchbox and saw there was only about a dozen of the red-headed matches. With no other option, he struck a match and dropped it into the post box. The flame flared a little and then died. He tried repeatedly until there were only four matches left. He felt in his pockets, and the only thing he had was a solitary tissue. He wrapped the tissue around the four remaining matches. He gripped all four together and struck them. He dropped the cluster of matches and the tissue into the post box and watched as the flare occurred. It lasted longer this time and didn't die. He saw a wisp of smoke emerge from the letterbox.

Without waiting to see the contents of the post box go up in flames, Nabin turned and walked away. He never saw that the small initial fire caused by the tissue had only burned for a minute or so before spluttering and dying completely. It had flared briefly and destroyed a couple of letters before singeing the edges of two or three others, his own included. The air was just too cold and damp for the contents of the post box to be set alight using a few safety matches and a tissue.

As he walked back to the family shop, he was watchful. The gang of youths that he had passed on the way were now nowhere to be seen.

He took out his keys and unlocked the front door of the shop before slipping quietly inside.

As he locked the shop door and took off his coat, he allowed himself a congratulatory smile that he had managed to destroy the worrisome letter. He would need to type another letter and send it in the morning. He would check on the burned-out post box before finding a different one to mail the letter to Valumart.

The scheme he had dreamed up, as he sat in the shed on his allotment worrying about his family, would soon pay off.

If everything went to plan, all his family's money troubles would soon be over.

53

11.30pm, 15 May 1988
Mansfield, Nottinghamshire

Sue woke with a start. She turned over in bed and quickly realised that Danny wasn't in bed next to her. She got out of bed, slipped on her silk dressing gown, and tiptoed into the nursery next door.

Her baby daughter, Hayley, was still sleeping soundly. Sue could hear soft, gentle snores emanating from the cot.

She quietly closed the door and made her way downstairs.

She found her husband seated at the dining room table.

He was wearing boxer shorts and gripping an empty coffee mug in his right hand. Sue could see he was staring at papers that were strewn all over the dining room table.

She stood behind him and massaged the powerful muscles that ran from his neck to his shoulders. She leaned forward, kissed him behind his right ear, and whispered, 'What are you doing, darling?'

Without turning to face her, he said, 'I couldn't sleep, so I made myself a drink.'

Sue took the mug from his hand and said, 'I'm awake now. Do you want a refill?'

He nodded, still staring at the papers.

Sue walked into the kitchen and boiled the kettle. She returned, minutes later, with two hot mugs of coffee.

She put the coffee mugs on coasters, sat down next to Danny and said, 'What are all these papers?'

'They're copies of the letters and envelopes typed by the lunatic who's poisoning people.'

'And what are you doing with them?'

'Do you remember Professor Whittle?'

'Yes, of course.'

'She once told me that detectives in the FBI sometimes try to imagine themselves as the killers they are hunting. Apparently, it helps them to understand their quarry better.'

'And that's what you're doing right now, is it? You do know that it's almost midnight?'

'I know it sounds ridiculous, but I'm ready to try anything. I need to understand this person better. Right now, I feel like I don't know anything at all about him or her.'

Sue took a sip of her hot coffee and said, 'Well, at least you know they're from the Nottingham area. Why else would they want a message placed in the *Nottingham Evening Post* personal ads column? I don't suppose the circulation of that newspaper stretches too far beyond the city.'

Danny looked at his wife and grinned. He snatched up the copies of the envelopes and began to examine the postmarks. He immediately saw that all the envelopes had been postmarked within the Nottingham area after they had been posted.

He put the papers down and placed both his hands on Sue's cheeks. Pulling her towards him, he kissed her hard on the mouth and said, 'Babe, you're a genius. I think you've just given me an idea how I can catch this maniac.'

'Good. Maybe we can go back to bed now. Hayley will be awake and wanting her feed soon, and I'm shattered.'

Danny gathered up all the papers and placed them back in his briefcase.

Sue looked at her husband. She could see the excited glint in his brown eyes and doubted he would be able to sleep.

She said, 'Come on, sweetheart, you need to rest. That idea will still be there in the morning.'

54

8.00am, 16 May 1988
Incident Room, Carlton Police Station, Nottingham

Danny heard the knock on his office door and shouted, 'Come in.'

Rob and Tina walked in. Rob said, 'You wanted to see us both?'

'Yes, grab a seat. I had an idea last night. Do you think it's possible for the post office to tell us where these letters were posted?'

Rob said, 'How?'

'From the postmark on the envelope. It was suggested to me that this maniac must be living somewhere in Nottingham. Why else would he want the messages placed in the *Nottingham Evening Post*?'

Danny paused, then said, 'I don't know anything about postmarks on letters. I wondered if there was some unique reference within that postmark that would tell us where the letters were posted.'

Tina picked up one of the copies of the envelopes and began studying the postmark that ran across the stamp, preventing its reuse.

She said, 'Well, there's a series of numbers and letters within the stamp, as well as the name Nottingham. So maybe it's possible.'

'Those numbers and letters are the same on every envelope.'

Rob said, 'And maybe the closest we'll get is that they've all been posted in Nottingham city. Have you any idea how many post boxes there are in this city?'

Danny said, 'That's what I want you to find out this morning. I want you to visit every sorting office. Start with the ones in the city, and gradually work your way out. I know it's a long shot, but it's worth trying. Even if we only narrow it down to an area of the city, it's a start.'

Tina said, 'Even if we can use the postmark to establish where the letters have been posted, what then?'

'We watch the post boxes. It's obvious this person is a creature of habit. If he, or she, has used the same post box to send all the letters so far, the chances are they'll use the same one again. It must be convenient for them; they probably live or work near to this particular post box. Just see what you can find out, but I need you to work fast. If it's possible, and we can narrow it down, I want to be in position to set up observations as soon as we can. If further letters are posted, it may be possible to photograph and identify the suspect.'

Tina said, 'Yes, we could do that ... but how will we know which individual has posted the letter to Valumart?'

'Well, we can't intercept and open the mail ourselves, but what we can do is photograph each person who posts a letter. Then we take the letters from the post box, when it's emptied, and deliver them alongside post office workers to wherever they are addressed to. The detective would be in possession of an album of photographs of the people who had posted the letters. It would be down to the recipient of the letter to then identify the person who had posted them the letter. It would be a long, staff-intensive operation, but eventually we would be left with the letter to Valumart and an image of the suspect. It will then be down to us to identify and arrest the suspect.'

Rob said, 'Will we have enough time to do all that?'

Danny shrugged. 'First things first. Let's see if we can identify which post box or boxes have been used. If the plan is feasible, we may have to goad this maniac into sending further letters to Valumart head office.'

The two detective inspectors stood up, and Rob said, 'We'll get the whole team visiting the various sorting offices this morning. That way, we'll cover the ground quickly and establish if your idea is feasible or not.'

'Thanks. Keep me informed of any progress.'

55

9.00am, 16 May 1988
Ransom Road, St Ann's, Nottingham

Nabin walked with his head down and the hood of his coat up. It was drizzling with a light rain, and the air felt damp. He hated the weather in this bloody country. He never felt warm.

The letter to Valumart was in the inside pocket of his coat. He had retyped it that morning and omitted all the details of the money drop.

The rest of the content was identical to the letter he had destroyed the previous night.

As he approached the junction of Ransom Road and Cromer Road, he could see the red post box. It looked unscathed. He cursed inwardly as he walked slowly towards the junction.

He peered inside the slot of the post box and could just make out some of the letters in the bottom. He could see that nearly all of them remained undamaged. There was a smell of scorched paper, but that was all.

Looking around, he could see that Ransom Road was now extremely busy, with vehicles and pedestrians. There was no way he could do anything about the post box now. Once again, he cursed. This time out loud. Why the fuck hadn't he stayed to make sure the post box had been destroyed?

He stepped back and leaned against a wall. He needed to think.

It didn't really matter if the details of the drop were in the first letter. He could always change the arrangements. It would probably be better to let Valumart and the police think one thing, and then do something completely different.

He would need to prepare an alternative.

When he had been planning the cash drop, he had come up with several different ideas. There was one location he had thought of that he knew could be used very effectively. He would need to put a few things in place first, though.

Feeling much more confident, he stepped forward and posted the new letter. It wouldn't hurt for Valumart to get the message twice. They might even take his threats more seriously. He would soon know the answer to that, though. He had given them forty-eight hours to place the message in the personal ads column, confirming that they had the money in place.

56

10.00am, 17 May 1988
Nottingham Police Headquarters

Danny had finished outlining the details of his proposed plan to Adrian Potter. The detective chief superintendent looked troubled by what he had heard.

After a lengthy delay, he eventually said, 'I can see what you're trying to achieve, but don't you think there's a significant risk in trying to delay the pay-out?'

'There's a risk in everything we do. I'll know later today if the post office can help us identify the post box he's using. I just think this is our best chance to catch the bastard.'

'I appreciate that, but this person has already killed six people because he thought he was being ignored. What's to say he won't place further contaminated products if we delay further?'

'I can't answer that, and I fully understand the risk. But if the post office can identify the post box, I'll need that brief delay to organise the observations teams.'

After another lengthy pause, Potter said, 'Very well. Get those post boxes identified. Hopefully, it won't be dozens.'

'Thank you, sir. As soon as I know if the plan's feasible, I'll organise the observations teams and draft another message for the personal ads column. I'll say in the message that it's taking longer than envisaged to get the money together, and that we need another twenty-four hours. Hopefully, such a short delay won't have any consequences.'

'Let's hope not. I dread to think what those consequences could be. I'm still not totally convinced of the wisdom of this, Chief Inspector. I want to know as soon as you hear anything from the post office. I'll make the final call when I know exactly how many post boxes are involved. That will be all.'

57

11.30am, 17 May 1988
Delaney House, Stevenage, Hertfordshire

Detective Chief Inspector Jacquie Wallace walked into the reception area at Delaney House. She said to the receptionist sitting behind the huge counter, 'DCI Wallace, from Hertfordshire police. I'm here to see Theodore Scott.'

The receptionist scanned her notepad. 'Please take a seat. Mr Scott will be down shortly. Can I get you a tea or a coffee?'

'No, thanks.'

Jacquie turned and walked across the marble floor, to the cream-coloured leather sofa on the far side of the foyer. She sat down, wondering why she had been asked to see Mr Scott.

She didn't have to wait long for the answer.

The lift doors opened silently, and an anxious-looking Theodore Scott strode across the deserted foyer towards her.

He was holding several clear plastic poly pockets.

Jacquie stood to meet him. Theodore said, 'Please sit down. Thank you for coming so promptly. These arrived in this morning's post.'

He sat down next to Jacquie and handed her the poly pockets. The clear plastic envelopes contained two typed letters and two envelopes. The experienced detective read the letters, her expression becoming more and more worried as she scanned the text.

She said, 'What happened to this envelope?'

'The scorching, you mean? It was like that when it arrived. Looks like somebody's tried to burn it. It still got here okay, though.'

'Have you contacted the police in Nottingham yet?'

'No. I wanted you to see them first.'

'Is Steve Dawson still in Nottingham?'

'Yes.'

'Is there a telephone I can use? Preferably one where we won't be overheard?'

'Yes, of course. Come up to my office.'

The detective followed the American executive into the lift. He pressed the button for the top floor. There was silence inside the lift as Jacquie quickly read the letters for a second time.

The lift doors opened, and Scott said, 'My office is this way.'

Jacquie followed him along a corridor and into his exquisitely furnished office. She asked, 'Do you have a contact number for Steve?'

Scott picked up a leatherbound Filofax from his desk and read out the number for Dawson's hotel room.

The phone was answered on the second ring: 'Steve Dawson.'

'Steve, it's Jacquie Wallace.'

'Good morning, Detective. To what do I owe the pleasure?'

'Two more letters have arrived at head office this morning. The content is quite disturbing. I'm going to contact the incident room in Nottingham, speak to DCI Flint and fax him over copies of the letters and the envelopes. I think it would be a good idea if you go to the incident room straight away. There are certain aspects to the letters that you're not going to be happy about. You'll need to discuss the best options with DCI Flint. I don't want to discuss them over the telephone. Just get yourself to the incident room as soon as you can.'

'Will do.'

Jacquie ended the call, turned to face Scott, and said, 'Who opened the letters?'

'My secretary.'

'We'll need to obtain her fingerprints for elimination purposes. There may be prints on the letter.'

Scott tutted loudly and said, 'Okay.'

'Have you taken any steps towards organising the cash demanded in the letters?'

'That's already been taken care of. There's five hundred thousand pounds, in used twenty-pound notes, sitting in the safe at the Nottingham superstore.'

'Is DCI Flint aware that the cash is already in place?'

'No. The only people who know it's there are Steve Dawson and the manager of the store, Owen Bradley.'

'How long has Bradley been employed by Valumart?'

'Over ten years. He has a very bright future within the company. A rising star, shall we say. Why do you ask?'

'It's just very unusual for an extortionist to stipulate exactly who should make the cash drop. This person has made it clear in the letters that only Owen Bradley must be allowed to hand over the cash.'

Scott shrugged. 'I wouldn't read any significance into that,

Detective. Bradley's a well-trusted employee of this organisation.'

'How do you think he'll react to being asked to carry out the drop?'

With a resigned sigh, Scott said, 'I really haven't a clue.'

Jacquie held up the poly pockets and said, 'I'll need to take possession of these and get them up to Nottingham for forensic analysis. I'll send a detective over later today to obtain your secretary's fingerprints.'

In his lazy American accent, Scott drawled, 'Do you really think that's necessary, Detective?'

'I do. Now, I need to get back to headquarters and speak to DCI Flint. Could you show me the way out, please, Mr Scott?'

58

12.30pm, 17 May 1988
Incident Room, Carlton Police Station, Nottingham

Danny, Rob and Tina were discussing the enquiries that had been carried out with the post office.

Rob said, 'We've now spoken to every sorting office in the city. We got lucky at one of the first ones we visited, in Carrington. They were able to help us quite a lot. Unfortunately, all they could tell us was that the letters were all posted in the Sneinton or St Ann's area of the city.'

'Can't they be any more specific than that?'

Rob shook his head. 'Sorry, boss. The guy in charge at Carrington said even that's pushing it. The letters could have been posted anywhere in or around those two areas of the city.'

'Roughly how many post boxes are there in those two districts?'

'I can tell you exactly. There are twenty-seven post boxes in Sneinton and another thirty-four in St Ann's.'

Danny felt crushed.

'So that's that,' Rob said. 'Keeping observations on that many isn't feasible.'

He was about to say something else, when the telephone on Danny's desk began to ring.

Still feeling a little disgruntled at the news from the Royal Mail sorting offices, Danny snatched up the phone and said abruptly, 'DCI Flint, Major Crime Unit.'

'Danny, it's Jacquie Wallace from Hertfordshire CID.'

'Hello, Jacquie. What can I do for you?'

'Two more letters have been received at Valumart's head office this morning.'

'Two?'

'Yes. They're virtually identical, except one gives details of a potential money drop, and the other doesn't. I've contacted Steve Dawson and asked him to come into your incident room to discuss the options moving forward.'

'Where are the two letters now?'

'The original letters and envelopes have all been packaged and exhibited by me. They're currently with a police motorcyclist, who's on his way to your incident room as we speak. I've arranged for elimination prints to be taken from the staff member who opened the mail at Delaney House. They'll have been obtained by this evening, ready for comparison to any prints your Scenes of Crime personnel may lift from the letters.'

'Can you fax me a copy of the letters and the envelopes, please?'

'I'll do that as soon as I come off the phone.'

'Thanks. Apart from the cash drop anomaly, is there anything else in the letters?'

'The main concern for me is that the extortionist has insisted the cash drop is made by Owen Bradley.'

'The store manager?'

'Yeah. I thought that was a bit strange.'

Danny was thoughtful for a second. Then he said, 'Did you mention that to Steve Dawson?'

'Not over the telephone.'

'Good. I'll talk to him about that. Anything else?'

'You'll see for yourself when I fax you the copies, but it looks like one of the letters, the one with the cash drop details, has been burnt.'

'I don't understand. What do you mean, burnt?'

'The edges of the envelope and part of the letter itself have been scorched. It's as though somebody has tried desperately to destroy it and failed.'

'How can you fail to destroy a letter with a flame? And why would you want to?'

'I've asked myself the same questions, and all I can come up with is that maybe there was something in the first letter that he regretted writing.'

'Details of the cash drop, maybe?'

'Possibly. I wonder if he's thought better of giving too much notice of his intentions, after posting the letter. If that was the case, he could have attempted to set light to the contents of the post box, to prevent the first letter being read.'

'That's possible, I suppose.'

'Did you find anything else out while you were at Valumart head office?'

'They've already got the cash organised for the drop.'

'The half a million pounds?'

'Yep. It's all in the safe at the superstore in Nottingham. Apparently, only Owen Bradley and Steve Dawson are aware it's in there. Five hundred grand in unmarked twenty-pound notes. I'll send you the fax through now, so you can read the letters and see the burn marks for yourself.'

'That's great. Can you make sure the elimination prints are sent to the incident room once they've been obtained, please?'

'No problem. I spoke to Steve Dawson about an hour ago, so he should be at your incident room soon.'

'Thanks, Jacquie. Talk to you later.'

Danny hung up and said, 'Rob, there's a fax on its way from Hertfordshire. Can you take it off the machine, please? Two more letters have arrived at head office this morning.'

Rob nodded and went to retrieve the fax.

Tina said, 'Obviously, I could only hear half the conversation. What's been burnt?'

'One of the letters has scorch marks on the envelope and on part of the letter. DCI Wallace thinks the post box could have been set alight.'

'I can check on that, boss. Damage to a post box or the mail inside would have to be reported by the postman collecting the mail.'

'Good thinking. Get onto that.'

As Tina stood to leave, Rob walked back in clutching the faxed copies of the letters and envelopes.

She said, 'Can I see the envelopes?'

Rob handed over the fax copies, and Tina quickly scanned the postmarks.

She handed them to Danny. 'The postmarks are identical to the other letters.'

Danny looked for himself before saying, 'Make those checks and see what you can find out about any damage caused to post boxes.'

'I'm on it, boss.'

As Danny began to read the content of the letters, there was a knock on his office door.

Danny shouted, 'Come in.'

The door was opened by DC Fran Jefferies. She said, 'Sir, Steve Dawson's waiting in the incident room. He says he needs to speak with you urgently.'

'Okay, Fran. Show him in, please.'

A few seconds later, the door opened again, and Steve Dawson walked in. He saw Rob sitting there and said, 'Is it a bad time?'

Danny said, 'Not at all. It's a bit of a squeeze in here, that's all. I take it you've spoken to Jacquie Wallace?'

'Yes. She phoned me this morning about new letters.'

'I've just received copies. Have a look at them and tell me what you think.'

Danny handed the letters to the head of security, who read them carefully. He read them both twice before saying, 'Very bizarre.'

Danny said, 'In what way?'

'Owen Bradley to make the cash drop. What's that all about?'

'I was hoping you could enlighten me.'

'I've no idea. Whoever's doing this seems pretty determined that it's got to be Bradley who makes the drop.'

'Do you think he'll be up for doing it?'

'I'll talk to him. He does seem the nervous type to me, though, so I wouldn't count on it.'

Tina walked back into the office and said, 'There was a small fire at a post box, reported yesterday morning. Two letters were destroyed, and several others had sustained some minor damage. Those letters with minor damage were posted on.'

'Where's the damaged post box?'

'It's located at the junction of Ransom Road and Cromer Road, in St Ann's.'

'In the catchment area that covers the postmarks?'

'Yes, boss.'

'Is the post box still functioning?'

'Yes. The debris from the burned letters was swept out, and the post box is still in use.'

Danny was thoughtful for a few moments. Then he said to Dawson, 'I understand you've now got the cash in place to meet the demands made by the blackmailer?'

Dawson nodded. 'I organised it last week. After getting authorisation from Sir Donald Waring himself.'

'As you can see in the letters, we've been given forty-eight hours to place a further message in the personal ads to let this maniac know that we agree to his terms and have everything in place.'

Tina said, 'These letters were posted on the sixteenth, so we've only got another twenty-four hours.'

'I want to place a message in the personal ads tonight that states we need more time to arrange the money. I want to try to delay making the cash drop for a further twenty-four hours so that we can get round-the-clock observations organised to cover this post box on Ransom Road.'

Dawson said, 'The money's available now. Surely any delay over making the cash drop's a bit risky?'

'There's no denying that to delay carries an element of risk. I'm hoping that because that delay will only be minimal, he, or she, will accept it.'

Dawson shrugged. 'It's your call, Detective.'

Danny picked up the telephone and dialled a number from memory. After a brief delay, he said, 'Sir, it's DCI Flint. We've now identified the likely post box being used by the suspect. I want your permission to go ahead with the operation I outlined to you this morning.'

There was a brief silence, and then Danny said, 'Thank you, sir. I'll start getting things organised.'

He hung up and said, 'Rob, I want observations teams

covering that post box from all angles. I want the obs posts manned twenty-four-seven, and I want every officer in position before the box is emptied at five o'clock this evening. I want them in possession of cameras from the Technical Support Unit that have a date and time stamp facility. Once the post box is emptied, I want good-quality photographs of anybody who subsequently posts a letter. Can you sort all that in the time?'

'Shouldn't be a problem, boss.'

Tina said, 'I'll crack on with obtaining the camera equipment and organising staff, if Rob wants to get out on the ground organising the observation posts.'

Rob said, 'Sounds like a plan. I'll need to see what the street lighting is like at that location. If it's crap, we may struggle to get photographs of any quality at night.'

'Let's hope the street lighting is adequate,' Danny said. 'Okay, let's get things organised quick as we can. I'll draft the message to be placed in the personal ads and go and see the editor at the *Evening Post* personally. I want this message in tonight's early evening edition.'

He paused, then turned to Steve Dawson. 'Steve, I want you to talk to Owen Bradley. Firstly, I want you to find out if there's any reason he can think of why he's being asked to do this cash drop. And secondly, is he up to doing it? We need to know if he's got the courage to carry it out. Although we'll have him under surveillance throughout, he needs to know that he could be putting himself in harm's way.'

'No problem. I'll talk to him and get back to you.'

'Thanks, Steve.'

The office emptied, leaving Danny alone with his thoughts. He knew it was a huge gamble to delay making the cash drop, but it was one he was prepared to take, to try to catch this madman.

59

3.00pm, 17 May 1988
Valumart Superstore, St Ann's Well Road, St Ann's, Nottingham

Owen Bradley jumped when Steve Dawson knocked once on the door with his fist before walking straight into his office. There was something about the brutish-looking Dawson that made the store manager nervous.

Hoping that the expression on his face hadn't betrayed that nervousness, Bradley stood up and said, 'Mr Dawson, what can I do for you?'

Dawson didn't reply at first. He held Bradley's gaze for a long time and then said in a low growl, 'You can tell me what the hell is going on.'

'Excuse me?'

'Two more letters have arrived this morning, and the

maniac writing them has insisted that you deliver the cash to him, personally.'

A heavy silence hung in the air, and Bradley slumped back in his chair. Finally, the store manager said, 'I don't understand.'

Dawson raised his voice. 'Listen, Bradley! A request like that is as rare as rocking horse shit! So what's going on?'

'Nothing's going on. What do you mean, they asked for me personally?'

'The letters state that the only person who can make the cash drop is you. He names you in the letter.'

'I can't do that. It could be dangerous.'

'Yes, it could. But more to the point, how does he know your name?'

'I don't know. There was a lot of publicity when the store opened. Lots of photographs were taken of me and my family.'

The realisation of what he had just said suddenly registered with him, and he asked, 'Oh my God! Do you think he knows about my family?'

Dawson sat down in the chair opposite the now-panicking store manager and, in a quieter voice, said, 'Let's not get ahead of ourselves. You said photographs were taken of you and your family. Who took them?'

'There were big spreads in all the local newspapers, covering the store opening. Head office thought it would be a good idea for the public to personally connect with the new store's manager. It was the head of public relations who instructed me to involve my family. There were several shots of me, my wife, and my two daughters standing next to the sheriff of Nottingham as he cut the ribbon to open the store.'

'Did you keep a copy?'

Bradley began to rummage through the drawers in his

desk, and after a few minutes searching, he said, 'Here it is. I don't know why I kept it.'

He handed the newspaper over. He could see the expression on Dawson's face. It screamed what he already knew himself: He had kept the paper because of his overinflated ego.

He blustered, 'I wanted a copy to show my two girls when they're older.'

The head of security scanned the article below the photograph. Then he said, 'You and your family are all named in this article. Did you realise that?'

A look of panic descended on Bradley's face, and he said, 'I saw the names were there, but I never thought it was a problem before. It's wrong. What the hell were they thinking? I couldn't give a toss about them printing my name, but it's out of order to name my wife and kids.'

'This extortionist is insistent that you make the cash drop. Can you think of a reason why that would be the case? Have you upset somebody over a personal matter recently?'

Bradley racked his brains.

Yes, he had fired employees, but nothing had been too nasty. There was certainly nothing in his private life he had to worry about. He was a faithful husband and a doting father. Having extramarital affairs wasn't his thing at all. His family meant everything to him.

He made eye contact with Dawson and said, 'Hand on heart, there's nothing. It must be this bloody newspaper article.'

Dawson was quiet for a while; then he said, 'How do you feel about making the drop?'

'I don't think I can do it.'

'You may not have a choice.'

'It's way too dangerous. I'm a supermarket manager, not a

member of the SAS, for Christ's sake! I've got my wife and kids to think about.'

'I understand that. The police have assured me they would have you under surveillance the entire time, so the risk to your own safety would be minimal.'

'I don't know.'

'There's something else to consider here, Owen.'

The sudden use of his Christian name by the head of security unnerved him.

He remained silent for a few seconds before saying quietly, 'And what's that?'

'The powers that be, at head office, haven't been at all impressed by your handling of this whole sorry mess. Don't think for one second that anybody believed your bullshit story about the secretary not telling you about the letters. We all know you dark-holed them. Out of sight wasn't out of mind for this maniac. People have died – *children* have died – as a direct result of your inaction and ineptitude.'

Bradley was close to tears. He whined, 'I didn't realise what would happen. I thought they were from a nutjob.'

'They were. But this nutjob doesn't mind killing people, does he, Owen?'

Bradley slumped forward, holding his head in his hands.

Dawson licked his thin lips and said coldly, 'I would hate for all this to become common knowledge. How do you think the public would respond? This could be your one and only chance to make amends.'

Without looking up, Bradley spluttered, 'What do you mean?'

'I'm sure head office would be very impressed if you pushed concerns for your own safety to the back of your mind and stepped up for the organisation.'

There was a long silence.

When Bradley finally looked up, there were tears in his eyes. 'I don't have a choice, do I?'

The head of security shook his head. 'This is how I see the situation. You deliver the cash, and you remain as manager of this store. You refuse to do what the extortionist wants, potentially putting even more of our customers' lives at risk, and you'll be history.'

Bradley shook his head.

Dawson pressed on, 'Think of all the hard work it's taken for you to achieve this position. Think of your future and how you're going to provide for your young family.'

Suddenly, Bradley snapped. He screamed, 'Alright, alright!' There was a second's pause; then he said quietly, 'I'll make the fucking cash drop.'

Dawson allowed a cruel smile to form on his lips. 'Good man. You know it makes sense.'

60

7.30pm, 17 May 1988
Hungerhill Road, St Ann's, Nottingham

Nabin Panchal paced back and forth in his bedroom. As he stomped up and down, he read the message in the personal ads again and again. Each time he read it, his mood became angrier.

The rage built within him until his head was filled with dark thoughts.

How dare they?

Their arrogance knew no bounds. Trying to play him like he was some halfwit.

It was obvious that they hadn't learned a thing. He was not a man to be ignored. He had given them forty-eight hours to be ready, and it still wasn't enough for them.

He screwed the newspaper up into a tight ball and hurled it across the room. With the blood pounding in his temples, he sat down in front of his typewriter. His fingers hammered down heavily on the keys, and his rage was transferred onto the paper as he typed another letter to Valumart.

They would pay a high price for their ignorance. As a direct result of their ineptitude and greed, someone else would suffer.

61

9.00am, 18 May 1988
Valumart Superstore, St Ann's Well Road, St Ann's, Nottingham

There had been no problems for Nabin when he placed the bottle of Valumart's own-brand apple juice on the shelf of the supermarket.

Earlier that morning, he had taken the previously purchased bottle of apple juice from the fridge at home and made the short walk to his allotment. In the privacy of his shed, he had drunk a quarter of the juice. He was expecting the apple juice to be sweet, but it was sharp, and he screwed his face up at the harsh taste.

He had then topped the bottle back up with the liquid he had extracted from the stewed-down *Brugmansia* plants. Once he had topped up the bottle, he had tightened the lid and given the contents a good shake.

Secreting the slim bottle into the inside pocket of his heavy coat, he had set off on foot to the Valumart superstore.

The colour of the liquid was ever so slightly darker than the apple juice in the other bottles.

He had slipped the bottle from his parka coat pocket onto the shelves without noticing the discrepancy.

Once the item was on the shelf, Nabin had immediately walked out of the superstore. He kept his head down and the hood of his coat up as he walked past the security guard.

As he walked along St Ann's Well Road, he thrust his hands deep into his pockets. He touched the letter in his pocket and felt the rage start to swell inside him. The letter had been typed the previous night after he had read the message in the *Evening Post* outlining the delay. Consequently, unlike the others he had sent, this letter was full of hatred and anger. It gave a much truer picture of the cold-hearted, twisted individual he had become.

In the letter, he had warned that other contaminated goods would now be placed on the shelves of a Valumart supermarket somewhere in the UK. It also made clear that unless a further message was placed in the newspaper within twenty-four hours, stating that his demands had been met in full, then further contaminated items would be deposited at various locations.

Nabin knew that somebody could die if they consumed the toxic apple juice. The guilt he felt was virtually non-existent compared to the anger he experienced whenever he thought of his own family and how life had been so unfair to them.

It was a pleasantly warm spring day, and the thick parka coat he had worn to avoid the CCTV cameras inside the store now felt cumbersome. The brisk walk had made him hot, and he had started to sweat. He pushed the hood of the coat back off his head and undid the buttons. The air immediately felt cool around his head.

He was about to take off the woollen gloves he was wearing, to help him cool down even further. But then he remembered that he would still have to handle the envelope when he posted the letter.

He turned a corner and began walking along the already busy Ransom Road towards the post box. As was his habit, he kept looking around to make sure nobody was following him as he reached the junction of Ransom and Cromer Roads.

He posted the letter and quickly removed the gloves, stuffing them back into his pocket.

In his hurry to post the letter, Nabin had failed to spot the white van with the Severn Trent markings on the side panels, parked thirty yards away on Cromer Road.

He didn't feel like going to the shop, so he made a detour and began walking back towards the allotments. It was the one place he knew where he was guaranteed to find solace.

62

9.20am, 18 May 1988
Cromer Road, St Ann's, Nottingham

DC Jagvir Singh and DC Sam Blake were trying to make the best of a bad job. They had been stuck in the back of the observations van parked on Cromer Road for just over four hours.

They had been driven onto the plot at five o'clock that morning. As soon as they had set up the Nikon camera, the other van, containing colleagues who had watched the post box overnight, had been driven off. It was driven by the same detective who had brought their own vehicle to its current location.

From the position in which the van had been parked, the two detectives had an excellent view of the post box. The Ford Escort van had been disguised as a Severn Trent water company vehicle. As well as the plates on the side panels displaying the Severn Trent logos, there were two small apertures at the rear of the van that the camera could slot into, to take any photographs required.

Their brief that morning had been a simple one.

They were to observe the post box at the junction of Cromer and Ransom Roads and take as many photographs as possible of anybody posting a letter. They had been instructed to obtain good-quality photographs of the person making the delivery, and close-up shots of the letter if possible.

A physical description of anybody making a delivery was also to be written into the observations log, alongside the time and the number of letters posted.

The two men had decided to take it in turns and swap over every hour. One would rest while the other maintained the obs.

The action had been slow.

Since being driven into position, they had only seen one person post a letter.

It was now Jag's turn to stare at the post box. He glanced down at the camera and, for the fiftieth time that morning, checked there was a full film inside.

He stifled a yawn and heard a voice behind him say, 'Don't worry, mate, only another four hours to go.'

Without looking at Sam, Jag said, 'I don't know if I can stand another four hours in here. My arse has already gone to sleep.'

'From the look of you yawning all over the place, I reckon the rest of your body's trying to catch up, mate.'

Jag replied sarcastically, 'Very funny.'

Suddenly, movement at the junction caught his eye.

He said, 'Now this geezer's definitely clocking points. His head's on a fucking swivel.'

Sam looked through the other aperture as Jag prepared the camera, and said, 'Has he got a letter?'

The camera started to whirr as Jag took shot after shot of the suspect. 'Oh yeah, and there it goes, into the post box.'

'Did you manage to get a shot of the letter?'

'Don't think so. I took some, but I think his hands were in the way. Did you notice he'd got woollen gloves on, and it's already quite warm outside today?'

Sam finished making a note of the man's physical description and clothing, and noted the time the letter was posted. The last thing he jotted down was the man's direction of travel as he left the area.

He said, 'Was it just the one letter, mate?'

'Yeah. Pretty sure it was just the one.'

'Well, that's two letters posted in four hours. Hope it stays this quiet.'

'You idiot, Sam! You know what happens whenever you use the Q word!'

Sam grinned. 'Sorry, mate.'

63

2.00pm, 18 May 1988
Hallward Library, Nottingham University Park, Nottingham

Jimmy McLeish was exhausted.

The second-year medical student had been out all night at a party before sitting through a three-hour presentation in one of the university's stuffy lecture theatres that morning.

He strolled wearily into the library, flicked his long, brown hair off his face, and plonked his tall, skinny frame down into the soft chair. He stifled a yawn before retrieving his notepad and three reference books from his bag. The last things he took from the Nottingham Panthers ice hockey rucksack was his pencil case and a bottle of Valumart's own-brand apple juice.

He had dashed into the superstore on the way to the bus stop from the flat he shared with three other students in

Sneinton. He had grabbed the apple juice, paid, and run out of the store. He was just in time to catch the bus that would take him to University Boulevard.

Still in a semi-intoxicated state, he had almost fallen asleep on the bus; it was only the driver's sharp braking that had jerked him awake at the right stop. He had jogged through the campus grounds to the lecture theatre and been one of the last to arrive.

The lecture, on the method and complications that could arise during the removal of the tonsils, had been heavy going. The lecture theatre had been packed with eager medical students, and he had received disapproving glances from some of them over his unkempt and scruffy appearance.

Jimmy didn't give a shit what he looked like on the outside. As his father always said, "It's what's between the ears that matters, son."

He had been blessed with an enormous capability to learn, from a very early age. He had always been a loner who didn't make friends easily, and this had helped him to devote his life to his studies.

A brilliant student at the grammar school he attended, he had been tipped to earn a place at Oxford or Cambridge. In the end, he had opted for a career as a surgeon and had chosen the prestigious medical school at Nottingham University. He had coasted through the first year and gradually, over time, had embraced the student lifestyle. Parties and heavy drinking sessions were now a regular occurrence for the farmer's son from the central highlands. City life was an exciting new experience for Jimmy.

He stared at the scribbled notes he had made during the lecture and felt a twinge of regret about the heavy drinking session the night before. He took a deep breath, opened the reference books and began to write out the formal notes he would use to revise the subject properly. He used a combination of the scribbled notes he had made and passages from the reference books to make the final draft of study notes.

The university library was his favourite place to study. It had none of the distractions that his communal flat had. It was warm, and the chairs were comfortable.

After working solidly for an hour, Jimmy picked up the bottle of apple juice he had purchased that morning, and drank a third of its contents. The taste was sharp, almost bitter. He wondered if it was the legacy of his drinking the night before that had made the fruit juice taste so bad. Whatever the reason, he didn't appreciate the awful aftertaste, so he screwed the lid tightly on the bottle and placed it back in his rucksack.

He resumed his work, and after another fifteen minutes had passed, he began to experience severe pain behind his eyes. He put his pen down and rubbed his eyes.

The pain was stubborn and began to spread to his temples. He felt flushed and began sweating. He tried to close his reference books, but his arms felt strangely heavy. He couldn't co-ordinate the movements in his hands, which were now shaking badly.

His vision became blurred, and he felt nauseous.

His arms dropped to his sides as he lost all control over his limbs. Starting to panic, he opened his mouth to speak, but no sound came out.

As darkness closed in around him and he lost consciousness, he fell sideways from the chair, clattering down heavily onto the parquet flooring. He ended up lying face down on the hard floor, with blood starting to trickle from the deep gash he had sustained to his forehead.

64

3.30pm, 18 May 1988
Incident Room, Carlton Police Station, Nottingham

Rachel Moore was alone in the incident room, finishing up a report on the interviews she had carried out with relatives of the Judd family. There was nothing suspicious to report.

The telephone began to ring, and Rachel picked it up immediately. 'DS Moore, MCIU.'

'DS Moore, it's DC Jane Pope, from Lenton CID. I've just been to a possible drugs overdose at the university. I think it could be linked to the deaths you're currently investigating.'

'Is the person dead?'

'No. The victim's a second-year medical student by the name of James McLeish. He's currently unconscious and on the Intensive Care Unit at the Queen's Medical Centre.'

'Have they given you a prognosis?'

'All they'll say is that the next twenty-four hours will be critical.'

'Why do you think it's linked to our investigation?'

'It's something I found when I was going through McLeish's property.'

'Go on.'

'There was a half-empty bottle of Valumart's own-brand fresh apple juice in his rucksack. I remembered it was fruit juice from Valumart that was used to kill all those people.'

'Okay, Jane. What have you done so far?'

'When I arrived at the hospital, the consultant informed me that he had completed all the usual tests and was struggling to identify exactly what drugs the student had taken. I told him what I had found, and what my suspicions were. He immediately took a sample from the bottle for testing.'

'So where's the bottle and the rest of the contents now?'

'With me. I've bagged it up ready for forensic testing.'

'Good. Are you still at the hospital?'

'Yes.'

'Stay there. I'll be with you in the next thirty minutes.'

'No problem.'

Rachel put the phone down and walked along the corridor to Danny's office. She knocked once and walked in. 'Sir, there's been an incident at the university that could be another case of scopolamine poisoning.'

Danny grabbed his jacket. 'Who's with the body, on scene?'

'The victim's still alive. He's a medical student and is currently being treated in the ICU at Queen's Medical Centre. DC Pope from Lenton CID is at the hospital. She called it in to us.'

'Let's go and see for ourselves. Have you got a vehicle?'

'Yes, boss.'

As they made their way out of the office, Rachel said,

'Jane Pope found a half-empty bottle of Valumart apple juice in the student's property and told the consultant. He couldn't establish what drugs the student had overdosed on, so he's taken a sample from the apple juice to test.'

Danny cursed under his breath and mumbled, 'Not another one.'

65

4.30pm, 18 May 1988
Intensive Care Unit, Queen's Medical Centre, Nottingham

The journey from Carlton Police Station to the Queen's Medical Centre had been a nightmare. It was the beginning of rush hour, and the traffic congestion through the city was heavy. The steady rain that was falling hadn't helped to speed their progress.

Danny and Rachel now stood outside the intensive care unit, waiting for the consultant to emerge. DC Pope had told them, on their arrival, that the consultant had been back inside the unit, trying to stabilise James McLeish for the last twenty minutes, and that he hadn't said a word to her as he had rushed back into the unit.

After what seemed an age, the consultant stepped back out into the corridor. Danny said, 'I'm DCI Flint from the Major Crime Investigation Unit. Are you treating the overdosed student from the university?'

The consultant said, 'Professor Greg Bowen. I'm the ICU consultant working today. The answer to your question is yes, I'm trying to stabilise Mr McLeish. And no, he hasn't overdosed. Our pathology lab fast-tracked the apple juice your detective gave me. Thanks to her telling me that it could be scopolamine he had ingested, the lab staff were able to do a rapid analysis. Her suspicions were correct. The laboratory found extremely high levels of scopolamine toxin in the sample of apple juice your detective gave me. It appears that this young man was poisoned.'

'I'm already investigating the deaths of six people caused by this toxin. What's the prognosis for this young man?'

'It's still far too early to give you a likely outcome, Detective. Mr McLeish was suffering from acute tachycardia and was unconscious when he presented. Now I know the toxin involved is scopolamine, I've been able to start him on a course of drugs to combat the tachycardia and address all the other symptoms that accompany this dangerous condition. I won't know what damage has been done until he regains consciousness – if he regains consciousness. It really is touch-and-go right now. Let's see how he responds to the treatments. The next twenty-four hours are going to be critical. Now I really must get on.'

'I'm sorry. Don't let me hold you up. Thanks, Professor Bowen.'

The consultant didn't look back, but waved a hand in acknowledgement as he rushed down the corridor.

Danny turned to Rachel and said, 'We need to establish exactly where McLeish purchased this apple juice. Start with the same Valumart superstore. Check their CCTV system. See if you can find him selecting and buying the fruit juice, then work back from there. If we're lucky, it might have been purchased this morning. Once you've identified him, you can look back and try to spot whoever it was who placed the bottle or bottles of apple juice on that shelf. I want every bottle of this apple juice removed from their shelves immediately. If you can't find anything on their CCTV, I'll need to hold another press conference to recall this product nationally.'

'Okay, boss.'

Rachel turned to DC Pope. 'Have you been able to see McLeish yet?'

'Yes. I saw him when he first arrived in ICU. I was allowed into the unit to take possession of his clothing and property.'

'I'll see if the nurse in charge will let me in so I can see him for myself. If they won't, will you be able to give me a good enough description for me to identify him on CCTV?'

'I think so, and I have all his clothes and property with me. He was carrying a very distinctive Nottingham Panthers ice hockey rucksack, which will be easily picked up on a CCTV system.'

Rachel approached the door to the ICU and rang the bell. A staff nurse appeared at the door. After a brief conversation, the nurse opened the door and allowed the detective to enter the unit to have a look at James McLeish.

Danny said to Jane Pope, 'That was quick thinking to remember the scopolamine toxin. You might just have saved that young man's life. Well done.'

'Thank you, sir.'

'I remember you. I interviewed you for the last vacancies we had on the MCIU?'

'You did, sir. It was you and DI Cartwright who interviewed me. Unfortunately, I didn't quite make it that time. I was told I'd been put on the reserve list. I'll apply again in the future.'

'We currently have another vacancy that I need to fill urgently. Did you say you're on the reserve list?'

Jane Pope beamed and said, 'Yes, sir.'

'Are you able to remain here until further notice? I'd like to be kept informed with regular updates on McLeish's condition.'

'If you can clear it with my DI at Lenton, no problem.'

'Leave that with me. I'll call the ICU if there's a problem, so you can resume your duties. If you don't hear from me, take it that you're able to remain. You've already got the number for the incident room, haven't you?'

'Yes, sir. How often would you like an update?'

'Every hour. It doesn't matter if there's no change; I want to know.'

'Okay, no problem, sir.'

Rachel came back out of the ICU and said, 'I'm ready. I know what he looks like now. I'll just have a quick look at this rucksack and the clothing you've seized, Jane, and then I'm all set to go.'

Jane said, 'I'll walk back to the car park with you. I put all the exhibits in the boot of my car for safekeeping while I was up here.'

The three detectives made their way back downstairs to the car park. The exhibits were handed over and the relevant labels signed for continuity.

Jane Pope said to Danny, 'I'll get straight back upstairs, sir.'

'Thanks. I take it you would be interested in filling that vacancy?'

'Definitely.'

'I'll get things organised and be in touch.'

As she walked away, Jane Pope said, 'Thanks, sir.'

Rachel placed all the exhibits in the boot of their car, turned to Danny and said, 'What vacancy?'

'DC Pope only just missed out on the last round of interviews I did for the MCIU. She was placed on the reserve list, so is eligible to start with the Unit straight away. I think I've just found your replacement.'

Rachel grinned. 'But you always told me I was irreplaceable.'

'Did I? It's funny, but I don't remember ever saying that. Come on, you've got a few hours' worth of CCTV footage to wade through at Valumart.'

66

6.00pm, 18 May 1988
Valumart Superstore, St Ann's Well Road, St Ann's, Nottingham

Nabin Panchal sat in his rusting, dirty Ford Escort van. He was waiting patiently in the car park of the Valumart superstore. He had positioned the van so he had a clear view of both the staff entrance into the store and the exit of the staff car park.

On the passenger seat next to him was a copy of an old *Nottingham Evening Post* newspaper. It had been left open at an article covering the grand opening of the new superstore.

In the centre of the article was a large photograph showing a smiling Owen Bradley with his wife and children. They were all standing next to the sheriff of Nottingham. The sheriff was dressed in his black ceremonial robes, festooned with the gold chains of office. He was holding a very large pair of scissors poised above the red ribbon, ready to make the cut that would officially open the store.

Finally, Nabin's patient vigil was rewarded, as he saw Owen Bradley walk out of the staff entrance. He stared at the store manager as he walked across the staff car park and got into a brand new, metallic grey BMW saloon.

Nabin growled under his breath, 'Look at you, with your fancy fucking wheels.'

Nabin turned the ignition key in his own vehicle. It made a horrible noise as the engine barely turned over. On the third attempt, it spluttered into life just as the headlights of the BMW came on.

He followed the BMW as it was driven out of the staff car park, keeping a reasonable distance. Luckily for Nabin, Owen Bradley wasn't a fast driver. It was no problem for his rusting van to keep pace with the sleek BMW as it was driven sedately through the city.

After a forty-minute drive out of the city and through countryside, both vehicles were approaching the town of Loughborough.

Nabin cursed, looked nervously down at his vehicle's fuel gauge and mumbled to himself, 'How much bloody further?'

The indicator on the BMW started to flicker. He saw the car being driven off the main road and into a new estate. This was a residential area. Maybe the journey was finally coming to an end.

He hung further back and followed the grey car into the new housing estate. He watched as Bradley manoeuvred his car onto the driveway of a stunning, five-bedroom detached house.

Nabin quickly stopped the van, turned off the lights and switched off the engine. He saw the front door of the house open and two young girls bolt towards the grey BMW. As

Bradley got out of the car, the two young girls leapt on him, squealing with delight.

Nabin picked up the newspaper from the passenger seat. He stared at the photograph, then at the attractive, blonde-haired woman who also emerged from the house. This was Owen Bradley's house, and the kids and the woman greeting him were definitely his wife and children.

Nabin had seen enough.

Watching the happy family revelling in their lavish, opulent lives, which had been achieved at the expense of his own family's welfare, sickened him.

He wrote the address of the house: 55 Darwin Crescent, Dishley, Loughborough, onto the newspaper, above the photograph of the grand opening, before throwing the newspaper back onto the passenger seat.

He would return later, after dark, and take the photographs he would need for the next part of his plan. First, he needed to find a petrol station.

67

8.30pm, 18 May 1988
Incident Room, Carlton Police Station, Nottingham

Danny was alone in his office. He was feeling the pressure and stress of another long, traumatic day. He put his pen down on the desk and reached for his jacket slung over the back of the chair.

It was time to go home.

As he began to stand, the telephone on his desk began to ring. He slumped back in his chair, still clutching his jacket.

He snatched up the phone. 'DCI Flint.'

'Sir, it's DC Pope.'

The urgency in the young detective's voice instantly caused a look of grave concern to appear on Danny's face.

He said, 'What's wrong?'

'McLeish started to regain consciousness, and the staff nurse came out to tell me. She asked if I wanted to go into the intensive care unit. As I walked in, it seemed like all hell broke loose. All the monitors at the side of McLeish's bed started sounding alarms at the same time. I heard one of the nurses at his bedside shout, "He's crashing!" and then the staff nurse ushered me back out of the room.'

'Is McLeish dead?'

'No, sir. That all happened forty minutes ago. The staff nurse has just been back out to inform me that they've managed to stabilise him again after the consultant placed him into an induced coma. She's just explained to me that doing this should help his recovery. Apparently, he had regained consciousness too soon, and his body couldn't stand the shock.'

'So what now?'

'The consultant's going to supervise McLeish's gradual withdrawal from the induced coma in twenty-four hours' time.'

Danny physically felt a wave of relief course through his body. Thank God. James McLeish was still alive.

'Thanks for keeping me informed so promptly, Jane. Would you ask the staff nurse to contact the force control room of any further changes in McLeish's condition, please?'

'Will do.'

'You may as well go home now and get some rest. He'll be stabilised in that coma, so I don't anticipate any changes overnight. Good work today. I'll get your transfer on to the MCIU organised. I want you here as soon as possible.'

'Thank you, sir.'

Danny put the telephone down. As he put his jacket on, he started to beat himself up. He felt exhausted, and his head was filled with accusing questions.

Why did I delay payment to the extortionist? What if, as a result of that delay, James McLeish loses his life?

Danny muttered a barely audible prayer and hoped that the next twenty-four hours would have a favourable outcome for the young student currently on life support.

68

7.00am, 19 May 1988
Incident Room, Carlton Police Station, Nottingham

Danny had managed to snatch a few hours of fitful sleep before making the drive back into the city. He was now back at his desk, talking to Rob Buxton and Tina Cartwright, who had joined him in his office. The three detectives were discussing the outcome of the observations carried out on the post box at the junction of Cromer Road and Ransom Road.

Rob said, 'There was a total of thirty-nine letters posted throughout the twenty-four-hour collection period. There were two collections made by post office staff. The morning collection netted twelve letters, and the afternoon one, a further twenty-seven.'

'Thank God it's not a busy post box. Have the post office held all the letters?'

'Yes, sir. They're all ready and waiting for us at the

Carrington sorting office. I spoke to the postmaster at Carrington first thing this morning, and he informed me that one of the letters is addressed to Delaney House in Stevenage, Hertfordshire.'

'Valumart's head office?'

Rob nodded. 'The very same.'

Danny punched the air. 'Yes!'

He looked at Tina and said, 'Did the observations teams manage to get photographs of everyone posting a letter?'

'They did. Those negatives are still with our photographic department, but they should all be developed within the next hour. It's taking a while because we need thirty-nine copies of each person photographed.'

'As soon as the photographs arrive, I want you to allocate your teams to start hand-delivering the mail to the various addresses. By this evening, at the latest, I want to have identified which person posted each of those thirty-nine letters. By a process of elimination, that should leave us with a photograph of the person who posted the letter to Valumart's head office. Let's get cracking.'

The two detective inspectors stood to leave the room. As Rob reached the door, Danny said, 'Rob, I want the letter addressed to Valumart back here. I'll contact Steve Dawson, ask him to come into the incident room, and get permission for him to open it here. It will save a huge amount of time if we can learn what's in that letter at an early stage.'

'Will do, boss.'

Tina said, 'What about the observations on the post box? Currently, we still have detectives watching it. We could do with them back here to help go through these letters.'

'The observations must be maintained. Talk to the special operations unit and utilise their staff for the obs if possible. It's vital that we continue to watch that post box.'

As Rob and Tina left the office to start organising the

huge undertaking of trying to identify which of the people photographed had posted the letter to the head office of Valumart, an exhausted-looking Rachel Moore walked in.

Danny could see how red-rimmed and bloodshot her eyes were. He asked, 'Have you been home?'

She shook her head. 'Not yet. I've just come from the superstore. I've been viewing all their CCTV with Josh Booth. He was good enough to stay all night, as well.'

'Why's it taken so long?'

'There are so many cameras. We've sat and watched hours of images. My eyes are knackered.'

'Have they withdrawn all the apple juice?'

'They've done more than that. They've taken every fruit juice they sell from the shelves as a precautionary measure.'

'Good. Did you find McLeish?'

'Yes, boss. That was the easy bit. I spotted him after an hour or so. He looked in a hurry. He dashed into the store, virtually jogged to the drinks aisle, grabbed a bottle of apple juice and then dashed to the checkout. He was in and out of the store within five minutes.'

'That's great. So it's definitely the same superstore being targeted again?'

'Yes, sir. Once I'd identified McLeish, that was when the hard work started. Josh started to work methodically through each of the cameras in the store. We viewed the entire twenty-four-hour period that preceded his entrance.'

'Bloody hell, Rachel. No wonder you look shattered. Did you find anything suspicious?'

'The only thing that looked remotely suspicious was spotted by Josh, initially. He noticed that the same person had walked up and down the aisle, where all the drinks are displayed, on three separate occasions.'

'Can we identify this person?'

Rachel shook her head. 'We couldn't positively identify

the person other than to say he was male and of south Asian heritage. He had the hood of his coat up all the time he was in the store. I've obtained a still photo from the CCTV that shows the best image we have of him. It shows just the lower half of his face. He's definitely an Asian male.'

'What about timings? How long was the time between this man walking up and down the drinks aisle and McLeish grabbing the bottle of apple juice?'

'There's a gap of around an hour and a half, that's all.'

'Was the supermarket, especially the drinks aisle, busy during that time?'

'Not really. No more than usual.'

'Did you actually see this man place something on the shelves?'

'No. But that doesn't mean he didn't have the opportunity to do so. There were a couple of occasions when he stopped right next to the fruit juices, but the view of the camera was blocked by another customer. We went over and over that footage, trying to spot him putting something down. The full view of his actions was blocked by other customers every time.'

'Okay. What was it about this man's conduct that made him stand out as suspicious?'

'He wasn't shopping, boss. He was just walking around, loitering almost. We couldn't pick him up at any of the check-outs, either.'

'Are you telling me he didn't buy anything after all that time in the shop?'

'Not that we could see.'

Danny was thoughtful: *Either this man is an accomplished shop thief, or he's a genuine suspect.*

'Rachel, I want you to make sure the photograph of this male is on the briefing board in the incident room. He could be a genuine suspect, and I want every effort made to identify him as soon as possible. We need to either implicate or eliminate him from this enquiry.'

'I'll do that, then go and see Rob to get briefed on the letters enquiries.'

'No, you won't. I want you to go home and get some rest. You look exhausted. Good work, Rachel.'

69

7.00pm, 19 May 1988
Valumart Superstore, St Ann's Well Road, St Ann's, Nottingham

Owen Bradley felt physically drained and mentally exhausted. The stress of the impending cash drop was beginning to weigh heavily on his mind. He closed the door of the staff entrance and took two deep breaths of the balmy evening air. It would be starting to get dark soon, and he still had to negotiate the forty-minute drive home.

Feeling a little invigorated by the fresh air, he walked towards his car in the staff car park. As he approached his car, he noticed something had been stuffed beneath one of the windscreen wipers. He removed the typed note and read it.

Beneath your car is a black bag.
Open it and read the instructions inside.

Bradley squatted down and peered beneath his car. He could just about make out the black bag that had been stuffed behind the front wheel. He retrieved the bag and stared at it. It was a long black nylon grip bag.

He unlocked the boot of his car and placed the bag inside. Very cautiously, he unzipped the long bag. It was empty apart from an A4-size manilla envelope. The envelope had Bradley's full name and home address typed on it. He removed the envelope from the bag and closed the boot. He quickly glanced around the empty car park before sitting in the driver's seat of his car. He stared at the envelope for a long time before he plucked up the courage to open it.

As Bradley opened the envelope, several photographs tumbled out. He gathered them up and stared in horror at what he was seeing. They were all photographs of his house that had been taken at night. The curtains were still open, and the photographs showed his wife and children inside the house.

He reached inside the folder and found another typed note. He read the contents.

We know where you live, Bradley.
We are watching your family.
We know Valumart have already informed the police.
If you talk to the police about this letter or attempt to move your family, we will kill them.
Fill this bag with newspapers and keep it hidden in the boot of your car.
You will be contacted with further instructions later.
If you tell the police, your family will die.

Owen Bradley couldn't quite believe what he was reading.

This gang of lunatics obviously knew where he and his family lived. The photographs proved that. His blood ran cold at the thought of evil men hiding in the shadows, watching his wife and children.

He couldn't take his eyes from the photograph of his wife and children, smiling inside the house, totally unaware they were being watched by men intent on killing them.

He slumped forward, resting his forehead on the steering wheel, and began to sob.

He remained like that for ten minutes.

Suddenly, he let out an anguished cry and sat up straight, wiping the tears from his bloodshot eyes.

He realised that he had no choice. He had to do everything to protect his family. That was all that mattered. It was Valumart's money, and it was their fault that his family had been put in danger like this. He cursed the public relations woman who had insisted that he and his family be photographed at the opening ceremony.

His wife and kids should never have been involved.

Owen Bradley had reached a decision; he would co-operate fully and do whatever he was instructed, to protect his wife and kids.

Fuck Valumart and fuck the police.

As he drove his BMW out of the staff car park, he was too preoccupied to notice the grinning man sitting in a battered, white van, watching his every move.

70

10.00pm, 19 May 1988
Hungerhill Road, St Ann's, Nottingham

Nabin sat in front of the typewriter on the small desk in his bedroom.

He felt good and had a smug grin on his face. It had been so satisfying watching Owen Bradley's reaction when he had read the letter and seen the photographs of his wife and family. He had been very fortunate to get the photograph that showed the man's wife and kids playing inside the house. He knew what effect that single picture would have.

He was busy typing the next letter he intended to send to Valumart. This letter would be different. It contained a new set of instructions for the cash drop. He had always intended to discard the original plans, because he knew the police would make plans to catch him as he attempted to retrieve the cash.

He had spent hours refining the plan, which would not

only allow him to extort the huge sum of money from the supermarket chain, but would also allow him to collect that cash without being caught by the police.

Nabin had always been convinced that the Valumart organisation would involve the police, but he was satisfied that his plan to terrorise the store manager would work. He was even more convinced after seeing Bradley's reaction as he looked at the photographs. He had seen him crying uncontrollably in his car. He had seen first-hand the man's fear at losing what he held most dear.

What man wouldn't do everything he could to protect his family from unknown, would-be assassins?

Nabin knew that feeling only too well himself. Everything he was now doing was driven by an overwhelming need to protect and provide for his family. That same desire had changed him completely as a person. He now felt detached from reality but still in total control.

He knew he had the store manager exactly where he wanted him.

Nobody was watching the family of Owen Bradley. It was all an elaborate deception to make Bradley think he was up against a gang of desperate criminals.

He finished typing the letter, folded it and placed it inside the envelope. He would only post the letter when he saw the message in the personal ads column confirming that everything was now ready.

He stepped away from the desk and lay down on his bed. Interlocking his fingers, he placed his hands behind his head and let out a contented sigh.

His plan was starting to fall together. Very soon, all his family's money troubles would be over, and they would be able to move away from this dreadful city.

71

10.00pm, 19 May 1988
Mansfield, Nottinghamshire

Danny was at home, watching the late-night news on the television. He was swirling the ice cubes in his almost empty whisky tumbler. Sue had already gone to bed, as she had an early start in the morning.

He drained his glass and was about to switch off the television when the telephone began to ring. As he stepped into the hallway to answer the phone, he automatically glanced at his watch. A call at this time of night had to be work related.

He snatched up the phone and said quietly, 'Danny Flint.'

The control room inspector said, 'Apologies for ringing you at home so late, sir. I've just had the ICU staff nurse at the Queen's Medical Centre on the phone. She was calling about a patient by the name of James McLeish. Apparently, there's a note on his records to contact you immediately if there was any change in his condition.'

Danny felt the blood in his veins instantly turn to ice. 'Go on.'

'The message was that McLeish has been brought out of his induced coma and has remained in a stable condition. Early indications are good. Tests are still being carried out, but the staff nurse said the young man is showing no signs of any cognitive impairment. I've got a number for you to call at nine o'clock tomorrow morning. Have you got a pen, sir?'

Danny grabbed the pen that was kept by the notepad next to the phone, and scribbled down the number.

He said, 'Thanks,' and put the phone down.

He walked slowly back into the lounge. His sense of relief was palpable.

Ever since he'd been informed of the young man's collapse, the thought of James McLeish dying as a direct result of his decision to delay making the cash drop had weighed heavily on his mind.

He poured another measure of whisky into the tumbler and swallowed it, draining his glass.

His sense of relief intensified as the alcohol from the single malt coursed through his veins.

72

6.00am, 20 May 1988
Incident Room, Carlton Police Station, Nottingham

Danny and Rob stood in front of the large board in the incident room.

Rob said, 'Everyone has worked tirelessly all day yesterday and through the night. The progress we've made has been brilliant. As you can see on the board, each of the letters and envelopes now has the photograph of the sender next to it. We were successful in thirty-six cases, but still have three letters and senders outstanding.'

He pointed to the three letters and envelopes at the bottom of the board and said, 'These are the outstanding letters. One is addressed to a woman in Leicester. We haven't been able to find anyone at that address. One is to an address in Barnsley, South Yorkshire. Again, we've had no reply at that address so far. The other outstanding letter is the one sent to Valumart's head office.'

'Do we still have people watching these two outstanding addresses?'

'Both the address in Leicester and the one in Barnsley are being kept under surveillance, so we'll know the moment somebody returns.'

'This is great work, Rob. So who do we have left, photograph-wise?'

'The three photographs at the bottom of the board are the people still outstanding and, therefore, our chief suspects.'

Danny took a step closer to the large board and stared at the three photographs.

The first was of a white, middle-aged female. She wore wire-rimmed spectacles, and her dark hair was cut short. Dressed in a smart business suit, she looked like a professional woman.

The second was of an Asian male in his thirties. He was quite short and stocky. There was nothing remarkable about the man.

The third was of a white male, again in his thirties, with a shaven head. He was dressed casually and wouldn't have looked out of place on the terraces at a football match.

Danny broke his gaze and looked at Rob. 'Do the observations teams watching the post box have copies of these three photographs?'

'Yes, boss.'

'We're getting close, Rob. I can feel it. I want a surveillance capability put in place as well. If any of these three individuals return to post anything else in that post box, I want them followed, housed and identified.'

'I've already started the arrangements for surveillance, boss. One phone call and the surveillance team can be in position.'

'Good work. Let's get them in place as soon as possible.'

Rob returned to his desk and picked up the phone. Danny

took the three suspects' photographs from the board and walked back to his office.

He sat down and carefully placed the photographs on his desk in front of him. He then picked up the latest letter that had been sent to Valumart and read it again. It made for chilling reading:

Because of your delay and greed, someone else will suffer.

Danny stared at the three photographs and muttered under his breath, 'Which one of you three is such a cold-hearted, callous bastard?'

His eyes were drawn to the middle photograph.

There was something strangely familiar about the unremarkable man.

73

11.00am, 20 May 1988
Nottingham Police Headquarters

Danny sat down opposite Detective Chief Superintendent Potter and said, 'We've made significant progress in this enquiry and have now narrowed the search down to three very good suspects.'

He explained how the observations at the post box and the interception of the posted mail had revealed the three suspects. He handed Potter the photographs and said, 'We're working hard to identify these three people.'

Potter studied the photographs for a couple of minutes before saying, 'How confident are you that one of these three people is responsible for the poisoning deaths?'

'We now know that it was one of these three people who posted the letter to Valumart's head office, demanding money with menaces. It's got to be one of them.'

'Apart from trying to identify these people, what are you doing?'

'I spoke to the editor of the *Nottingham Evening Post* first thing this morning, and I've arranged for another message to be placed in the personal ads column.'

'Saying what?'

'This message will let the extortionist know that Valumart have received the letter he posted, that they are ready to pay the cash demanded, and are awaiting the time and date to make the drop.'

'When will this message go out?'

'The editor has assured me it will be placed in this evening's early edition.'

'And how is the young man from the university?'

'I had a lengthy conversation with Professor Bowen, the ICU consultant, at nine o'clock this morning. James McLeish is now fully awake and off all life support. He's being moved from the intensive care unit to a ward later today, as soon as they've found him a bed.'

'Prognosis?'

'It's very good. The consultant expects him to make a full recovery.'

'That's good news. The decision to delay making the payment the first time of asking was always a risky one. But it seems to have worked and flushed the suspect out.'

'We were extremely lucky, sir. The professor informed me this morning that the only reason McLeish survived ingesting this poison was because of his proximity to emergency medical care when he collapsed. He was only a couple of minutes away, and the doctors were able to intubate him very quickly, to increase the oxygen in his blood. Even then, it was only thanks to the expertise of the intensive care unit staff that the student survived his ordeal.'

Potter remained tight-lipped and silent.

Danny continued: 'Professor Bowen also informed me there was one other major factor that enabled young McLeish to survive.'

'Which was?'

'The fact that DC Pope was sharp enough to remember the cases we were investigating, and realize that the toxin in the apple juice could be scopolamine. The information she provided enabled the hospital to make an early confirmation of the poison. This subsequently allowed the medics to provide the correct treatment regime to combat the effects of the powerful toxin that much faster.'

'A lucky escape all round, Chief Inspector. If that young man had died as a result of the decisions made in this room, the shit would really have hit the fan.'

Danny was shocked at the senior officer's callous, selfish assessment of the situation. He said, 'His mother and father are travelling down from Scotland today to be with their son. I'm just pleased he's survived and will suffer no adverse effects in the future.'

Potter said coldly, 'Quite.'

Danny paused, then said, 'DC Pope is on the reserve list for the MCIU, after the last round of interviews. I think she would be an ideal candidate to fill the vacancy left by DS Moore's promotion. Can I request that she be transferred onto the MCIU as soon as possible?'

Potter was thoughtful for a few seconds, then said, 'I can see that you were impressed by her actions yesterday. Do you think she would cope working on the MCIU?'

'I wouldn't have put her on the reserve list if I didn't think that, sir.'

'Very well. I'll arrange for her transfer. You need to have your team up to strength.'

After a brief pause, he continued, 'If there's nothing else, I won't keep you, Chief Inspector. I appreciate you still have a lot of work to do.'

Danny placed the photographs of the three suspects back into his briefcase and stood up.

As Danny reached the door, Potter spoke again. 'Make sure you use the time we bought to catch this maniac.' He paused before parroting the chief constable's comment: 'I want no more deaths. Understood?'

Danny nodded. 'Yes, sir.'

74

4.15pm, 20 May 1988
Ransom Road, St Ann's, Nottingham

Ransom Road was already busy with rush hour traffic heading out of the city. Nabin strolled casually along the pavement, dodging other pedestrians, who all appeared in a hurry to get wherever it was they were going.

He had been wandering up and down the bustling road for over fifteen minutes. Patiently waiting for the van that delivered the evening newspapers to arrive at the newsagents on the corner. As soon as the van had made its delivery and driven off, Nabin had ducked inside the small shop.

He purchased the early evening edition of the *Nottingham Evening Post* and stepped back out onto the street. He leaned against the wall of the newsagents and flicked through the pages. Once he had found the page containing the personal advertisements column, he greedily scanned the contents.

When he saw there was a message from 'Happy Chap', he grinned. He tore out the column containing the message before discarding the rest of the newspaper into a nearby waste bin.

As he walked along Ransom Road, he began rereading the message from 'Happy Chap'. He had his head down, so he stuck close to the building line to avoid bumping into anyone.

The message he had been praying to see was there in black and white. It was confirmation that he was now being taken seriously. He could feel his grin growing wider as he read the message again.

Everything is now ready, Baby Doll.
Awaiting details of the time and date for our special meeting.
Happy Chap.

He thrust the torn paper into his coat pocket and quickly donned a pair of black woollen gloves. Fifty yards ahead, he could see the red post box at the junction of Ransom Road and Cromer Road. As he approached the post box, he took out the typed letter from the inside pocket of his parka coat and slipped it inside the post box.

He smiled as he walked away. Everything was now in place for the final part of his intricate plan. He was only a few telephone calls away from becoming a wealthy man, and all his family's worries over money would be a thing of the past. He knew the police would be watching as he collected the money, but he was confident he could outwit them.

He had no idea they were already watching his every move.

75

4.30pm, 20 May 1988
Ransom Road, St Ann's, Nottingham

The detectives from the regional crime squad surveillance units had been alerted by the officers in the observation van as soon as the Asian male had approached the post box.

The two officers from the Special Operations Unit who were inside the van had been convinced that they were looking at the same man who had previously been photographed posting a letter.

They had followed their briefing instructions and informed the surveillance team, who had then followed the suspect on foot from the post box.

It had been a very short surveillance.

After posting the letter, the suspect had walked along Cromer Road towards Hungerhill Road. At the junction, he had turned left and began walking along Hungerhill Road.

The surveillance team had followed at a discreet distance until the suspect reached the junction of Hungerhill Road and Aster Road. The man had walked into the small grocery shop located on the junction.

Detective Sergeant Tom Casey quickly deployed detectives to cover every possible exit from either the shop or the shop's backyard.

After fifteen minutes, the suspect had not emerged from the shop. During the surveillance, he had displayed no obvious anti-surveillance techniques. In fact, he'd appeared oblivious he was being followed.

Tom Casey was sitting in an unmarked vehicle fifty yards from the junction. He turned to his driver and said, 'He's been inside for almost twenty minutes now. Either he's somehow given us the slip, or he lives there. Walk down and buy something. I need to know if he's still in there.'

As the detective made his way down the road, Tom began checking with the other members of the surveillance team. It was soon clear that the suspect hadn't emerged from the shop.

Ten minutes later, the detective returned and got in the car, clutching a plastic carrier bag. He said, 'He's nowhere to be seen in the shop, but there's an internal door that leads to what looks like a flat upstairs.'

'Who served you?'

'A young Asian woman.'

'So it's possible our man lives above the shop.'

'I couldn't see any way he could've slipped past us. I could only see two doors. There's the front entrance to the shop, and another door that leads out into the backyard.'

'Great. I need to let DCI Flint know what's happening; then we need to get our positions sorted. We need to make sure we've contained these premises properly. I don't want him slipping out without us being all over him.'

76

5.00pm, 20 May 1988
Incident Room, Carlton Police Station, Nottingham

Danny had been informed of the developments at Hungerhill Road by DS Casey. He had ordered the crime squad surveillance team to remain where they were, and to place both the shop and the suspect under twenty-four-hour surveillance.

For once, manpower was not an issue. He had all the staff he needed. He had also received word from the observations team that the last collection from the post box at Cromer Road had just taken place. All the letters posted during the last twenty-four-hour period at that location, including the one from the suspect, would now be en route to the sorting office in Carrington to be processed prior to delivery.

He had taken the decision to maintain the twenty-four-hour observations on the post box. He wanted to keep an open mind. It was still possible that either of the other two suspects in the remaining photographs could be the extortionist. He was frustrated that his detectives had still not been able to speak with anybody at the two outstanding addresses.

He picked up the telephone and dialled the number for Steve Dawson's hotel in the city. After being put through by the hotel receptionist, Danny heard the security man's voice. 'Hello, Steve Dawson.'

'Steve, it's DCI Flint. There's been a couple of significant developments this afternoon. Can you meet me at the Carrington sorting office tonight at ten o'clock? One of our three suspects has been seen earlier today, posting another letter at Cromer Road. If there is a letter addressed to your head office in with the collected mail, it would save us a lot of time if we could intercept and open it straight away. All the letters from the Cromer Road post box will have been separated by ten o'clock.'

'No problem, Danny. I'll see you there.'

Danny put the phone down and walked into the main incident room. He sought out Rob Buxton. 'I'm meeting Steve Dawson at the Carrington sorting office at ten o'clock. Are you okay to stay on duty tonight?'

'I'll make a quick phone call home, but yeah, no problem.'

'If there is a letter addressed to Valumart within the mail posted at Cromer Road, I'm going to ask Steve Dawson to open it straight away. Depending on the demands made, there may be a lot of things to organise tonight. It could be a late one.'

With a half-smile, Rob said, 'Nothing new there, boss.'

77

6.00pm, 20 May 1988
Valumart Superstore, St Ann's Well Road, St Ann's, Nottingham

It had been another long and stressful day for Owen Bradley. He was just about to switch off the lights in his office when the telephone started to ring. For a split second, he thought about ignoring it. Something inside him made him walk back to his desk and pick up the telephone.

He snatched up the receiver and said, 'Bradley.'

There was silence.

He repeated his name and then said, 'Who is this?'

A man's voice growled, 'Sometime in the next twenty-four hours, you will be asked by the police to make the cash drop.'

With the merest hint of a tremor in his voice, Bradley repeated, 'Who is this?'

'I'm the man controlling the people who are watching your precious wife and children. If you do exactly as I tell you, they'll live. If you try to include the police any further than they already are, your family will die. Do you understand?'

Owen Bradley swallowed hard. 'Yes, I understand. What do you want me to do?'

'The police will give you a bag that looks similar to the one already stashed in the boot of your car. The police will have received a letter that contains instructions telling them how the cash is to be delivered. You will be delivering the cash, and I want you to follow those instructions exactly. Do you understand?'

'Yes.'

'Have you filled the bag in the boot of your car with newspapers?'

'Yes.'

'Good. Only when I've recovered the bag containing the cash will your family be safe. I repeat, you are not to inform the police of my contact with you. If I suspect for one second you've betrayed me, your wife and children will be killed. Is that clear?'

'Yes. I'm begging you, don't harm them. I'll do what you say, I promise.'

'Don't ever forget that we're watching you, as well as your family. We'll know if you try anything stupid. It will be your wife and children who suffer.'

The phone call was terminated as Owen repeated, 'Please don't hurt them. Please don't hurt them.'

The store manager slumped back in his chair and began to sob. He knew he had no choice but to do exactly what the gravel-voiced man had said.

78

10.00pm, 20 May 1988
Royal Mail Sorting Office, Carrington, Nottingham

The sorting office was a hive of activity. Post office staff were milling around, carrying sacks of letters collected from the various post boxes scattered around the northern half of the city.

Danny and Rob were standing alongside Steve Dawson, with their backs pressed against the wall. The last thing they wanted to do was cause an obstruction in this busy environment.

They were approached by an extremely harassed-looking man, who was in his early fifties and wearing a crumpled, ill-fitting suit.

As he approached, he said above the din, 'You must be the police. My name's Jim Scott; I'm the supervisor in charge tonight. I have your letters in a side room. Follow me.'

The three men followed Scott into the room, who pointed

at the pile of letters stacked on a table and said, 'Here they are, gents. I'd better see some identification before we go any further.'

Danny and Rob produced their warrant cards. Rob said, 'I'm DI Buxton, this is DCI Flint, and this man is Steve Dawson, the head of security for Valumart.'

Scott examined the warrant cards, then turned to Dawson and said, 'I'm sorry to be a pain, but do you have any identification, Mr Dawson?'

'I have my driving licence, if that's any good?'

'Ideally, I would have liked something with your photograph on, but as you're here with the police, I suppose your driving licence will suffice.'

As Dawson got his licence from his jacket pocket, Danny said, 'How many letters this time?'

Scott glanced at the details on Dawson's driving licence and said, 'There's twenty-three letters in all. The good news for you is that apart from a couple, they're all quite local.'

'May we?'

The supervisor nodded. As Danny and Rob stepped forward to examine the envelopes, Scott said quickly, 'You understand they can't be opened here; you'll have to do that with the addressee.'

The two detectives nodded and donned latex gloves.

Danny said, 'Mr Dawson has the authority to open any mail here that's addressed to Valumart head office.'

They flicked through the pile of letters until Danny found the one that was addressed to Delaney House, Stevenage, Hertfordshire.

Danny said, 'It's here, Steve.'

Rob handed the security chief a pair of latex gloves and said, 'You'd better put these on before you open it.'

Dawson donned the gloves and took the envelope from Danny. He carefully opened the envelope and placed the typed letter on the table. Rob slipped the letter and the envelope into clear plastic exhibit bags, and the three men began reading the letter.

Jim Scott said, 'Will you be sending detectives down here later to deal with these letters?'

Danny said, 'I'll have a team here first thing tomorrow morning.'

'I'll make sure the letters are secured away until they arrive. Do you need me to stay, as I've got a stack of work to do?'

'There's no need for you to stay, Mr Scott, and thanks for all your help tonight.'

Scott hustled out of the room, leaving the three men to discuss the contents of the letter.

Rob said, 'Well, this is all very different to the previous letter.'

Danny said, 'Not really. It's only the location of the first contact that's changed. They still want Owen Bradley to deliver the cash using his own car, and they still want the money placed in that certain type of bag. What do you make of that?'

'I can understand it. They know what Bradley looks like. They're bound to know what car he drives. I see it as just another layer of protection for them.'

'But what about the bag? Why do they want a specific type of bag?'

Rob shrugged. 'I don't know. I suppose it depends on what happens after that first contact between the extortionist and Bradley.'

Danny looked at Dawson and said, 'Is the cash for the drop still at the superstore?'

'Yes, it is. All the serial numbers on the notes have been recorded.'

'Is Owen Bradley still prepared to do the cash drop?'

'Like I told you, when I spoke to him before, he was very reluctant to get involved with anything so dangerous, but he's on board now. He'll do it.'

'Good. Get in touch with him tonight. I want you both to be at the incident room tomorrow afternoon at three o'clock. We've got a lot of work to do if we want to be ready for two o'clock on the morning of the twenty-second.'

79

3.00pm, 21 May 1988
Incident Room, Carlton Police Station, Nottingham

Danny's small office was packed.

Tina and Rob were standing at either side of Danny's desk, while Owen Bradley and Steve Dawson occupied the two seats in front of the desk.

Danny leaned back in his chair and said, 'Thanks for getting here on time. I want to go through with you both what's going to happen tomorrow morning.'

He looked directly at Owen Bradley and said, 'I need to know you understand fully what's being asked of you?'

The store manager nodded nervously.

Danny then turned to Rob and said, 'I see you've managed to get the type of bag stipulated for the cash drop.'

Rob held up the large black nylon-material grip bag with a shoulder strap and said, 'No problem. I picked this one up at the first camping shop I went into. I think it fits the description of what they wanted.'

Danny looked at Dawson and said, 'Steve, I want you to make sure the cash for the drop is brought here from the safe at Valumart tonight. You've seen the cash. Will it all fit into this bag?'

Dawson replied, 'No problem. The weight of that many banknotes is approximately twenty-five kilograms. A million pounds, in twenties, can easily fit inside an average-size suitcase, so we'll get half a million in this bag easily.'

Tina said, 'You sound like you've done this sort of transaction before?'

'No. I just do my research.'

Once again, Danny looked directly at Owen Bradley and said, 'Let's go through what we're asking you to do, Mr Bradley. If you think of any questions, ask them. Okay?'

Bradley nodded.

Danny said, 'At two o'clock tomorrow morning, you're to drive your own vehicle to the telephone box at the junction of Incinerator Road and Cattle Market Road. You're to park the car directly outside the telephone box with the window down. You must wait for ten minutes and then go inside the phone box. Do you know that location?'

'Not really.'

'Do you know where the Notts County football ground is?'

'Yes.'

'Cattle Market Road is the road that leads to the football ground from the main A60.'

'Okay, I know where that is.'

'I'll make sure DI Buxton has a map prepared for you before tonight's operation. In the meantime, study an A to Z map of the city, and familiarise yourself with the area.'

'Okay.'

'We've already searched the telephone box at that location, and it's empty. That means it's probable that the instructions will be called into the phone box. You must be prepared to be moved around the city. It's imperative that you understand the instructions you're given, and know how to locate the places you'll be sent to. I know it's not ideal, but an A to Z map will help you with this.'

Danny paused and looked at Bradley, who nodded nervously.

Danny continued, 'You'll be wearing a covert radio, with a throat mike and an earpiece. All you have to do is depress the switch in the palm of your hand and talk normally. You'll be able to hear the officers watching you through the earpiece. Avoid touching the earpiece.'

'If somebody's watching me, will they be able to tell I'm wearing this radio?'

'No. It will be completely hidden beneath your clothing. We'll need to know what instructions you are given so we can maintain our surveillance on you and prepare the ground for any new locations you are sent to. It's vital that you use the radio to repeat back any instructions you are given. Do you understand that?'

Bradley shook his head. 'I don't know; it all sounds very risky.'

Danny looked at the store manager. The man was obviously terrified at the prospect of doing the cash drop.

He said, 'Try not to worry, Owen. We'll do everything in our power to maintain your safety and minimise your risk. You'll always be under surveillance throughout the operation, and you'll have your radio to communicate with us. Okay?'

Bradley looked down at the desk and nodded.

Danny exchanged concerned glances with Steve Dawson before saying, 'Go with DI Buxton and sort out an A to Z map book. Then go home and get some rest. You'll need to be back here at nine o'clock tonight. Steve will meet you here with the cash, and we'll give you any final instructions. Try not to worry. Steve will be waiting for you at the superstore to make sure you can get back in after you've made the cash drop. It's going to be a long night, so try to get some rest.'

Rob said, 'Come on, Owen. I'll sort you out that map.'

Rob and Bradley left the office. Danny said to Steve Dawson, 'Is he going to be alright?'

'He's scared. Who wouldn't be? What he's being asked to do is well outside the comfort zone of a superstore manager.'

'That's true.'

'I think he'll be okay once he's out there doing it. He's not stupid. What about this suspect you're watching?'

Danny looked at Tina and nodded.

She said, 'Crime squad are maintaining observations on the target premises. There's been no movement overnight. The shop is open, but there are very few customers going in. There's been no sign of the suspect all day.'

Danny said, 'Thanks for coming in, Steve. I want you back here with the cash at nine o'clock tonight for the final briefing, please.'

'No problem.'

Danny waited for Dawson to leave, then said to Tina, 'How are you getting on with researching the target premises and the suspect?'

'We now know that the property's owned by the Panchal family. They own the shop and live in the flat above. They pay rates on both and are in arrears. We're still working hard to find out more details about them.'

'Keep on it. The more we know about our suspects, the better.'

'Will do.'

As Tina was going through the office door, Danny shouted after her, 'And let me know the second there's any significant movement at the target premises.'

80

3.00pm, 21 May 1988
Hungerhill Road, St Ann's, Nottingham

Nabin had deliberately slept in. His sister, Padama, had opened the shop today, for what it was worth. He knew he would need to be fresh and alert for what the night was about to bring.

He turned over in bed and looked at his alarm clock. It was now three o'clock in the afternoon. He adjusted his pillows and sat up in bed. He took a mouthful of water from the glass at the side of his bed and swilled it around his dry mouth before swallowing it.

He sat with his eyes closed and mulled over the plan. Everything had been put in place over the last three days. Apart from the two cardboard boxes, the items he would need were already in the back of his van. He had decided at the last minute against leaving the boxes in the van. He didn't want some thieving piece of shit to break into the van, thinking there was something worth stealing in the boxes. He would load those in at the last minute.

He had made a note of all the telephone numbers he would need.

He thought about Owen Bradley.

He was confident that the terrified store manager would do as he was instructed. It had been a stroke of genius to involve Bradley. It made his entire plan so much easier to carry out.

Nabin suddenly felt ravenously hungry. He grabbed his tatty dressing gown and went into the kitchen. His mother was sitting at the table reading. She stared at her unshaven son, still in his bedclothes, and said, 'Are you unwell, Nabi?'

'No, *maamii*. I have to work late tonight, and I've been feeling tired lately, so I just stayed in bed.'

Without saying another word, his mother returned to the book she was reading. He got himself a huge bowl of cornflakes, poured cold milk onto the cereal and sprinkled sugar on top before carrying his breakfast back to his bedroom.

There was nothing to get up for. He would stay in his room relaxing and going over his plans. He wouldn't need to leave the flat until one o'clock in the morning.

81

8.00pm, 21 May 1988
Darwin Crescent, Dishley, Loughborough, Leicestershire

Owen Bradley stood in the master bedroom of his luxurious home. The light was off, and the curtains were open. He stared out over the open countryside of Darwin Park, which was immediately behind the house.

The beautiful area of woodland and open spaces had been one of the main reasons he and his wife had decided to buy the house. They had thought It would be the perfect environment for them to raise their young children.

As he stared out into the darkness, that area of natural beauty had now taken on a sinister, menacing air. He strained his eyes, trying to see any sign of movement. He was searching for the men who were no doubt watching his house right now. Those unknown men, who threatened the very existence of the people he held most dear.

He felt a heavy sense of foreboding descend upon him. This was then replaced with a barely recognisable steely resolve. He knew exactly what he had to do to keep his family safe.

When the hard-faced detective had been briefing him earlier, there was a moment when he felt like blurting out his predicament. He was about to say something when an image had crashed into his brain. It was the photograph given to him by the monster blackmailing him. It showed his wife and children smiling happily inside their own home. It was enough to make him remain tight-lipped. He had chosen to say nothing.

He glanced at his watch; it was almost time for him to be leaving. He still had to drive to the police station in Nottingham. He had to be there at nine o'clock to meet Steve Dawson.

He glanced in both the children's bedrooms. They were already fast asleep. He felt bile rise in his throat and swallowed hard. He needed to stay strong for them. He walked downstairs and saw his wife standing by the fireplace in the lounge.

With just a hint of annoyance in her voice, she said, 'I just don't understand why you've got to go into work at this time of night. It's bloody ridiculous.'

He put his arms around her slim waist. 'I've got no choice, darling. It's that bloody head of security from Stevenage. He's got a bee in his bonnet about some figures that aren't adding up, and he wants to go over them with me tonight when the store's closed, so we don't get interrupted.'

She looked directly into his eyes and said, 'So long as this head of security isn't a twentysomething and blonde, with a gorgeous body.'

'Don't be daft.'

He pulled her close and squeezed her tight. 'There's only one woman I love, and I'm holding her right now.'

She chuckled and said, 'Right answer.'

He pulled away. 'I'd better get going. It's a long drive.'

'What time will you be home?'

'I honestly don't know. I think it's going to be a late session, so don't wait up. Close the door behind me when I leave, and make sure you lock up properly tonight. Put the deadbolts on. Love you.'

He closed the front door behind him and walked to his car parked on the drive. As he looked up and down the street, he heard the key turn in the door behind him.

There were no strange cars parked on the street. Just the usual cars of his neighbours, sitting on driveways.

Even though he couldn't see anything suspicious, he knew they were out there somewhere, watching his every move. He shuddered inwardly before starting the car and driving away from his precious family.

82

9.00pm, 21 May 1988
Incident Room, Carlton Police Station, Nottingham

Rob placed the black nylon holdall onto Danny's desk and unzipped it.

As soon as the bag was undone, Steve Dawson opened the suitcase he had brought with him, and began transferring bundles of twenty-pound notes into the bag. Each block of notes contained ten thousand pounds. There were fifty blocks in all.

Danny had never seen so much cash in one place before. He let out a low whistle and said, 'I hope this isn't the last time we see this lot.'

Steve Dawson said, 'I'm sure it won't be. I just don't see how this muppet thinks he's going to be able to get his hands on it. He must know the police will be involved by now.'

'I'm sure he does, and that's what's worrying me. He

knows, and he's still going ahead with it. He'll have something up his sleeve, that's for sure.'

'How good are your surveillance teams?'

'They're all very experienced detectives. Surveillance is ninety percent of the regional crime squad's work. They do it all day, every day.'

Dawson placed the last block of notes in the bag, zipped it up again and said, 'Well, that sounds reassuring anyway.'

Danny said, 'I'm more concerned about Owen Bradley. We're asking an awful lot of him; do you think he's up to the task?'

'Would you prefer it if I did the cash drop? I could always drive Bradley's car to the contact point.'

Danny considered the idea, then said, 'I don't think we can take that risk. The extortionist obviously wants Bradley to do it for a reason. I don't think I can afford to jeopardise the whole operation with such a late change. No, it will have to be Bradley. I just hope he remembers what he's got to do.'

'He will. He's an intelligent guy, smart as a whip. He'll be okay.'

The head of security lifted the bag from the desk. Rob said, 'How's the weight?'

'It's heavy, but not unmanageable. Has there been any news on your suspect?'

Danny said, 'There's been no movement all day.'

'Can't you just nick him?'

'For what? Posting a letter? We still haven't been able to confirm the identities of the people posting the other two outstanding letters. Until we can say for certain that our suspect is responsible for posting the letters, he's just one of three suspects. I know the sighting of him posting a further letter makes him the favourite; it's still not definite. Observations teams have been known to miss things in the past. No, we'll keep him under surveillance until we're ready and have the evidence to arrest him.'

Danny paused and said, 'If he is our man, he'll be on the move soon enough, to collect this cash. And when he does, that's when we'll have him.'

The door opened, and a very nervous-looking Owen Bradley walked in.

Danny said, 'Are you happy with the covert radio? Do you know how it operates?'

Bradley nodded.

'And you've got your A to Z map book?'

He held up the small book and nodded again.

Rob said, 'It's time you were both leaving. You've got to be at the superstore at ten o'clock. They might be watching the store.'

Steve Dawson picked up the heavy grip bag and said, 'Come on then, Owen, let's get this done.'

83

1.15am, 22 May 1988
Hungerhill Road, St Ann's, Nottingham

Detective Sergeant Tom Casey squinted through the windscreen of the car. Luckily, it was a dry night, so vision from the car was quite good. He was sure he had seen movement near the gate, in the rear yard of the corner shop.

He turned to his colleague in the driver's seat and said, 'Did you see that?'

Detective Constable Mac Winters stared at the rear of the shop. 'Sorry, Sarge, I didn't see a thing.'

Tom Casey wound the window down a little. He could clearly hear a scuffling sound emanating from the yard.

He whispered, 'There's something going on, Mac. Get ready.'

The words had barely escaped his mouth when the wooden gate that led into the yard opened slowly, and the suspect emerged onto the street. He walked to the Ford Escort van that was parked five yards from the gate, and unlocked the back doors.

Tom Casey already knew that the van was registered to the target premises. He spoke softly into the radio: 'All units stand by. We have movement at the target premises. The suspect is out to his vehicle. Stand by.'

Tom heard a series of clicks on the radio as the other detectives acknowledged his message.

Having unlocked the rear doors, the suspect turned and walked back into the yard. He emerged seconds later, carrying a large cardboard box. He placed the box into the back of the van before repeating the process with another box.

As soon as the two boxes were in the van, the suspect closed the doors and walked to the driver's door.

Tom heard the van's engine splutter into life at the third attempt, and he said, 'All units. Suspect is now in the vehicle. Target vehicle is a white Ford Escort van, registered number Charlie Five Three Eight November Delta Echo. Repeat, Charlie Five Three Eight November Delta Echo. Stand by for direction of travel.'

Tom could hear the engine of the battered van spluttering in the cold. A cloud of exhaust fumes billowed from the rear of the vehicle as the engine reluctantly warmed up.

After a few minutes, he heard the revs change and saw the vehicle being driven away from the kerb.

Tom grabbed the radio and said, 'Target vehicle is right right onto Hungerhill Road. Charlie One has the eyeball. Convoy check.'

As other surveillance vehicles slotted in behind Tom Casey's vehicle, they gave an update on the back-to-back radio channel they were using for the surveillance. They would alternate positions, taking it in turns to be directly behind the target vehicle as they followed the Ford Escort van through the city.

Tom grabbed another radio, which was tuned into the frequency used by the Major Crime Investigation Unit. He said, 'DS Casey to DCI Flint.'

There was a brief delay before he heard, 'From DCI Flint, go ahead.'

Tom said, 'Boss, the suspect's on the move. He's in the white Ford Escort van that's registered to his address. We're currently travelling through the city centre heading towards the main A60, London Road. Over.'

'Stay with him, Tom. I want regular updates.'

84

1.30am, 22 May 1988
Queen's Medical Centre, Nottingham

Nabin drove steadily through the city; there was no rush. Traffic in the city was light at that time of the morning, and he still had plenty of time before he needed to make the first phone call.

After a fifteen-minute drive, he steered the van into the grounds of the Queen's Medical Centre. He followed the perimeter road until he saw the sign for the multi-storey car park that remained open all night.

He drove to the top of the six-storey car park and reversed the van into deep shadow. He switched off the engine, got out of the van and listened intently. He could hear no other vehicles in the car park. It was deathly silent.

He opened the rear doors and took out the mannequin he had retrieved from a skip a week ago. The mannequin had no bottom half, and he dressed it with his own parka coat. He sat the dummy in the front driver's seat, keeping it in place with the seat belt. He placed the hood of the coat over its head and stepped back to check it out.

He closed the van door and walked away from the vehicle, then looked back. From a distance, it looked as though the driver was still sitting in the vehicle.

He removed everything he would need from the van and locked it before making his way stealthily down each of the levels. His progress was slow, but eventually he came to the first floor.

On each of the levels above, there were grilles in place to prevent people leaping to their deaths from the car park. On the first floor, there were no such suicide-prevention fences in place. Using the shadows, he made his way to the very back corner of the first floor.

Groping in the darkness, he ran his hand along the wall until he felt the rope. He had tied the rope in place three days before. He yanked it hard, to make sure it was still secure, before climbing over the three-foot wall.

He slid silently down the rope until his feet touched the ground. Before moving off, he squatted down and listened intently. There was still no sound from the car park.

He began making his way into the thick woods and shrubs that backed up against the car park. After a couple of minutes searching the undergrowth, he found what he was looking for. He breathed a sigh of relief when he found the tatty, second-hand pushbike. He had stashed it in the woods at the same time as he had secured the rope. The bicycle was a vital piece of equipment if his plan was to succeed.

After three days of being stashed under a bush, exposed to the elements, the pushbike was now soaking wet. Using the sleeve of his black fleece-lined hoody, he wiped the worst of the damp from the saddle. He pushed the bicycle through the woods until he came to a footpath at the side of the River

Leen. The river was little more than a small stream at this point.

Once on the footpath, Nabin checked the tyres, mounted the bicycle and pedalled away from the car park. It was hard going on the soft, muddy footpath, but he pedalled steadily until he saw the bridge that marked the point where the river joined the Beeston Canal.

He stopped and looked up at the bridge that crossed the canal. It was all clear, so he rode the bicycle down onto the towpath that ran alongside the canal. The surface of the towpath was much firmer than the muddy footpath at the side of the river, so he made good progress as he rode towards Dunkirk.

After five minutes, he saw the red telephone box that was situated at the bottom end of Cloister Street, near the towpath.

He placed the bicycle against the fence that bordered the quiet cul-de-sac from the canal, then climbed over. He squatted down and carefully looked up the quiet street. All the nearby houses were in darkness. The street was as silent as the grave.

He glanced at his watch; it was almost two o'clock. He walked to the telephone box and stepped inside. He took out a handful of coins and the scrap of paper he had written the series of numbers on. In a couple of minutes, it would be time for him to make the first call of the night.

85

1.45am, 22 May 1988
Queen's Medical Centre, Nottingham

'DS Casey to DCI Flint. Over.'

'From DCI Flint, go ahead. Over.'

'We've followed the suspect to the multi-storey car park at the Queen's Medical Centre. It's impossible for us to follow him inside in the vehicles, so I've sent a footman into the car park to see what's happening. Over.'

'Have you got all the pedestrian entrances covered? Over.'

'Affirmative. I've got units covering all the vehicle and pedestrian exits. Over.'

'Have you heard from your footman yet? Over.'

The surveillance radio crackled into life, and a voice barely more than a whisper said, 'From Mac. The target vehicle's now parked on the sixth floor. The suspect's still sitting in the driver's seat. Over.'

Tom relayed the update to Danny, who said, 'Can your man get any closer? Over.'

Tom picked up the surveillance radio and said, 'Tom to Mac. Can you get any closer to the target vehicle? Over.'

'Negative. It's bloody risky where I am now. If I try to get any closer, he'll spot me for sure. Over.'

'Okay, Mac. Stand by. Over.'

Once again, Tom relayed the message he had been given by his footman to Danny, on the other radio.

Danny said, 'It's your call, Tom. If you think it's too risky, call your man back and continue watching all the exits. At least we know where he is. Over.'

'I'm going to call him back. It sounds way too risky up there. The last thing we need is for him to get spotted by the suspect. If there's any movement, I'll update you immediately. Over.'

'Okay, Tom. For your info, the package is now on its way to the first contact point and is being tracked by your colleagues. Keep me informed of any changes your end. Over.'

86

1.55am, 22 May 1988
Cattle Market Road, Nottingham

As instructed, Owen Bradley had parked his grey BMW right beside the telephone box on Cattle Market Road. In the distance, he could see the hulking shape of the Meadow Lane Stand at Notts County's football ground. The buildings in the area were all industrial, and at this early hour, the street was deserted. The white street lights dotted along the road gave off very poor lighting, and Bradley felt nervous as he waited alone in the darkness. He had opened the window of the car about an inch, just enough to hear if the telephone began to ring.

He now had two almost identical black nylon grip bags in the boot of his car. One bag contained half a million pounds in used twenty-pound notes, and the other was stuffed with shredded copies of old newspapers.

He felt physically sick as he thought about what he was

involved in, and what could happen to his precious family. He knew what he was about to do was totally wrong, but he had to try to ensure the safety of his family.

Earlier, as he had driven through the deserted streets of the city, he had seen no sign of the police surveillance teams that were supposed to be watching his every move. Either they were extremely good at what they did, or they had already lost him.

Sitting alone in his vehicle on this gloomy, deserted street, Bradley felt vulnerable and afraid.

The noise of the telephone ringing galvanised him into action. He jumped out of his car, stepped inside the phone box and lifted the receiver.

He heard a voice say, 'Do not speak until I tell you to. When you speak, just answer yes or no. Do you understand?'

Bradley pressed the switch in the palm of his hand and spluttered, 'Yes.'

'Go to the telephone box at the junction of Castle Marina Road and Lawrence Way. Do you know where that is?'

'Yes.'

'Be there in ten minutes for further instructions.'

The phone went dead, and Bradley got back in his car. He reluctantly pressed the switch in his palm again and whispered, 'Phone box. Junction of Castle Marina Road and Lawrence Way.'

He turned on the ignition and glanced down at the A to Z map. He quickly located Castle Marina Road and steered the car away from the kerb. He only had ten minutes to get to the next phone box.

87

2.10am, 22 May 1988
Cloister Street, Dunkirk, Nottingham

Nabin Panchal waited until his watch said exactly ten minutes past two before dialling the second number on his list of three.

The telephone was answered immediately, and Nabin thrust coins into the payphone to connect the call. He heard a breathless voice say, 'Yes.'

Nabin could hear the rising panic in the man's trembling voice. He said, 'Bradley, your family are safe, for now. Do you want them to stay that way?'

Bradley stifled a sob and said, 'Yes.'

'Then keep doing exactly as I say, understood?'

'Yes.'

'There's another telephone box on Harrimans Lane. Do you know where that is?'

'Yes, I think so.'

Nabin barked, ‘Only say yes or no! Do you know where that is?’

‘Yes.’

‘Opposite that phone box is a parking area. Reverse your car until the boot is next to the waste bin that’s at the side of that parking area. Do you understand?’

‘Yes.’

‘Be there in fifteen minutes. Don’t be late.’

Nabin hung up the phone and smiled. He could hear the fear in the store manager’s voice, and he knew the man would continue to comply.

So far, so good.

88

2.10am, 22 May 1988
Castle Marina Road, Nottingham

Detective Inspector Jo Thomas was leading the regional crime squad surveillance team tasked with following Owen Bradley as he attempted to make the cash drop.

She was the front seat passenger in a vehicle behind a queue of other parked cars on Castle Marina Road. From her position, she could see the telephone box at the junction of Castle Marina Road and Lawrence Way, about fifty yards away. She had observed Bradley as he sprinted from his BMW to the telephone box to answer the ringing telephone. She had heard the store manager, through the covert radio he was wearing, say 'yes' several times, but that was all she'd heard him say.

Her driver had started the car as soon as the grey BMW

pulled out of Leonards Way and back onto Castle Marina Road.

She turned to him and said, 'What the fuck is Bradley playing at? Why is he just saying "yes"? They weren't the instructions he was given.'

She barked out instructions to the rest of the team and said finally, 'Try to stay with him, at all costs.'

She grabbed the radio on the dashboard, which was tuned into the radio channel being used by the MCIU, and said, 'DI Thomas to DCI Flint. Over.'

Danny snatched the radio from his desk and said, 'From DCI Flint. Go ahead. Over.'

'Sir, I think we may have a problem. The package is not relaying any information on locations. We're doing our level best to stay with him, but he's driving at speed and ignoring red traffic lights. Over.'

'You must stay with him, Jo. We can't afford to let him out of our sight for a second. Over.'

Jo Thomas looked at her driver. 'You heard the man; fuck the red lights. Get closer and stay with him.'

89

2.25am, 22 May 1988
Harrimans Lane, Dunkirk, Nottingham

After a frantic fifteen-minute drive, Owen Bradley arrived on Harrimans Lane. He saw the red telephone box and the parking area opposite. As instructed, he reversed his car into the parking area until the boot was almost touching the waste bin.

As soon as he turned off the car engine, he heard the telephone in the phone box start to ring. He jumped out of the car, sprinted across the lane and yanked open the door.

Depressing the switch in the palm of his hand, he snatched the phone from the cradle and said, 'Yes.'

The menacing voice said, 'I see you've parked as I told you. Good.'

Bradley stared out of the phone box, straining his eyes to catch a glimpse of his tormentor.

He couldn't see anything.

The voice said, ‘In ten minutes’ time, take the bag containing the newspaper from the boot and start walking, very slowly, along the footpath. Do you understand?’

Bradley had noticed that the road effectively ended where the phone box was located. Beyond that point, Harrimans Lane became little more than a tarmacked footpath. He looked out of the phone box, down the footpath, and could see that it had dim white lights spaced every hundred yards or so. It was bordered on one side by trees and shrubs that led down to the Beeston Canal, and on the other side by a high wire fence that guarded ramshackle industrial units.

He said, ‘Yes.’

‘After two hundred yards, you’ll see another path that leads off to the left and down to a bridge over the canal. Walk down to the bridge and place the bag on the middle parapet. Wait there, with the bag, for another ten minutes. Do you understand the instruction?’

‘Yes.’

‘When you remove the bag from the car, leave the boot unlocked and slightly open. Do you understand?’

‘Yes.’

‘After waiting the ten minutes on the bridge, leave the bag where it is and return to your car. Walk slowly at all times. Do you understand?’

‘Yes.’

‘Once you get back to your car, drive straight to the superstore. Only when we have the money, and we see you arrive at the superstore, will I call off the men watching your family. Do you understand?’

‘Yes.’

The phone went dead.

Bradley glanced at his watch as he walked slowly back to his car.

He looked back along the lane, the way he had arrived. In

the far distance, about one hundred yards away, he could see a lone vehicle parked on the quiet lane. He wasn't sure, but he thought he could see people sitting in the car.

He sat back in his car and waited. As soon as the ten minutes had passed slowly by, he got out and unlocked the boot. He unzipped both bags and made sure he was removing the right one.

He placed the bag at his feet and then gently closed the boot, leaving it unlocked and half an inch open.

With a rising sense of trepidation, he started walking. His eyes were darting back and forth along the dimly lit footpath, his mind imagining a sadistic thug hiding behind every tree or shrub, waiting to ambush him.

90

2.35am, 22 May 1988
Harrimans Lane, Dunkirk, Nottingham

Detective Inspector Jo Thomas was sitting in her vehicle, one hundred yards away from where Bradley's car was now parked.

She had watched as the store manager raced across the lane and into the telephone box.

As she heard his brief transmissions over the radio, she turned to her driver and said, 'What the hell is he doing, with all this "yes" shit? Is he deliberately doing that, or has he just bottled it?'

The experienced RCS detective sitting next to her said, 'If you ask me, it's deliberate. I reckon he's been told to answer either yes or no. This is one crafty bastard we're dealing with.'

DI Thomas saw Bradley walk from the telephone box and sit back in his car. 'Now what's he doing?'

Nothing happened for ten minutes; then she watched the

store manager get out of his car, walk to the boot, open it and remove the black bag.

'Where's he going now?'

'Looks like he's been told to walk from here, boss.'

She snatched up the radio and ordered two detectives in another vehicle to get out and follow the store manager on foot. She barked another order as the two men moved swiftly to observe Bradley. 'Get as close to him as you can, but be careful. I always want the package under observation. Do not let it out of your sight. Move!'

91

2.40am, 22 May 1988
Incident Room, Carlton Police Station, Nottingham

Danny cut a frustrated figure as he listened to the radio signals from the Regional Crime Squad surveillance teams. It was difficult not to interfere and talk to them directly, but protocol demanded he wait until the officers conducting the surveillance contacted him.

He sat with Rob and Tina in his office, exchanging worried glances at the latest developments. The MCIU radio suddenly burst into life: 'DI Thomas to DCI Flint. Over.'

Danny snatched up the radio handset and said, 'Go ahead, Jo. I've been listening to your signals. Over.'

'I've got two detectives out on foot; the subject and the package are still in view, but this is extremely risky. They're very exposed. Over.'

'Understood. I know there's a risk of them showing out,

but you've got to keep the package in sight. Have you had any update from DS Casey? Over.'

'Negative. Over.'

'Can I contact him direct? Over.'

'Yes. But be very brief. I may need air priority at any moment. Over.'

'Understood. Over.'

Danny then said, 'DCI Flint to DS Casey. Over.'

'Go ahead. I was listening, sir. Over.'

'I need an update on the suspect. I want to know if he's still in his vehicle, or if he's given you the slip. Over.'

'Stand by. Over.'

Without being asked, DC Mac Winters slipped out of the car and began to make his way through the shadowy, multi-storey car park.

After four minutes, he reached the same location where he had observed the suspect in his vehicle before. He peered into the shadows and could still see the suspect sitting in the driver's seat of the battered Ford Escort van.

He retreated down the levels of the car park, quietly got back into the surveillance car and said, 'He's still there, Sarge. He hasn't moved.'

Tom Casey said into the radio, 'DS Casey to DCI Flint. Over.'

Danny said, 'Go ahead, Tom. Over.'

'Suspect is still sitting in the target vehicle at our location. Over.'

'Received that. Maintain your positions. Over.'

Danny put the radio down and turned to Rob. 'What the fuck's going on? What are we missing here?'

Rob shrugged. 'He's either working with an accomplice, or we're off the mark altogether.'

Danny didn't respond. He was worried. Something about this whole thing felt very wrong.

92

2.40am, 22 May 1988
Harrimans Lane, Dunkirk, Nottingham

As soon as he had terminated the last call to Owen Bradley, Nabin had ridden the pedal cycle along the canal towpath towards Harrimans Lane.

Using the towpath was perfect. He could make good progress and was out of view of the roads, away from any prying eyes.

As he rode, he carefully scanned the trees at the side of the towpath for the sign he had left two days ago.

He saw the white ribbon he had tied to the trunk of the rowan tree. He braked and brought the pushbike to a stop next to the ribbon. He quickly hid the pushbike off the towpath and made his way through the undergrowth, up the banking and away from the canal.

He moved stealthily, being careful not to disturb the thick

vegetation too much. After what seemed an age, he could finally see the store manager's BMW parked next to the waste bin.

From the darkness of the woods, he watched as the store manager got out of the car and opened the boot. He saw him remove the black bag and then close the lid of the boot.

Nabin smiled to himself as he saw Bradley leave the boot half an inch open.

From his position in the bushes, he could clearly see the fear etched onto the man's face. He watched Bradley looking around, scanning the area. It was obvious the panic inside him was bubbling just below the surface.

As soon as the store manager started walking down the dimly lit footpath away from his car, carrying the black bag, Nabin made his move.

He crawled forward on all fours until he was next to the waste bin.

He was about to reach up and open the boot of the car when he heard footsteps to his right. He slunk back into the bushes and saw two men creeping past his position. They were clearly following the store manager at a discreet distance and were obviously detectives.

He waited patiently for the two men to clear his position before creeping forward once more. He calculated that Bradley would now be approaching the bridge over the canal.

He had to act.

He reached up from behind the waste bin and lifted the boot of the BMW. He raised it just enough to retrieve the black bag that remained in the boot. Holding the bag in one hand, he carefully closed the boot with the other and retreated into the woods. Once under the cover of the trees and shrubs, he unzipped the bag and checked the contents.

A smile passed his lips as he saw the bundles of twenty-pound notes. He zipped up the bag and made his way back down the banking to the canal towpath. He slipped the bag over his shoulders, retrieved the pushbike from the bushes and began cycling back along the towpath, towards the hospital.

93

2.40am, 22 May 1988
Incident Room, Carlton Police Station, Nottingham

Danny, Rob and Tina listened anxiously to the radio signals on the Regional Crime Squad channel. They could hear the frantic messages between the detectives as they attempted to maintain a foot follow on Owen Bradley and the bag containing half a million pounds.

Danny couldn't stand it any longer. He snatched up the MCIU radio and spoke directly to Detective Inspector Jo Thomas. 'What the hell's happening, Jo?'

Danny could hear the tension in the detective inspector's voice when she said, 'Something's wrong. All we're getting from the subject is "yes", nothing else. We've still got eyes on the subject, but it's a nightmare trying to follow on foot without showing out. We're doing everything we can to maintain it.'

'Where are you now?'

'I'm still with the subject's vehicle on Harrimans Lane.'

'Where's the subject?'

'The subject is standing on a bridge that spans the Beeston Canal. He still has the package with him. That has been placed on the parapet at the centre of the bridge.'

'Does your surveillance team still have eyes on the package?'

'Yes. I've got two men on the ground who are eyes on.'

The radio that was being used for the surveillance once again sparked up as one of the detectives watching Bradley reported that the store manager had now left the bridge and was making his way back along the footpath towards Harrimans Lane.

Using the MCIU radio, Danny asked, 'Where's the package? Is it still with the subject?'

DI Thompson relayed Danny's question. The answer from the detective on the ground was brief. 'Negative. The subject has left the package on the bridge.'

Danny said, 'Jo, they've got to stay on the package. Somebody else can pick up the subject when he returns to his vehicle. Stay with the package.'

'Will do, sir.'

Danny threw the radio down onto his desk in frustration. 'This is fucked up! I need to be out there, on the ground. There's something very wrong going on here.'

94

2.55am, 22 May 1988
Queen's Medical Centre, Nottingham

It had taken Nabin fifteen minutes to ride the pushbike along the canal towpath and the muddy footpath at the side of the River Leen. He was hampered by the heavy bag flopping about on his shoulders, and by the time he saw the multi-storey car park loom into view, his thigh muscles were burning, and he was out of breath.

He got off the pushbike and lowered it gently into the canal, avoiding any splash.

Adjusting the strap on the black bag, so it felt tighter on his shoulders, he made his way through the trees and the undergrowth, towards the rear of the car park. He walked along the back wall until he found the rope dangling from the first floor.

It took all his strength to haul himself up the rope with the bag on his shoulders. Once inside and on the first floor, he squatted down, got his breath back, and listened for any sound.

The car park was still and silent.

Nabin made his way slowly up each level, sticking to the shadows and moving silently. When he reached the top floor, he again squatted on his haunches and paused in one of the many dark shadows. He scanned every corner of the car park. Only when satisfied he was alone did Nabin move forward to his van.

He unlocked the rear doors of the vehicle, opened the two large cardboard boxes that were inside, removed the bag from his shoulders, and unzipped it. Smiling broadly, he transferred the bundles of twenty-pound notes from the bag into the two cardboard boxes.

He quietly closed the rear doors of the van and unlocked the driver's door. He removed the mannequin, then took off the parka he'd dressed it with. He slipped the coat over the top of his fleece jacket and put the hood up.

The last thing he had to do was to dispose of the mannequin and the black bag. He walked to the balcony, reached up and forced the mannequin through the small gap at the top of the fencing. The space was just wide enough to squeeze the tailor's dummy through.

He let go and heard it fall into the shrubs and undergrowth at the rear of the car park. He did the same with the black bag before getting in the driver's seat, closing the door, and starting the engine.

Feeling satisfied that his careful planning had come to fruition, he drove his rusting van slowly out of the car park.

95

3.00am, 22 May 1988
Queen's Medical Centre, Nottingham

Detective Sergeant Tom Casey heard the clapped-out engine of the van before he saw the vehicle emerge from the main exit of the multi-storey car park.

He snatched up the radio and said, 'All units. We have movement at the south exit of the car park. Target vehicle is on the move, passing our position now. Suspect is the driver, no passengers visible. We have the eyeball. Convoy check.'

As DC Mac Winters drove after the van, keeping a discreet distance, Tom Casey could hear the other vehicles in the surveillance team all getting into position, to alternate the actual pursuit of the target vehicle.

Satisfied that the surveillance team were all in position, Tom picked up the MCIU radio and said, 'DS Casey to DCI Flint. Over.'

Danny had heard the initial radio message on the RCS radio and snatched up the MCIU handset. ‘From DCI Flint. Go ahead. Over.’

‘Sir, we finally have movement at the car park. The suspect is in the target vehicle and driving slowly through the city. Direction of travel is back towards Sneinton. Over.’

‘He’s been in that car park for one and a half hours. What’s he been doing? Over.’

‘He was just sitting in the van. I wonder if he was expecting someone to turn up, who didn’t show. It’s all a bit weird. Over.’

‘Did any other vehicles enter or leave the multi-storey while you were there? Over.’

‘Negative. Over.’

‘Stay with him and keep me updated of any stops he makes. Over.’

‘Will do. Over.’

96

3.30am, 22 May 1988
Incident Room, Carlton Police Station, Nottingham

Danny and Rob were listening intently to the RCS radio signals as the surveillance team followed the target vehicle slowly through the city. He was impressed by the professional and smooth way the team operated. Every three or four minutes, the vehicles exchanged places so the same vehicle was never behind the target vehicle for too long.

He heard Tom Casey's voice on the MCIU handset. 'DS Casey to DCI Flint. Over.'

'From DCI Flint. Go ahead. Over.'

'The target vehicle is now parked outside the suspect's premises. Suspect is out of the vehicle and at the back doors of the van. He's unloaded two cardboard boxes and taken them back into the yard of the premises. He's locked the target vehicle and has gone inside the property. Property is now in darkness. Over.'

'Thanks, Tom. Stay on the suspect's premises and keep me informed of any further movement. Over.'

'DCI Flint to DI Thomas. Over.'

'From DI Thomas. Go ahead. Over.'

'Do you have an update on Bradley? Over.'

'He's back in the car park of the superstore. He's leaning against his car, talking to Steve Dawson. Over.'

'I want them both back here at the incident room as soon as possible. Over.'

'Understood. Over.'

'Do we still have eyes on the package? Over.'

'Affirmative. The package is still on the bridge. Over.'

'Okay. I want officers deploying 360 around the package. Whatever way they decide to approach it, I want it covered. Over.'

'Already done, sir. We have officers deployed on the canal towpath now, in case the approach is by water. Over.'

Danny turned to Rob and said, 'We need to speak to Owen Bradley and find out what the hell was going on out there.'

'At least we still have eyes on the cash, boss.'

Danny had an uneasy feeling in the pit of his stomach. The entire operation hadn't gone the way he had envisaged. Why would the extortionist leave a bag containing half a million pounds unattended for so long? It just didn't make any sense. Anybody could walk by, at any moment, and pick it up.

Something wasn't right. Danny knew instinctively that Bradley had the answers.

He looked at Rob. 'As soon as Owen Bradley gets here, we need to sit him down and debrief him, hard. He's got the answers to what's going on here. I'm sure of it.'

97

3.45am, 22 May 1988
Hungerhill Road, St Ann's, Nottingham

Nabin stared at the two cardboard boxes on his bed.

He still couldn't quite believe that his plan had worked. Apart from the two heavy-footed detectives he had seen on Harrimans Lane, there had been no sign of the police. He had managed to easily outmanoeuvre them, and now he had his reward.

He opened the boxes and looked in wonder at the bundles of twenty-pound notes. He didn't bother counting the cash; he just began wrapping the bundles of notes with clingfilm until he had ten blocks of fifty thousand pounds each. They would be easier to move that way.

He opened the loft hatch that was in his bedroom and pulled down the ladder. He carried each of the bundles up into the loft and hid them beneath the insulation felt.

After he had placed the last of the bundles under the

insulation, he inspected the loft. There was no sign anything was hidden there. Feeling satisfied, he replaced the ladder and closed the hatch.

Carrying the two empty cardboard boxes back downstairs and into the shop, he heard his mother's nervous voice from the flat above. 'Who's there?'

'It's only me, *maamii*. Nabi.'

He walked back up the stairs to the flat and saw his mother in the kitchen. She looked worried.

She clasped both her hands on his cheeks and said, 'Where have you been, Nabi? I heard you go out earlier; I've been worried sick.'

He gently moved her hands from his face, stepped over to the sink and filled the kettle with water. 'I had to go out to meet somebody, that's all. It was a chance to buy some cheap stock for the shop.'

'Did you get it?'

'No, *maamii*. He didn't show up.'

As he put instant coffee in two cups and waited for the kettle to boil, he said, 'I don't know why I bothered. It was a waste of time and fuel for the van.'

His mother stepped over and said, 'Sit down; I'll make the coffee. Have you been up in the loft since you got back?'

He took the mug of hot coffee from her. 'No. It will be the bloody pigeons again. I'll go up in the loft later, after I've had a sleep, and see if I can do something to stop them getting in.'

'Thanks, Nabi. You're a good boy, but I worry for you.'

'I worry for all of us, *maamii*. I'll make things right again. We'll soon have money to spend again, *baabujii* will be home from the hospital, and we can all move from this awful place.'

'I know you will, son. I'm taking my coffee to bed. Don't stay up too long, Nabi; you look tired.'

'I won't, *maamii*. Night, night.'

98

4.00am, 22 May 1988
Incident Room, Carlton Police Station, Nottingham

Danny cut a worried figure, sitting at his desk. He looked at Rob and said, 'Where the hell's Bradley? He should have been here by now.'

Before Rob could answer, there was a knock on the office door, and Steve Dawson walked in.

Danny said tersely, 'Where's Bradley?'

Dawson said, 'He's getting a hot drink. He'll be through in a minute.'

'What's happening, Steve? Has he said anything to you on the way here?'

'He hasn't said a thing. But he's hiding something. I'm sure of it.'

'Why do you think that?'

'There's just been something about his demeanour ever

since he got back from the cash drop. He was scared stiff before he went, but he's almost euphoric now.'

Rob said, 'I'll go and fetch him in.'

As Rob stood and opened the door, Owen Bradley walked in.

Danny said, 'Grab a seat, Owen.'

As soon as the store manager had sat down, Danny said, 'What happened out there? You didn't say anything to us on the radio. We couldn't follow you.'

'I did everything I was asked to do.'

'How is just saying yes doing everything you were asked to do?'

'The voice on the phone instructed me to just answer with a yes or no, so that's exactly what I did. I knew you were watching me and would still be following me. That's the reason I drove slowly between the telephone boxes.'

'Slowly? You were speeding through red lights. How is that slowly?'

'I only had a certain time to get to the next contact point.'

Steve Dawson said, 'You must be relieved it's all over.'

Bradley nodded.

Dawson persisted, 'You certainly don't look as worried. You were crapping yourself before you went out.'

'Like you said, I'm just glad it's all over.'

Danny said, 'What's all over, Owen? Are you talking about the cash drop or something else?'

Bradley looked up, and for the first time, he made eye contact with Danny.

Danny could see the tears welling in the store manager's eyes.

Bradley spluttered, 'I had to protect my family. That's all that matters.'

'Protect your family from what, exactly? Talk to me, Owen.'

A look of resignation spread over the store manager's face, and he said quietly, 'It doesn't matter anymore; they're safe. The gang were watching my family until they picked up the cash. My wife and kids will be safe now.'

'How will they be safe now? The cash is still where you left it.'

'No, it isn't.'

Danny turned to Rob and said, 'I want officers deployed to this man's home address immediately. Let's make sure his wife and kids are safe.'

Rob nodded and hurried out of the room.

Danny leaned forward and stared across the desk at Bradley. 'Start talking.'

'The bag I left on the parapet of the bridge is full of shredded newspaper. I left an identical bag, containing the cash, in the boot of my car.'

'Shit!'

Danny snatched up the crime squad radio on his desk and said, 'DCI Flint to DI Thomas. Over.'

'DI Thomas to DCI Flint, go ahead. Over.'

'Recover the bag from the bridge. I need to know what's inside. Do it now. Over.'

'Sorry, boss. Can you repeat your last? Over.'

'There's been a development here. Recover the bag immediately and tell me what's inside. Over.'

'Stand by. Over.'

Danny could hear Jo Thomas barking orders over the radio; then there was a pause. After a few minutes, the radio crackled back into life. 'DI Thomas to DCI Flint. Over.'

'Go ahead. Over.'

'Sir, the bag's been recovered. It's full of newspaper. Over.'

99

4.15am, 22 May 1988
Incident Room, Carlton Police Station, Nottingham

Rob walked into Danny's office and said, 'Local officers are at Bradley's home address in Loughborough now. His wife and children are all safe.'

'Thank God for that. The bag that had been left on the bridge is being brought to the incident room by DI Thomas. Apparently, it's almost identical to the one the cash was in, but this one is full of newspaper.'

Rob let out a low whistle. 'Bloody hell.'

'This is rapidly turning into a nightmare. I want Bradley arrested and interviewed under caution. I want to know how this has happened. I want to know how he was contacted and exactly what he was told by whoever contacted him. Does he know them? Are they ex-employees? Get into his ribs, Rob. His family are safe, so he should speak freely now. I want to know everything he knows. We've got half a million quid in the breeze, and we need to try to recover it fast. I'll organise a section of Special Ops to raid our suspect's premises. We've got nothing to lose now. It's our only chance of recovering the cash.'

'I'm on it.'

Rob left the room, and Danny picked up the telephone. He dialled the number for the control room and said, 'Inspector, this is DCI Flint. I want a full section of the Special Operations Unit travelling to the incident room at Carlton Police Station for a briefing in one hour's time.'

'C Section are on call. I'll start contacting them straight away. Is it for an armed raid?'

'No, they won't be armed. I need premises searched in the city, as a matter of urgency. I want them here, ready to be briefed, at no later than 5:15.'

'Yes, sir.'

Danny put the phone down and picked up the Crime Squad radio. 'DCI Flint to DS Casey. Over.'

'Go ahead, sir. Over.'

'Any movement at the target premises? Over.'

'No, sir. There's just the one light on, in the flat above the shop, but no movement. Over.'

'I want to know the instant anybody tries to leave that location. Over.'

'Yes, sir. Over.'

Danny put the radio back on the desk, sat back in his chair and rubbed his temples. He suddenly felt drained. It had been a long day, and the stress of the situation was almost intolerable.

He now had half a million pounds missing and still no hard evidence to connect his only suspect to either the missing money or the fatal poisonings. The sooner Special

Ops arrived, raided the property and detained the suspect, the better.

He tried not to think past that. The thought of finding no evidence, or no money, at the suspect's property filled him with an ice-cold dread.

100

5.30am, 22 May 1988
Incident Room, Carlton Police Station, Nottingham

Danny and Tina had just finished briefing the Special Operations Unit and the MCIU staff about the impending raid, when Rob Buxton and Glen Lorimar walked in, having finished their interview with Owen Bradley.

Danny told Sergeant Graham Turner, who was leading the SOU section, to stand by.

He looked at Rob and said, 'What did Bradley have to say?'

'Bradley's convinced it's a gang behind all of this. They contacted him by leaving a bag under his car in Valumart's car park. The black bag was almost identical to the one we used for the cash drop. It contained typed instructions, as well as Polaroid photographs of his home. A couple of these photographs showed his wife playing with the kids inside their house.'

'Does he still have these instructions and photographs?'

'He says they're hidden in the bottom drawer of his desk at work.'

'I want them recovered as soon as possible. We'll need to submit them for forensic testing.'

'I've tasked DC Baxter and DC Paine to travel to the supermarket. Staff are already in store, so they'll be able to gain access to his office.'

'Good.'

'What else did he say?'

'He blamed Valumart for putting him and his family in such a dangerous predicament. They had insisted he include his family for the publicity photographs when the store was opened. The public relations woman in charge had wanted to portray an image showing that although the new superstore was huge, it was still a family store.'

'So he blames them for putting his family in harm's way?'

'Yes.'

'And what did he say about tonight's events?'

'He was instructed to leave the bag full of cash in the unlocked boot of his BMW when it was parked on Harrimans Lane.'

'Have you asked Phil Baxter to check Bradley's car at the supermarket?'

'He contacted me as I was walking back up to the incident room. The car's been thoroughly searched. It's empty.'

'Let me get this straight. While we were all watching a bag stuffed with newspaper, this crafty bastard has got clean away with half a million quid.'

Rob nodded. 'Whoever's behind all this has really thought things through.'

Danny shook his head. 'Unbelievable.'

Glen Lorimar said, 'Boss, the location where Bradley parked his car on Harrimans Lane isn't a million miles away from where the crime squad were watching our suspect for one and a half hours.'

'Do you think he somehow managed to slip past them?'

'It's unlikely. The crime squad are the best at what they do. But DI Buxton said they weren't watching him all the time he was in the car park. They just plotted up on the exits, so I suppose it's possible he somehow managed to get by them.'

'Would one and a half hours be long enough for him to get from the car park to Harrimans Lane and back?'

'Easily.'

Danny turned to Rob. 'Get some staff back to the car park and search the area where the suspect's van was parked.'

'Yes, boss.'

Danny had made his decision.

He looked at Sergeant Turner. 'There's nothing new to tell you and your staff. I want your team travelling to the address on Hungerhill Road. We'll follow you there, and once you've gained entry, I'll detain the suspect on suspicion of demanding money with menaces. He hasn't been out of the property since he returned, so there may still be evidence inside the target premises. Let's move.'

101

5.45 am, 22 May 1988
Hungerhill Road, St Ann's, Nottingham

Nabin lay on his bed, feeling exhausted. His eyes felt heavy, and he was fighting drifting off to sleep. He had listened to his mother pottering around in the kitchen, wishing she would return to her bedroom. He didn't want to have another awkward conversation with her about his nocturnal activities.

He needed to leave the flat again and didn't want to answer the inevitable questions about why he needed to go out again so soon and at such an ungodly hour.

There was one last thing he had to do before his immaculate plan was complete. He needed to make the short trip to the allotment before any of the other growers arrived, as he had to destroy all evidence of the *Brugmansia* plants he had cultivated in his greenhouse. With the plants gone, as well as any of the remaining liquid he had extracted from them, there would be nothing to connect him with the recent deaths in the city.

It was a vital element of the plan, and part of him cursed that he hadn't gone straight to the allotment on the way back from the QMC. As he had driven back through the deserted streets, he had thought it best to hide the cash first rather than risk leaving the van on the street unattended, with half a million pounds inside.

Finally, he heard his mother going into her bedroom.

It was time to go.

He carefully closed his bedroom door and tiptoed down the stairs. He grabbed his boots, his coat and the keys for the van, then tiptoed inside the shop.

As he laced up his boots, he allowed a grim smile of satisfaction to play on his lips as he thought of all the meticulous planning and preparation he had carried out to get to this point.

The police were idiots. He had enjoyed outfoxing them and demonstrating his superior intellect.

Nothing could stop him now.

He threw on his thick parka, slid the top bolt across, unlocked the door and opened it.

102

5.50am, 22 May 1988
Hungerhill Road, St Ann's, Nottingham

'Stand still, don't move!'

The voice belonged to Sergeant Graham Turner of the Special Operations Unit. He stepped forward and grabbed a shocked Nabin Panchal by the arm as other black-clad officers streamed into the shop beyond them.

Graham Turner gripped the arm of the suspect, who appeared totally stunned by their presence and made no attempt to break the tough sergeant's grip or otherwise resist.

Graham spun the suspect around and placed handcuffs on his wrists, with his arms behind his back. As soon as the handcuffs were applied, Danny stepped forward and said, 'Nabin Panchal, I'm arresting you on suspicion of demanding money with menaces.'

Panchal listened as the detective cautioned him. He said nothing but allowed a sly smirk to form on his lips.

Danny was annoyed at the smirk, put his face close to the suspect's, and growled, 'Who else is in the property?'

'Just my elderly mother and my sister. Is this some kind of pathetic, sick joke? What money? What menaces?'

Danny turned to Rob Buxton. 'Take him to Carlton and get him booked into custody. I'm staying here to supervise the search and talk to the family.'

There was a sudden commotion in the flat above the shop; Danny heard loud footsteps running down the stairs. The interior door that led from the flat into the shop burst open, and a young Asian woman shouted, 'Nabin, where are you going? What's happening?'

As he was being hauled away by Rob Buxton, Nabin shouted back, 'Don't worry, Padama. This is all a stupid mistake by these idiot policemen. Look after *maamii* until I get back. This won't take long.'

Rob dragged Nabin to the car, opened the door and sat him on the back seat. DC Glen Lorimar climbed in the car and sat next to the suspect.

Danny turned to Rachel Moore and said, 'Take her back upstairs to the flat and talk to her and the mother. Find out where the old man is, sharpish. We need to locate him as soon as possible; he may be involved in all this.'

Rachel nodded and began to walk through the shop, towards a very frightened Padama.

Danny said, 'And while you're at it, ask her about her brother's recent behaviour and what their financial situation is. Have you seen the shelves in this shop? They're almost empty of stock. I need some answers fast.'

Rachel said, 'Will do, boss.'

She then gently took hold of Padama's arm and spoke to the young woman. 'Come on. Let's go and find your mum; she'll be worried.'

Danny looked at Graham Turner. 'He wasn't expecting that, was he?'

'Not at all. For a few seconds, he was like a rabbit in headlights.'

'Let's go upstairs and have a look round the flat.'

As they walked slowly up the stairs, Graham said, 'I've deployed a pair of officers to search each room. PC Naylor will bag and tag any exhibits we recover and maintain the search record.'

Danny had worked alongside the Special Operations Unit on many occasions and trusted their professionalism, especially when it came to searching.

He walked behind Graham, up the stairs and into the pokey flat. The two men walked into what was obviously Nabin's bedroom. Danny immediately saw the Olivetti portable typewriter, paper and envelopes.

One of the SOU officers was in the process of placing the light blue typewriter into a brown exhibit bag.

Danny said, 'Don't forget, gents – I want every scrap of paperwork you can find. I want all letters, bank statements, accounts, everything.'

The two men nodded and continued with the search.

Graham said quietly, 'We've got this in hand, sir. We all heard the briefing, and we know what we're looking for. There's really no need for you to stay and supervise. It's going to take us a good few hours to complete this search properly. Don't forget we've got the shop and the van outside to also search.'

Danny nodded. 'Okay, Graham. I just need the evidence to nail this bastard. I swear he was laughing at me when I nicked him.'

'I saw the smirk too, boss. Don't worry, I'll keep you updated as soon as we find anything significant.'

Rachel then walked into the bedroom and said, 'The

mother has just told me her husband is a patient at Mapperley Hospital, after suffering a complete nervous breakdown.'

'Ask them both to get dressed and take them to Carlton Police Station. I want you to interview them properly, and we can't do that here. Don't arrest them unless you have to. Tell them you want them to come to the station to assist us with our enquiries, and that the sooner we get to the bottom of what's happening, the sooner Nabin will be released.'

'Okay, boss.'

'I'll arrange some transport and come back with you.'

Danny walked slowly down the stairs and back into the shop part of the property. Looking behind the counter, he saw the two cardboard boxes that the regional crime squad detectives had watched the suspect load into his van, only to unload them again on his return.

Intrigued as to what might be inside, Danny opened the boxes. He was shocked to see they were both empty.

Why the hell did this guy take two empty cardboard boxes all the way to the QMC and back?

103

9.30am, 22 May 1988
Incident Room, Carlton Police Station, Nottingham

Danny was sitting at the back of the incident room. Facing him were Tina Cartwright, Rob Buxton, Rachel Moore and Andy Wills.

He was exhausted and starting to feel irritable.

He snapped, 'Let's make this quick. I want to know what progress we've made. Andy, you go first.'

Andy Wills said, 'I've been to the multi-storey car park at the QMC. I spoke to DC Winters from the crime squad, and he showed me where the suspect had parked his van. I can understand why they didn't want to stay watching the suspect up there; it's totally exposed. The van was parked at the rear of the car park, on level six. There was nothing in the area where the van had been parked, so we made a systematic search of all the floors.'

'Anything?'

'On the first floor of the car park, also at the rear, I found a rope that had been secured to the parapet. The rope led down to the wasteland immediately behind the car park. There are none of the security grilles on this level. You know the ones I mean; they're there to stop people committing suicide by jumping.'

Danny nodded impatiently. 'Exactly what's behind the car park?'

'It's an area of bushes, trees and rubbish. It's totally wild and overgrown.'

'What's on the other side of the overgrown area?'

'On the far side is a footpath that runs alongside the River Leen.'

'Is it feasible that our suspect could have made his way on foot from there to the cash drop?'

Andy nodded. 'The footpath leads on to the towpath of the Beeston Canal. That's where the drop was made.'

'I want a full search of that area of undergrowth carrying out.'

'I thought you would, boss. I've already arranged for a further section of special ops lads to carry out the search. They've been at it for about an hour, but it's heavy going.'

'Have they found anything yet?'

'I contacted them for an update just before we started this debrief. They've recovered a black nylon holdall and half a mannequin.'

'That's interesting. Is the black nylon holdall like the one used for the cash drop?'

'They say so, boss.'

Danny felt himself relaxing. He was surrounded by extremely hard-working, gifted detectives who weren't afraid to use their initiative. He had to trust in his team.

He said, 'That's good work, Andy.'

Rob said, 'The mannequin is interesting, too. Do you

remember the surveillance team said the suspect hadn't moved a muscle in the van? What if he used the mannequin to make people think somebody was sitting in the van?'

'While he slipped down the rope and out the back of the car park?'

'It's definitely feasible.'

Danny looked at Rachel. 'How are you getting on with the mother and sister?'

'I've teamed up with Fran to talk to them. We're making progress, but it's slow.'

'Did you establish what caused the father to have a breakdown?'

'Mum doesn't want to talk about it at all, but Padama, the daughter, has told me his illness was caused by the business failing. You saw the empty shelves; the shop is going under.'

'How come?'

'It was doing really well, and they were making good money, but it has been in dire straits ever since the Valumart superstore opened. They just can't compete with the low pricing of everything the supermarket sells. Padama also told me they are well behind on their mortgage repayments and face eviction. Her dad couldn't cope with it all, so Nabin has been trying to salvage the situation and find a way out.'

'That's very interesting. What have they said about Nabin?'

'Neither of them wants to talk about Nabin. It's like pulling teeth trying to get them to open up to us at all.'

'You've got to push them harder. Find out exactly how Nabin has been trying to salvage their situation. What's he been doing? Has he met anybody? Keep pushing. I want to know his background; we still don't know anything about him.'

'Will do, boss.'

Tina Cartwright said, 'I know a little more now, boss. I've

been researching the family all morning. They were part of Idi Amin's forced exodus of Asians from Uganda, in the early seventies. That's why records here are scant in detail. I've spent the morning trying to get an idea of their lives while they were still in Uganda. It seems they had a very different lifestyle there. From the research I've carried out so far, Nabin was a gifted scholar who studied as a horticultural biologist. He had been tipped for great things until the family were expelled from the country. His father is also an extremely intelligent man. He was a professor of biochemistry in Uganda.'

Danny interrupted, speaking to Rachel. 'Use this information. Let's see if we can put some flesh onto these bare bones. Find out where Nabin went to university. What did he specialise in? Where was the father a professor? Let's dig deeper. Don't forget, we already know that the toxin used to kill all these people can be plant-based. It looks like our suspect isn't just a disgruntled shopkeeper. He could also be someone eminently qualified to produce such a toxin. Good work, Tina. Keep digging.'

Danny looked at Rob. 'How was Panchal when you booked him into custody?'

'He was confident, cocky almost. He looks totally untroubled by it all. He keeps saying we've made a massive mistake, but he isn't being an arsehole about it. He's not screaming to make a complaint or anything. He just says we've got it all wrong.'

Danny was thoughtful for a couple of minutes; then he said, 'You and Glen can't do much more until we know what the search has yielded. Has his solicitor arrived yet?'

'Yeah. She's downstairs and has been told why her client's under arrest.'

'Okay. I want you and Glen to go back downstairs and carry out a preliminary interview with Panchal. Just question him about his movements overnight. I want you to let him know that we've had him under round-the-clock surveillance, and that we've been watching his every move. That way, you'll get a feel as to how he's going to respond in interview. It might also knock some of that cockiness out of him.'

'Will do, boss.'

'Good work, everyone. Any questions?'

Rachel Moore said, 'I saw the coat the suspect was wearing when he was arrested. I've compared it to the one he was wearing at the post box, and with the coat being worn by the Asian male suspect on the CCTV at the supermarket. It looks identical.'

'I take it we've seized the coat?' Danny asked Rob.

Rob nodded. 'Standard procedure. All his clothing has been seized and bagged as possible evidence.'

'Rachel, before you go and speak to the mother and daughter again, get in touch with Tim Donnelly. I want that coat fast-tracked for forensic examination. Let's see if we can positively identify it as being the same coat. Anything else?'

There was silence.

'If there's nothing else, let's meet back here in an hour's time. We should know what we've got from the searches by then.'

104

10.15am, 22 May 1988
Cell Block, Carlton Police Station, Nottingham

Nabin Panchal walked back into the cell and sat down on the hard bench. The interview with the two detectives had been brief. He had been instructed by his solicitor to answer all questions with 'no comment'. She had told him, in the private consultation prior to the interview, that the detectives were on a fishing expedition and had provided her with no real disclosure yet. Her advice was simple: Say nothing.

The questions were banal and easily batted off. He had stuck resolutely to the instruction and had said 'no comment' to every question.

He had tried hard to show no emotion throughout the interrogation. He knew the detectives would be looking for any reaction, however small. Even when they had informed him he had been under surveillance, he managed to maintain an ice-cool demeanour.

He was confident his careful planning had outwitted the police. This was reinforced when he thought about the detectives blundering along the footpath in the dark, following the store manager.

He smiled to himself as he recalled their clumsy efforts to move stealthily. If they had been watching him, they would have known where he was, and wouldn't have needed to send men out to watch the store manager.

He lay down on the hard bench and closed his eyes.

The police had nothing.

105

11.00am, 22 May 1988
Incident Room, Carlton Police Station, Nottingham

Danny was prowling up and down in his small office, like a caged tiger. He was impatient for news of the search. He walked into the incident room and saw Rob and Glen Lorimar going through a stack of paperwork.

He walked over and said, 'What have you got there?'

Rob said, 'One of the SOU lads just brought it in so we could make a start prepping for interview. It's all the documentation recovered from the suspect premises so far.'

'Anything interesting?'

'We're still going through it, but so far, we've got the letter paper and envelopes that were found next to the portable typewriter. We can have them forensically tested and hopefully matched to the paper and envelopes used by the extortionist.'

'Have they almost finished the search?'

'Just about. The lad said they've just got the outbuildings, the loft space, and the van left to search.'

'And this is all we've got?'

'We have all the family's bank statements and the accounts for the shop. As we suspected, their financial situation is dire. There's also a letter from the Nottingham Building Society informing the family that they only have until the end of June to make the outstanding mortgage payments, or the property will be repossessed.'

'Is that it?'

Glen Lorimar held up a piece of paper and said, 'There's this.'

'What's that?'

'A letter from the allotment society. It's about Nabin's overdue invoice for the communal manure order.'

'Does he have an allotment?'

'His name is on the invoice for the manure, so I think he must do.'

'Where are these allotments?'

'The letterhead says St Ann's Well Road. I didn't realise there were any allotments there.'

Danny was thoughtful for a moment. Then he said, 'Glen, can you get me a photocopy of this letter, please.'

Glen took the invoice and said, 'Will do.'

Danny looked at Rob and said, 'Keep going through the paperwork; you might find something else you can use. God knows we need something. All this waiting around is killing me. I'm going to get a breath of fresh air. If anything changes, I'll be on the radio.'

Just then, Glen returned with the photocopied letter and handed it to Danny.

Danny looked around the incident room and saw Tina Cartwright staring at one of the computer screens.

He said, 'Will that keep, Tina?'

'It's more research on the family, so yes, it will keep. What's up?'

'Grab some car keys and your coat. We're going to have a look at an allotment.'

106

11.15am, 22 May 1988
St Ann's Well Road Allotments, Nottingham

Tina had parked the car on St Ann's Well Road, near to the metal gates that led into the allotments.

The gardens were surrounded by a high hawthorn hedge and were invisible from the road. Danny had driven along this road a thousand times and never realised there was this oasis of greenery right in the centre of the city.

The high metal gates were topped by spikes and a coil of barbed wire to deter intruders. Danny pushed on the gate. It was closed but not locked, and swung open.

The two detectives walked along a pathway that was bordered on both sides by immaculately tended vegetable patches. On one such garden, they saw a middle-aged woman busily hoeing weeds from between rows of beetroot seedlings.

Danny took out his warrant card and approached the woman. 'Good morning. Sorry to interrupt your labours. We're looking for a man named Nabin Panchal. Do you know him at all?'

The woman leaned on her hoe and smiled. 'We all know Nabi. He's been like a breath of fresh air to these gardens. He's such a helpful man and so knowledgeable. He certainly has green fingers, that one. Why, what's wrong?'

Danny showed the woman his identification card and said, 'We're from the CID. There's nothing wrong; we're just making some routine enquiries. Which is Nabin's allotment?'

The woman propped the garden tool against the canes holding her runner beans up, and said, 'It will be easier for me to show you where it is. This way.'

The detectives dutifully followed the woman through the allotments until they were near the very far end of the gardens.

She pointed at a very large, neat plot with row upon row of healthy plants and said, 'All this is Nabi's. Do you see what I mean about his green fingers? His plants always look so healthy. The amount of produce he grows and gives away is unbelievable.'

All Danny could focus on was the greenhouse and the large shed at the far end of the plot. He turned to the woman and said, 'Are the buildings his as well?'

'The greenhouse and the shed are both his.'

'Does anybody else ever work on his allotment?'

'Never. I don't think Nabi would like that. For all his generosity, he's quite a shy, sweet man. No, everything you can see is all his own hard work.'

Danny looked at Tina and said, 'Get this lady's details. We'll need a full statement from her later.'

While Tina took the woman's contact details, Danny walked along the path to the greenhouse. The door was unlocked, so he opened it and looked inside. He was confronted by tall plants with broad, emerald green leaves. There were cascades of white, trumpet-shaped flowers hanging from the plants.

Tina approached the greenhouse and said, 'Angel's Trumpets.'

Danny spun around. 'What?'

'Don't you remember the pictures of the *Brugmansia* plant we saw. Its common name is Angel's Trumpets because of these pendulous white flowers.'

Danny felt a familiar surge of adrenalin coursing through him and instantly forgot how tired he had felt moments earlier.

With real excitement in his voice, he said, 'Let's have look in the shed.'

There was a heavy padlock securing the door to the shed. Tina said, 'It's going to take a couple of hours, but we really should get a warrant.'

She paused and then said in a conspiratorial whisper, 'However, if we found the building in an insecure state, we would be obliged to check the property was okay, and make sure that the intruder wasn't still inside. There was a spade inside the greenhouse. We could use that.'

Danny grinned and retrieved the spade from the greenhouse. He took one last look around him, to make sure no one was watching, and then smashed the hasp holding the padlock from the door. With the lock forced, the door opened easily.

The two detectives stepped inside and looked around. The shed was neat and tidy; everything was in its place. Danny picked up a book from a wooden trestle table. It was a book on the cultivation of tropical plants. The corner of the page had been turned down on the chapter referencing *Brugmansia* plants.

Tina said, 'Look at this, boss.'

Danny turned and saw her pointing to an old plastic lemonade bottle that was half-filled with a brackish brown liquid.

Danny took the radio from his pocket and said, 'DCI Flint to Sergeant Turner. Over.'

'Go ahead, sir. Over.'

'I need your section to join me at the allotments on St Ann's Well Road for another search commitment. Over.'

'I've just this second contacted the incident room, boss. We've struck gold in the loft at the flat. We've discovered a large amount of twenty-pound notes all wrapped in clingfilm. The notes had been hidden well. They were stashed in between the sheets of fibreglass loft insulation, between the rafters. We're in the process of recovering it now. Over.'

'That's fantastic news. How long before you could send me some staff to this location? Over.'

'I'll split the team and send five officers to you now. Over.'

'Inform your men that the allotment I want searched is at the very far end of the gardens. DI Cartwright is on scene, and I'm arranging for Scenes of Crime to attend. Your blokes will no doubt see all the activity when they get here. Good work, Graham. Over.'

Danny turned to Tina and said, 'I want you to stay here and supervise the search by the Special Ops lads. I'll get Scenes of Crime travelling to you straight away. I want everything photographed in situ before special ops start searching. I need to get back to the incident room. I think we've got the bastard.'

107

2.00pm, 22 May 1988
Incident Room, Carlton Police Station, Nottingham

Danny rubbed his eyes; they were red-rimmed and stinging. He had been awake over twenty-four hours, and he was flagging. He made himself yet another mug of strong black coffee and walked into the incident room.

He saw Rob and Glen with their heads together, talking about the impending interview with Nabin Panchal.

Danny said, 'I thought you would have made a start by now?'

Rob said, 'His solicitor's still in consultation.'

'How long does she need, for Christ's sake?'

'We finished giving her disclosure on our evidence forty minutes ago. To be fair to her, she has got a lot to go through with him, boss.'

'Who's the solicitor?'

'Her name's Navinder Khan. She's from the Khan and Associates law practice in the city. I haven't met her before, but she seems very switched on. She'll know her client's fucked. The amount of evidence we have connecting her client to these crimes is overwhelming. I'm not expecting anything other than a "no comment" interview, the same as the preliminary one we had.'

'You might get a prepared statement and then "no comment".'

Glen Lorimar was the most experienced interviewer on the MCIU. He looked thoughtful and said, 'You're probably right, boss. But I've been in a few interviews where it's worked completely the opposite way. When an accused is totally screwed by overwhelming evidence, remaining silent doesn't really help them. All they've got left is mitigation. Don't be surprised if he starts talking and coming up with a load of bullshit excuses for what he's done.'

The telephone rang and was answered by Fran Jefferies. After a brief conversation, she put the phone down and said, 'DI Buxton, that was the custody sergeant. The solicitor has finished her consultation. Nabin Panchal is ready to be interviewed.'

108

2.25pm, 22 May 1988
Cell Block, Carlton Police Station, Nottingham

Rob Buxton and Glen Lorimar were in an interview room sitting opposite Nabin Panchal and his solicitor, Navinder Khan.

There had been no prepared statement handed over by the solicitor at the start of the interview, and Panchal had remained silent, refusing to acknowledge the questions with an answer of 'no comment'. He had sat and stared down at the desk in front of him, refusing to raise his head.

Rob changed the tone of his questions, adopting a harsher manner. Pushing the boundaries of what was acceptable, he said, 'What I don't understand is how you can treat innocent people in such a cold-hearted, callous way. To you, they were nothing but collateral damage to your greedy ambitions. These were the same people who had welcomed you with open arms when you and your family were expelled from Uganda by Idi Amin.'

The change of attitude worked. For the first time, Nabin looked up and made eye contact with the hardened detective.

He stared at Rob and scoffed, 'This country didn't do us any favours. We're all British citizens; we all have British passports. We had the right to live and be accepted here.'

Rob was experienced enough to know when to remain quiet. He waited for Nabin to continue. He didn't have to wait long.

Nabin pointed his finger at Rob and said aggressively, 'In Uganda, my father was an important man, an educated man, treated with the honour and respect he deserved. He was rightfully revered for the amazing work he did.'

There was a pause; then he continued. 'Here, he couldn't get a job of any kind. Nobody was interested in employing him. I was treated the same way; that's your wonderful British welcome. In Uganda, I was a skilled, highly educated horticultural biologist. All I could do here was wash fucking dishes at an Indian restaurant in the city. Do you even know what a horticultural biologist is, Mr Policeman?'

Rob stared back and said, 'Somebody skilled in the cultivation and propagation of plants.'

Nabin sat back in his chair and clapped his hands sarcastically. 'Very good. Maybe you're not as dumb as you look.'

Ignoring the insult, Rob decided to play to the man's obvious ego.

He said, 'I've seen evidence of your skills at the greenhouse on your allotment. How the hell did you manage to grow healthy tropical plants in this country?'

'It was easy.'

'But where did you get the plants in the first place?'

'I grew them from cuttings I took at Kew Gardens, in London.'

'Why did you choose to grow that plant, the *Brugmansia*?'

'I chose it because I needed the "Devil's Breath." '

'The what?'

'The "Devil's Breath" is what you get when you extract the juice from the leaves and seed pods. There is a potent toxin to be found in them.'

'So you cultivated the plants from cuttings, and once they had grown into mature, healthy plants, you harvested the leaves and pods so you could extract the toxin.'

In the same sarcastic tone, Nabin said, 'Very good, Mr Policeman. I can see why they made you a detective.'

Rob ignored the attempt to rile him, and just said, 'How do you extract the toxin from the leaves and seeds?'

'It's a simple enough procedure. I put all the leaves and pods in a saucepan with a little water and stew it down over a low heat. It takes hours, but you end up with a soggy, brown pulp. I strained that pulp through a sieve, and you end up with a brackish liquid. That is the "Devil's Breath". I know you already have the liquid I extracted, so why are you bothering to ask me all these stupid, dull questions?'

'I'm hoping you'll give me one good reason why you did this terrible thing.'

There was a long pause while Nabin weighed up his options; then he said, 'Okay. Listen to me, and I'll tell you why. Even though we were treated like scum when we were expelled from our beautiful home in Uganda, and then again when we arrived here, we worked hard and tried to find our own path. None of us ever claimed benefits from the state or accepted handouts. We went from living in luxury, with servants to do our every bidding, to living the life of paupers. Still, we persevered and worked hard in the only shitty jobs we could get. We were merely surviving, and then we got the opportunity to buy the corner shop. My father ploughed everything we had, every scrap of gold he owned, into raising the deposit for the mortgage we needed to buy the shop. He was reluctant to take the risk, but I badgered him into doing it. I wanted a future.'

'Did the shop do okay?'

'At first, it did better than okay. It was extremely profitable, a little gold mine. We all worked long, hard, unsociable hours, but we made a good healthy profit. For the first time, we had real money to spend. We had that bright future.'

'So what happened?'

'Valumart happened.'

'I don't understand.'

'They could have built their fucking huge superstore anywhere, but they chose to build it just a few streets away from our little shop. Our flourishing little business died the day that superstore opened.'

'You blame Valumart for your business failing?'

'I blame them for much more than that. My father knew we would lose everything, and it broke him. His once-beautiful mind is now totally fucked, and it's all because of their corporate greed.'

'And you decided to make them pay?'

Rob could see the fire burning in Nabin's eyes as he replied, 'Yes, I did, Detective.'

He blinked hard before continuing. 'It was never my intention to kill anyone. I just wanted people to become sick enough to force Valumart into paying me the money I needed to take care of my family. It was all my fault, my responsibility. I had talked my father into buying the shop. I was the one who had to remedy the situation.'

'But you told me yourself, you're a skilled, highly educated horticultural biologist. Surely, you knew what the consequences of your actions could be?'

'I didn't. Nobody knows the exact amount of "Devil's Breath" to use. Each plant has a different strength of toxin. It's the reason why so many people die who ingest it. Some seed pods and leaves are stronger than others. I had to use an educated guess to try to get the levels right.'

'And you obviously failed.'

'I thought I had got the level right. When I tested it out, it was fine. The old lady survived.'

'What old lady?'

'I needed to test the strength of the liquid I had extracted, so I took a small bottle of it to a café in the city centre. I poured some into an old lady's cup of tea when she wasn't paying attention.'

'What happened?'

'She drank the tea and almost immediately became very ill. She collapsed, and the staff in the café called an ambulance. As far as I knew, the old lady didn't die. I never saw anything in the newspaper or heard anything on the news, so I assumed she was okay. After that experiment, I thought I had achieved the right level of toxicity.'

Rob was shocked at the cold, calculating manner in which Nabin described the events.

He said, 'If, as you claim, this old lady survived the poison you administered to her, why did all those other people die?'

Nabin shrugged. 'I really don't know. I could have got the amount I used wrong. The liquid could have got stronger as it fermented. It was just bad luck. I'm sorry for their deaths. That wasn't what I wanted.'

'But you knew the risks. You knew what could happen, and you still placed this deadly toxin on the shelves of a supermarket for innocent members of the public to buy and consume.'

'Yes, I did. I had to take care of my family.'

'As a direct result of your actions, other families – innocent men, women and children – have died. Doesn't that bother you at all?'

'I've said I'm sorry, but my family is the most important thing to me. Nothing and nobody else matters. I've said all I'm going to say. I won't be answering any more of your inane questions.'

Nabin resumed staring at the desk, effectively shutting the interview down. Rob persisted with a few more questions, but then brought the interview to a close.

109

10.00am, 24 May 1988
Nottingham Police Headquarters

When Danny finally got home, he had been exhausted. He had fallen into bed and slept solidly for over twelve hours. He had woken this morning feeling refreshed and energised.

It was a beautiful spring morning, and for once, he had enjoyed the drive into force headquarters.

He knocked on the door of Chief Superintendent Potter's office and waited until he heard Potter's reedy voice shout, 'Enter.'

Danny walked in. 'Good morning, sir.'

'Take a seat, Chief Inspector. Do you have an update for me?'

'Nabin Panchal has been charged with six murders, one attempted murder, and demanding money with menaces.

There may be a further charge of administering a noxious substance to come later.'

'Will the murder charges stick?'

'The lawyers are satisfied that Panchal administered the poison randomly, being reckless to the outcome. He's doomed by his own knowledge. He fully understood what that toxin could do. He knew it could be lethal, yet he still put it out there.'

'What about this bizarre test run he talked about?'

'I have detectives working around the clock to try to trace the old lady concerned. I'm confident that we'll find her. Once we do, and we've obtained her statement, the lawyers will decide whether to additionally charge Panchal with another attempted murder, or an administration of noxious substance charge.'

'What was his motive? Was it purely the money?'

'I think so, sir.'

Potter made a tutting sound and then said, 'I've listened to the tapes of the interview. The little remorse he showed during the interview was unfeeling and insincere. He appears to be an extremely cold, calculating, and highly intelligent individual. Couple all those things with an obsessive, evil character, and you've got a very dangerous man, capable of murder.'

'I would agree with a lot of those sentiments, but Nabin Panchal was a man driven by an overwhelming desire to step up and care for his family. He blamed Idi Amin for expelling the Asian community from Uganda. He blamed this country for not giving him and his father the opportunities to be employed in their fields of excellence. He blamed Valumart for ruining the family business and for making his father so ill. Basically, Nabin Panchal blamed everything and everyone but himself. At the end of the day, whatever was driving his behaviour, his actions have cost the lives of six innocent members of the public, including two young children. And it was all done for money.'

'Are Valumart satisfied with the outcome of the enquiry?'

'I think so. I've been in touch with Steve Dawson, and he informed me that the organisation hierarchy aren't looking forward to the negative publicity that will no doubt emerge at the forthcoming trial. They're happy that their stock is no longer contaminated, and customers can shop in safety.'

'I thought you'd lost their half a million pounds at one point, Chief Inspector.'

'To be honest, so did I, sir. Thank goodness I hadn't placed all my hopes on the surveillance operation. It was the observations on the post box that proved the key and identified Nabin Panchal.'

'Talking of the debacle that was the surveillance operation, what's going to happen to the store manager who assisted the extortionist?'

'Owen Bradley was acting under severe duress. He genuinely believed his own wife and young children were in imminent danger. I don't intend to charge him with assisting an offender. I think it would be counterproductive. We're far better off using him as a witness for the prosecution.'

'Agreed. Will the supermarkets be taking further measures to prevent similar attacks in the future?'

'That's already underway, sir. All the supermarkets have agreed to ensure that all fresh foodstuffs will be sealed in the future. That way, customers will know instantly if the food or drink they've selected has been tampered with.'

'Well, that's something positive to come out of this tragedy. It's been another complicated case solved by you and your team, Chief Inspector. The chief constable has asked me to pass on his congratulations.'

'Thank you, sir. I'll pass his message on to my team.'

'One other thing: DC Pope will be joining you on the first of June.'

'That's great. Thank you, sir.'

'Let me know if there are any problems as we approach Panchal's trial date.'

Danny knew that was his cue to leave, so he stood up and said, 'Will do, sir.'

EPILOGUE

11.00am, 10 June 1988
Mapperley Hospital, Nottingham

Padama Panchal placed her arm around her mother's shoulders, to comfort her. The older woman was sobbing quietly as she stared at her husband, who was propped up in the bed.

Aadesh Panchal was heavily sedated and barely conscious. On their way into the ward, the young nurse had informed them of their loved one's condition. She had said kindly that even though he looked out of it, they should try to talk to him, as he could still hear them.

Padama knew that it would be down to her to talk to her father. Her mother was deeply upset at seeing the man she loved more than life itself in this state, and couldn't bring herself to talk.

Padama smiled and said, 'I've come to tell you all our news, *baabujii*.'

She couldn't tell her father the truth; it would be too upsetting. So she said, 'Nabin's landed a brilliant job in London and has moved down to the city to live. He sends us money back each week.'

There was no reaction from her father. She leaned forward and gently wiped a line of spittle from his chin and continued with her fabrications. 'I've got other great news as well. We've managed to find a buyer for the corner shop. We're moving out this weekend.'

The reality was that the building society had repossessed the corner shop and the flat above, and they had been made homeless. They were fortunate that a charity housing association had provided them with a two-bedroom flat, in Southchurch Court, a high-rise tower block.

Their tiny flat was on the eleventh floor, but it was warm and comfortable, and it meant they had a roof over their heads.

There was one piece of news she could tell him that was the truth and was positive: '*Baabujii*, *maamii* and me both have new jobs, so we can earn some good money. We're both going to be working at the Valumart superstore. I'm going to work on the checkouts, and *maamii* has a job in the staff canteen. Isn't that great?'

There was still no reaction from her father.

She leaned forward and kissed him gently on his forehead. 'Get well soon, *baabujii*. We'll come and visit you again soon.'

The old man rocked gently back and forth, stared straight ahead, and said nothing.

WE HOPE YOU ENJOYED THIS BOOK

If you could spend a moment to write an honest review on Amazon, no matter how short, we would be extremely grateful. They really do help readers discover new authors.

ALSO BY TREVOR NEGUS

EVIL IN MIND

(Book 1 in the DCI Flint series)

DEAD AND GONE

(Book 2 in the DCI Flint series)

A COLD GRAVE

(Book 3 in the DCI Flint series)

TAKEN TO DIE

(Book 4 in the DCI Flint series)

KILL FOR YOU

(Book 5 in the DCI Flint series)

ONE DEADLY LIE

(Book 6 in the DCI Flint series)

A SWEET REVENGE

(Book 7 in the DCI Flint series)

THE DEVIL'S BREATH

(Book 8 in the DCI Flint series)

Printed in Great Britain
by Amazon

13801578R00239